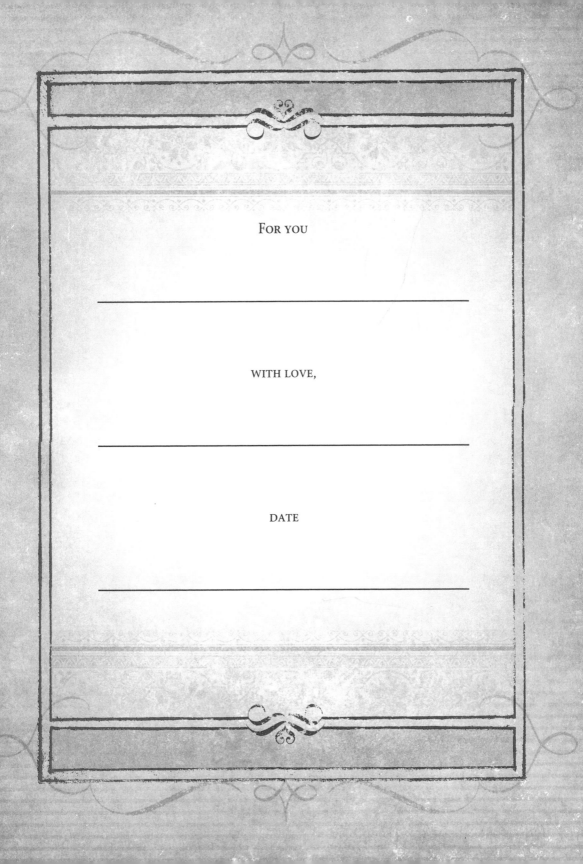

FOR YOU

_____

WITH LOVE,

_____

DATE

_____

DEDICATION

My life has been blessed beyond quantifying by the daily example of my
only surviving great aunt, Lois Wheeler Berry, who turned 104 in 2007.

She remains incredibly alert, witty, in tune with the Zeitgeist,
and prays for a long list of descendants every day of her life.

When escorted out to her car on a rainy day, she quipped to the clerk,
"When you're short like me, you're the last to get wet and the first to drown."

When asked, "Aunt Lois, how old do you have to be before you get old?"
she shot back, "'Old' is anyone who is fifteen years older than you are."
By that yardstick, "old" is currently anyone who is 119 years old.

She also loves our story collections, especially the *Christmas
in My Heart* story anthologies. Indeed, she loves them so much she reads
and re-reads them all year long and every year has me inscribe copies
of the newest collection to a long list of deserving descendants.

Consequently, I can think of no one who deserves this dedication more than

LOIS WHEELER BERRY
of
ANGWIN, CALIFORNIA

THE BEST OF
Christmas
IN MY
HEART

COMPILED & EDITED BY
JOE WHEELER

Timeless Stories to Warm Your Heart

HOWARD BOOKS
A DIVISION OF SIMON & SCHUSTER
New York   London   Toronto   Sydney

Our purpose at Howard Books is to:
· *Increase faith* in the hearts of growing Christians
· *Inspire holiness* in the lives of believers
· *Instill hope* in the hearts of struggling people everywhere

Because He's coming again!

HOWARD

Howard Books, a division of Simon & Schuster, Inc.
1230 Avenue of the Americas, New York, NY 10020
www.howardpublishing.com

The Best of Christmas in My Heart © 2007 by Joe Wheeler

First Howard hardcover edition October 2007
HOWARD and colophon are registered trademarks of Simon & Schuster, Inc.

For information regarding special discounts for bulk purchases,
please contact: Simon & Schuster Special Sales at
1-800-456-6798 or business@simonandschuster.com.

Edited by Chrys Howard
Cover and interior design by Greg Jackson, Thinkpen Design, LLC, www.thinkpendesign.com
Photography © 2007 iStockphoto

Manufactured in the United States of America

Library of Congress Cataloging-in-Publication Data

Christmas in my heart. Selections.
The best of Christmas in my heart / compiled and edited by Joe L. Wheeler.
p. cm.
1. Christmas stories, American. I. Wheeler, Joe L., 1936—
PS648.C45C4472 2007
813'.0108334—dc22
2007025637

ISBN-13: 978-1-4165-4222-3
ISBN-10: 1-4165-4222-1
10 9 8 7 6 5 4 3 2

ISBN-13: 978-1-58229-706-4 (gift edition)
ISBN-10: 1-58229-706-1 (gift edition)
10 9 8 7 6 5 4 3 2 1

Table of Contents

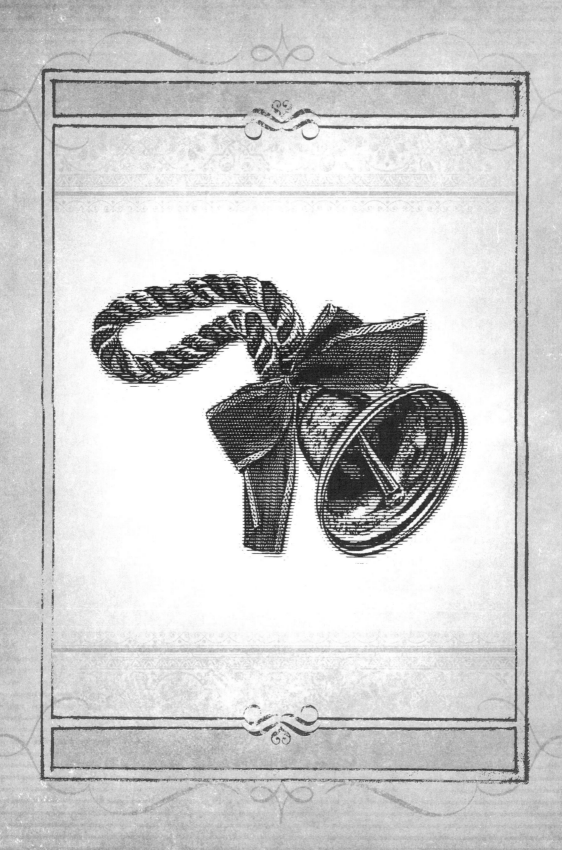

MY PATH TO CHRISTMAS STORIES

JOSEPH LEININGER WHEELER

Like Lucy Maud Montgomery's immortal heroine, Anne of Green Gables, Barbara was a voracious reader with a love for literature. Due to her near photographic memory, she could memorize thousands of pages of poetry, readings, and short stories. By the age of twelve, she was what some called an "elocutionist," a performer so mesmerizing, so dramatic, with such stage presence, that she was able to take control of any audience she addressed. In fact, she was only fourteen when she held her entire high school spellbound with Amelia Burr's "A Song of Living." Prophetically, it would become her life's signature poem. Sixty years later, in her "Cradle to the Grave" performance, invariably she would conclude with the same poem.

And how Barbara loved stories—*especially* Christmas stories! Timeless Christmas stories such as Parmenter's "David's Star of Bethlehem" and Sangster's "The Littlest Orphan and the Christ Baby," both so charged with emotion and feeling that when she concluded either one, both she and her audience would be weeping.

Barbara fell in love with a man named Lawrence. They would marry, become missionaries to Latin America, and have three children. She would homeschool them all: pouring into her children all that she was, all that it was possible for her to give.

Each of the three of us—Romayne, Marjorie, and I—owe a debt to this unforgettable woman we can never repay.

Our mother!

God, who sees the end from the beginning, was determined that Barbara's flame would continue to light up the darkness long after she was gone. That the stories she told—simple, heartfelt, and laden with values worth living by—would be entrusted to another.

THE CHOSEN ONE

In college I majored in English and history; I graduated, married my beautiful wife, Connie, and became a teacher. And as I kept turning life's corners, one constant followed—my love for stories, learned early on.

When I was a young teacher, especially, it became glaringly apparent that my students much preferred hearing a story to working on the rules of grammar. I decided to take advantage of this reality, and eventually I would see stories had become the centerpiece of my teaching career. Not just any stories, of course, and not just the kind of stories that literati gave their attention to—but rather the ones Mother raised me on: the stories *that touched the heart.*

Twenty-nine years into my career, another turn of events happened—not because I had willed anything to happen, but because a Higher Power willed them to happen. Because of what was to occur, I would learn the real definition of the word *epiphany*: It means that one moment, the train of your life is racing full-speed down a certain set of tracks—only minutes later, your train is racing full-speed down tracks in an *entirely different direction!* Sometimes the epiphany isn't discovered until later when you retrace your life journey: *Goodness! I didn't know! If that one day, if that one moment, had never been*—how different my life would have been!

Just so, I never saw it coming.

On a snowy December morning in 1989, I had no inkling that the next twelve hours would represent perhaps the most significant "switch box" of my career! After one of my classes that epochal day, one of our English majors, Naomi Snowdy, came up to me and said, "Dr. Wheeler, I'm so sick of dorm regulations and cafeteria food that I'm ready to go stark raving mad! Can I come home with you this weekend?"

I called my wife and quoted Naomi to her. She laughed and said, "Sure, I can remember feeling that way, too, during college. Tell her she's welcome."

So the stage was set. I can see it now as though it were yesterday rather than eighteen long years ago. We'd reached my Annapolis home, on the shores of the

Severn River. Naomi had unpacked, we'd eaten a delicious supper, the wind was howling outside, and the snow was slashing at our windows.

After dinner, exhausted from the long week, I leaned back in my big brown easy chair, across from a crackling fire and Naomi. She had a contemplative look in her eyes that I mistook for a look of blissful gratitude that she had a break with little to do, for that was what I was thinking.

Oh, it all started so innocently! She leaned toward me, and said softly, conversationally, "Dr. Wheeler, have you ever thought of writing a Christmas story?"

Unaware of my doom, and just as relaxed as she, I lazily answered, "Yes, I've thought of it."

"Well, why haven't you?"

"Oh, I will—someday."

I had not a clue about what was behind that ostensibly dreamy look in Naomi's eyes. But now, after all these years, I've finally pieced it together.

Naomi was in my creative writing class, the victim of many of my deadlines during the semester. I was completely blindsided by her reversal of roles as she sat up straight, lost the dreamy look, and barked out a question that was really a command: "Why don't you write it *tonight*?"

Tonight? I looked at her unbelievingly. *Surely she was just kidding.*

Inexorably she responded with, "Yes, tonight. It's going to snow all weekend anyway, so what else are we going to do? Besides"—and she gave me a malicious smirk—"I want to proof your story."

I couldn't believe it: sweet, soft-spoken Naomi turning out to be a tyrant in disguise! But try as I did to beg off, to get out of it, Naomi was as intransigent as Gibraltar . . . and my wife, Connie, was no help either. She just laughed and sided with Naomi, so it was two against one—no, make that three against one. My last hope was that the good Lord, in His great mercy, would grant me a severe case of writer's block—that way I wouldn't have to write the miserable thing. But God ganged up on me, too. Virtually instantaneously, He gave me a full-blown plot. All I had to do was flesh it out and write it.

So, I dutifully wrote all evening, all day Saturday, and part of Sunday. As fast as I completed a page, Naomi would snatch it out of my hands, read it, scribble viciously on it, and hand it back, saying, "Fix it!" . . . So that was my "relaxing" weekend. Eventually *we* finished. The story even had a name: appropriately, we titled it "The Snow of Christmas." The topic was a young husband who deserted his lovely wife and young daughter one Christmas.

In creative writing class that next Monday morning, Naomi took fiendish delight in regaling her classmates with the story of the weekend and she handed out copies of my story to everyone. That started a chain of dominoes that are toppling still. I gave out copies to colleagues, friends, and family—

Big mistake! For next Christmas season, people said, "Well, you wrote a Christmas story last year—so what's keeping you from writing one *this* year?"

So I wrote "The Bells of Christmas Eve," ostensibly for my American literature class. Since my students were reading Louisa May Alcott's *Little Women,* I wrote this Christmas romance, set in Switzerland (about a little-known interlude in Alcott's life), as a gift to them. It seems I had been chosen.

THE NEXT STEP

Again and again in life, I've seen it happen: *God never does anything by halves!* And I was about to experience the second half of a plan I knew nothing about. I took my creative writing class on a field trip to Maryland's largest publishing house, Review and Herald Publishing Association, in Hagerstown. Once the guide had my students safely in tow, I escaped. As I wandered around, I chanced to peer into the office doorway of then Acquisitions Editor Penny Estes Wheeler (I figured that with a last name of Wheeler she couldn't be all bad).

We small-talked for some time. Turned out she was already familiar with my writing in magazines and liked what she'd read. After a time she said, "Well, what have you been writing lately?"

Never one to miss an opportunity to share, I explained that I had written a couple of Christmas stories, explaining that they were centered around the true meaning of Christmas, not just around Santa Claus. And then I added that you couldn't read them without crying.

"But you've only written two?" she replied.

"Yes. But I've been collecting others all my life—in fact, I was *raised* on them," was my response.

That's all it took. Being very good at what she did, she leaned back and said, in just as deceptively casual a tone as Naomi had used a couple of years before, "You know, there's a real vacuum for that kind of story in the market today. Why don't you just package up your favorite stories and send them to us? We'll do the rest. Piece of cake."

Although it sounded so easy, I suspected I had a lot of work to do. Penny bulldogged me by mail and by phone until I assembled a big stack of Christmas stories and sent them to Hagerstown; happy to be done with my part, I all but forgot about it.

Several months later, I was jolted back to reality with a phone call. She said, "Joe, the committee has cried its way through your manuscript. We'd very much like to publish it."

From there on, events moved quickly—but no thanks to me. From the title of the book to the cover, which appropriately was created from one of the oldest type of illustrations known to man, the woodcut, to the interior, my good editor pushed the book through.

The finished book was beautiful. People loved its design, the Currier & Ives winter scenes that graced the covers and all; however, they loved the deeply moving stories even more. The collection was called *Christmas in My Heart,* and no thought went to doing more than one.

But gradually sales began to build. People realized that the collection was different from anything else available. When it went through two printings before Christmas, my editor got me on the phone and said, "Joe, can you put together another collection right away so we can rush it into print before next Christmas?" "Sure, no problem," I answered.

So it came to pass that our second collection bravely bore a "2" on its cover. It would not be a one-shot book after all; it would be a two-book series.

Right after *Christmas in My Heart* came out in 2002, I become convinced that I had to send a copy to Dr. James Dobson of the Focus on the Family ministry! I knew him to be a sentimentalist about tear-jerky stories, too. I inscribed a copy to Dobson and sent it off. He didn't respond, but one of his vice presidents did—she loved it! When Number 2 came out, I sent him another. Dobson didn't respond, but the same vice president did.

Late in '93, I came to my personal Rubicon—on the phone was my remorseless editor: "Joe, Number Two is selling so well, we're wondering if it's possible for you to put together a third collection of Christmas stories?"

The ball was now in my court. I was out of stories as well as illustrations for the covers. If the series was to go to three, I would have to seriously dig in and find the stories that would grace it. Fortunately, by now readers had begun sending me their favorite stories, their way of letting me know they wanted another collection. So I was able to put together a third collection. As for the illustrations, I began buying old books illustrated with woodcuts (most of these books were at least a hundred years old).

So it was that I belatedly moved from a passive role to an active one. For the first time I began to realize that I was part of something big. That it was big enough to commandeer the rest of my and Connie's lives: although, mercifully the full impact of that realization was withheld from us.

In the fall of '94, *Christmas in My Heart 3* came out, and I once again sent a copy to Dr. Dobson. In my naiveté I assumed that all you had to do was address a book to Dobson, mail it off, and he'd get it and read it. The reality is Focus had thirteen hundred employees; that over eighty Christian publishers barraged the ministry with their books. And that it took almost six hundred employees to answer mail and phone calls from people like me. The chances of getting through to the great man himself were almost nil. Yet, in spite of those facts, now came the third life-changing day. The telephone rang and a voice I'd never heard before was on the line. The voice turned out to be my correspondence friend at Focus on the Family, Diane Passno.

My relationship with the Focus on the Family ministry began when they asked to use one of my stories called "The Tiny Foot" by Frederic Lommis. They called again later and asked if the story could also be used on the air. Again I agreed.

But I still had no idea of what those two requests would *really* mean for me. I did remember that Diane Passno had warned me, "Joe, if Dr. Dobson ever really uses you, your life will never be the same again."

Truer words were never spoken. By the time that story had gone out to about three million homes and it had been read on the air around the world, life as I had known it was over. The series was a Gold Medallion finalist the next year and, before I long, it was 2006 and I was working on Book 16! Then through the concerted efforts of my agent and good friend, Greg Johnson, enough contracts were signed to allow my wife and me to leave the classroom and work on our books full time.

THE LEGACY CONTINUES

I am deeply humbled that God would go to so much trouble to get me on board. I have daily prayed for direction for my book anthologizing, and for God to gift me with the plots and characters of the Christmas stories that bear my name. When asked how I choose the stories for each edition, I answer that it's all a matter of the heart. Hundreds of stories are passed over for every one that makes it in. I feel strongly that life is too short for me to waste time on stories or books that fail to move me deeply or take me to places I've never been before. Most meet what black-belted Christmas story collectors have come to call The Kleenex Test—they ask, "Is this a five-Kleenex story, a four-, or a three-?" They know that, no matter how well the story may be written, no matter how famous an author may be, the single deciding factor will be the power of the story alone. Thus, if two stories are on my desk at the same time, one by Pearl Buck and one by a housewife and mother who has never shared a story outside her immediate family before, neither will have the edge: the story's emotional wallop alone will tip the balance.

And this is why I believe this new hardcover series—so lovingly and beautifully crafted— will be so eagerly recieved. The stories are like those my mother told to me—they touch the heart. If this is the first *Christmas in My Heart* book you've ever picked up, I'm confident it will be anything but the last. If you're already familiar with the series—*welcome home!*

A FEW BARS IN THE KEY OF G

CLIFTON CARLISLE OSBORNE

Just what was it about that strange postal card that made it so magical? That opened so many doors?

O f all the Christmas stories ever written, this one is unique in one respect: No one who has ever read it once will find it possible to forget. It reads like a Whodunit page-turner: once started, it is virtually impossible to stop before the end.

The story behind the story is almost as gripping as the story itself, for its origins appeared to be unknown. When the story first came to me in my childhood, it was hearing my elocutionist mother reciting it by memory. But she had no idea who had written it. Almost half a century later, when I first anthologized the story in *Christmas in My Heart 1*, I still had no idea who the author was. But soon, readers were mailing in other texts that revealed that my text was incomplete. By the time the story was featured in Doubleday's *Second Treasury of Christmas in My Heart* in 1996, I was able to piece together an expanded text (one I assumed was now complete), as well as finally identify the author as Clifton Carlisle Osborne. But the story was not over even yet! In December of 2005, another faithful reader of our series, George Radcliffe of Webster, NH, sent me the equivalent (to me, at least) of the Holy Grail: the complete original text of the story written by this British author (hadn't known that!), copyrighted first in Great Britain in 1902, and who received a prize of $2,160 [about $50,000 in today's money] by the publisher of *Black Cat Magazine*, who featured it as the lead story in their October issue of 1904. So here it is, "A Few Bars in the Key of G," the *complete* story, for the first time in 103 years!

Enjoy!

It was two o'clock, and time for the third watch on the night herd. These two facts gradually impressed themselves on the consciousness of John Talbot Waring, as he was thumped into wakefulness by the Mexican house wrangler.

Disentangling himself from his damp blankets, he sat up and groped for his boots; meanwhile viewing with that strange satisfaction which misery finds in companionship, the rough pounding process which was being repeated upon the mummy-like figure by his side.

The dim light of the smoky lantern swinging from the ridge-pole of the dripping tent revealed the rolled-up forms of a dozen audibly slumbering cowpunchers, crowded together like sardines in a box; it also made visible an expression of disgust on the features of Mr. Waring, while failing completely to disclose the whereabouts of his missing boots. The sense of touch, however, presently located them lying in a little puddle near the tent flap, and their owner was immediately engrossed in the backbreaking task of forcing his swollen feet into the sodden leather.

"Seems to me, Jack, you ought to know enough to take your boots to bed with you," remarked his neighbor, "Slim" Caywood, as he complacently produced his own high-heeled pair from their dry nest. "That mornin' last week up on the Pass, when you had to do a war dance in the snow while they was thawin' out, don't seem to have learned you nothin'."

Waring paused in his struggle long enough to express, in a few well-chosen words, his opinions of boots in general, and his own wet ones in particular. This relief to his feelings seemed to endow him with renewed strength, for, after a few more violent contortions, he accomplished his purpose, and unrolling his slicker, which had been serving temporarily as a pillow, enveloped himself in its clammy folds, and followed his tall fellow-victim of stern duty out into the drizzling rain.

There was a moon above the heavy clouds, but it might as well have been on the other side of the earth for all the assistance it gave in the operation of saddling two of the picketed horses. The herd lay to the north of the camp, and settling reluctantly into their soggy seats, the drowsy riders turned their horses in that direction, trusting to the instinct of the animals to find the cattle. The darkness was intense, and the wiry little beasts were obliged to pick their way cautiously over the rough ground lying between the camp and the spot where the herd had been bedded down for the night.

Presently the sound of a hoarse voice tunefully raised in a dismal minor melody came faintly to their ears, and as they neared the singer, they became aware that he was entreating the public to "take him to the graveyard, and place a sod o'er him," varying the monotony of this request by begging someone to "bury him not on the lone prairie." The effect of this mournful music was indescribably gruesome, and Waring found himself wondering with considerable impatience why cowpunchers invariably chose such gloomy themes for their songs, and then set them to the most funereal tunes imaginable.

Approaching carefully to avoid startling the cattle, the two riders separated, and relieving the tired watchers, commenced their dreary three hours' vigil, on opposite sides of the herd. The cattle were unusually quiet, needing little attention, and Waring had ample opportunity to reflect on the disadvantages of a cowpuncher's life, as he rode slowly along the edge of the black mass of sleeping animals. The rain dripped from the limp brim of his sombrero, and ran in little streams from the skirts of his oil-skin coat into his already soaking boots. The chill wind, sweeping down from the mountains, pierced his damp clothes, and made him shiver in the saddle. For the hundredth time within a week, Waring condemned himself as an unutterable ass for relinquishing the comforts of civilization for this hard life among the rough and dangerous slopes of Colorado.

He recalled his arrival on the range six months before, a tenderfoot, and the various tribulations he had endured incident to his transformation into a full-fledged cowpuncher. He remembered with a smile, the painful surprise occasioned by his first introduction to a pitching horse. Of the hardships and dangers which come to every rider of the range, he had experienced his share, and faced them bravely, thereby winning the respect of the rough, lionhearted men among whom he had cast his lot.

But all the weary months had been wasted: he had failed in his object; he could not forget. He was not the first to learn that one cannot escape memory by merely crossing the continent. It even seemed to him that, instead of growing more endurable with time, the soreness in his heart and the sting of regret increased with every passing day. He wondered if *she* felt the separation; if *she* cared. As his thoughts wandered back over the past two years, he recalled every incident of their acquaintance as distinctly as though they occurred but yesterday. The day he had first seen her, as she stepped gracefully out beside the piano to sing, at a musical he had attended; the song she had sung—

> *"The hours I spent with thee, dear heart,*
> *Are as a string of pearls to me";*

the sweet days which followed—their enjoyment together of symphony, oratorio, and opera. For both being amateurs of no mean ability, they had met (and loved) upon the common ground of their love of divine harmony.

He looked into the blackness of the night, and could see her as she appeared on that wonderful day when he had met her at the altar of Trinity Church, and spoken the words that were to bind them together through life. How beautiful she was, and how proud he had been of her as they walked down the broad aisle and out into the brilliant June sunshine, followed by the grand chords of Mendelssohn's masterpiece. He looked back at their wedding trip as a beautiful dream. The noble mountains of New Hampshire seemed to have been created as a setting for their happiness; the great hotels only to cater to their pleasure. How well he remembered the return to the lovely home he had prepared for her, and the first dear days within its walls. How happy they had been, and how he had loved her! *Had* loved her? He *did* love her. That was his sorrow. He realized now that as long as he had life, his whole heart would be hers alone.

And then the shadow had come over their home. He asked himself bitterly why he had not been more patient with her, and made allowance for her high spirits and quick temper. She was such a child. He could see now that he had been to blame many times in their quarrels, when at the time he had sincerely believed himself in the right. Should he go back to her, and admit that he was in the wrong? Never! The memory of that last day was too clear in his mind. The words she had spoken in the heat of her anger had burned themselves into his soul, and could not be forgotten. Waring straightened in the saddle, and the hot blood rushed to his face. He wondered now that he had been able to answer her so calmly. He recalled every word he had said:

"Your words convince me that we cannot live together any longer. I will neither forgive nor forget them. I am going away. You are at liberty to sue for a divorce, if you care to do so. Three years, I believe, is the time required to substantiate a plea of desertion." That was all. Without a word he had left her, standing white and motionless in the center of her dainty chamber, and gone from the beautiful home in white-hot rage, to come out here to the wildest spot he could find in the vain effort to forget.

He pulled down the dripping brim of his sombrero to shelter his face from the stinging wind, and resolutely turned his thoughts in other directions. He speculated vaguely on the condition of his considerable property, and wondered indifferently how his agents were managing it. His friends at the clubs—did they miss him? From them his thoughts strayed to the strange postal card he had received the day previous, and he began to puzzle his brain in the effort to decide who had sent it, and what it could mean. It had been directed in care of his attorney, and forwarded by the lawyer to the remote mountain post office where Waring received his mail. It was an ordinary postal card, its peculiarity consisting in the fact that the communication on the back was composed, not in words, but music—four measures in the key of G.

He had hummed the notes over and over, and though they had a strangely familiar sound, yet he could not place the fragment, nor even determine the composer. His failure to decipher the enigma annoyed him. It had a meaning, of that he was convinced, but what could it be? Who could have sent it? Among his friends were many musicians, any one of them might have adopted such a method of communication with him. He began to hum the phrase, as he rode round and round the cattle.

The wind was dying out, and the rain had ceased. On the eastern mountaintops a faint rose tint was dimly visible; another hour of monotonous watching, and then for a hot breakfast beside the campfire. Waring, abandoning the riddle of the postal, began to sing to pass the time, and his rich baritone rang out above the sleeping herd. The light stole slowly over the peaks, and chased the shadows from the plain. The camp awoke, and the men crawled shivering from the tent. The cook's fire whirled showers of sparks aloft. One by one the cattle stirred, rose, and commenced to graze. Waring still sang, carelessly passing from snatches of opera to lines of sacred harmony.

Suddenly, while in the midst of a passage from one of the great works of a master composer, he stopped short in surprise: *He was singing the notes on the card!* It had come to him like a flash. He tore his coat open and drew the postal from the inner pocket. There was no mistake. He had solved the mystery. Almost mechanically he reached for a pencil and wrote the words under the lines of music, added a signature, and gazed long and earnestly, his face a perfect kaleidoscope of changing expressions; then, with a wild shout, he wheeled his horse and rode furiously to the camp.

Pulling up with a jerk that almost lifted the iron-jawed bronco from the ground, he literally hurled himself from the saddle, and reached the Boss in two bounds.

"I must be in Denver tonight! I want your best horse quick!"

The Boss stared at him in astonishment.

"Why, man, it's a hundred and twenty miles. You're crazy!"

Waring fairly stamped with impatience. "It's only sixty to Empire," he cried, "and I can get the train there. It leaves at one o'clock, and I can make it, if you will lend me Star! I know he's your pet horse, and you never let anyone else ride him, but I tell you, Mr. Coberly, this means everything to me. I simply *must* get there."

Coberly scowled.

"You ought 'o know, Jack, that I won't loan Star; so what's the use o' askin'? None o' the other horses can get over there in that time, so you might 's well give it up. What in thunder's the matter with you that you're in such a confounded rush?"

Waring thought a moment, and then, drawing the Boss beyond earshot of the listening cowpunchers, spoke to him rapidly and earnestly, finally handing him the postal card. Coberly scanned it intently, and a change came over his face. When he looked up, it was with an expression of respect mingled with amazement, as he said:

"Why didn't you show me this first? Of course you can have the horse. Hi, there! Some o' you boys round up the horses an' rope Star for Mr. Waring. Jump lively!"

The men made a mad rush for their saddles and, in an incredibly short time, several of them were racing across the plain in the direction of the horses. Waring dove into the tent and began gathering his few possessions. Coberly plunged around outside, giving orders at the top of his voice.

"Roll up some grub for Mr. Waring, quick! Nick, you get his canteen an' fill it out o' my jug. Fly around now!"

A rush of hoofs announced the arrival of the horse and his escort, just as Waring emerged from the tent with his little bundle. A dozen hands made quick work of saddling, and with a hurried goodbye all around, he swung himself up and astride the magnificent animal, and was off on his long ride. He looked back and saw the boys in a group around the Boss, who was explaining the cause of his hasty departure. Presently a tremendous yell reached his ears, and he saw hats excitedly thrown in the air. He waved his hand in reply, and settled down in the saddle.

The long, pacing stride of Coberly's pet covered the ground in a surprising manner, and eight o'clock found twenty three miles behind his nimble feet, and the Bar Triangle

Ranch in sight. A five-minute stop, and then on across the gently rising country to the stage station at the foot of the great Continental Divide, fifteen miles away. It lacked twenty minutes of ten o'clock when Waring drew rein in the shadow of the giant peaks that towered above him. He unsaddled and turned the big thoroughbred into the corral. A half hour's rest would put new life into him. Twenty-two miles to the railroad, and nearly three hours in which to cover it. It seemed possible; but the great range must be crossed, and Waring knew that the ten miles of steep climbing to the snowy summit of Berthoud Pass meant more than twice that distance on the flat plain.

At quarter past ten, Star, refreshed by an energetic rubbing and a mouthful of water, was carrying him up the road, with no apparent diminution of power. Up, up they went, mile after mile, until the plain they had left was spreading out like a map behind him, and the thick forest had given place to a scattering and scrubby growth of pines. They were nearing timberline, and the piercing chill of the biting wind testified to the proximity of the snow-covered peaks. Two miles from the top Waring dismounted, and led his panting horse along the icy trail. The rarified air seemed to burn his lungs as he struggled up the remaining distance to the summit of the Pass, eleven thousand feet above the sea.

Twelve o'clock! He stopped, and anxiously examined the noble beast that had carried him so far and so well. The inspection reassured him. There was plenty of life and energy left in Star yet. Not without reason was he acknowledged the best horse in the county. One hour, and twelve miles to go, the first seven down the steepest road in the state. Could he make it? He *must*! A final pull at the cinches, and Waring was again in the saddle, racing down the dangerous path towards the sea of dark green forest that stretched far below.

Down sharp pitches and long slopes, around dizzy curves and through deep canyons, slipping, swaying, followed by masses of loose stones and gravel, they went, faster than ever than that trail was covered before. The iron-shod hoofs struck fire from the flinty rocks, as, almost sitting on his haunches, Star would slide twenty feet at a time down an unusually steep grade, recovering his footing with a staggering effort at the bottom. It was perilous work. They reached the timberline, passed below it, and plunged into the woods. A mile beyond, they flew past the stage at a mad pace, throwing a shower of mud over the astonished passengers.

Down at last to the level road they came, with five miles still to go. Star swung into a strong, easy lope, and his rider drew a long breath. Not till then had he realized the strain of that wild ride. Rounding a turn in the road, he espied a horseman approaching, and turned out to pass him. The stranger eyed him sharply as he drew near; and suddenly slipped out a six-shooter!

"Hold up there! I want to talk to you!"

For a moment Waring considered the chance of riding over the man, but for a moment only. The stranger looked too determined, and his aim was sure. He pulled up, raging.

"I suppose you want my money," he snarled. "Well, you're welcome to it if you'll leave me enough to pay my fare to Denver."

The other grinned.

"That's a good bluff, but it won't do. I'm the sheriff, an' what I want to know is where you're going with Joe Coberly's horse?"

"Oh, is that all you want?" said Waring, relieved. "Why, I've been working for Coberly, and he lent me the horse to ride over to catch the train." And he gathered up his reins to ride on.

"Hold on, young man!" and the sheriff raised his gun suggestively, "that yarn won't do. I know old Joe, an' I happen to know that he wouldn't lend that horse to his own brother, let alone one of his cowpunchers. I guess I'll have to lock you up till the boys come over after you."

Waring groaned.

"Look here, Mr. Sheriff, I'm telling you God's truth. Coberly let me take the horse because it was the only one that could get me over here in time to catch the train, and I had to be in Denver tonight, without fail."

His captor shook his head:

"It's no use, my friend; your story won't hold water. Why're you in such a tearin' hurry anyway?"

Waring remembered the postal card; he reached into his breast pocket and produced it. "That is my reason for haste," he said, " and that is why Coberly let me take the horse," and he added a few words of explanation.

Keeping his captive covered with the muzzle of the revolver he carried, the officer rode closer and took the card. As he read it, his face lighted up, and he lowered his gun.

"That's all right, youngster. I'm sorry I stopped you. I don't wonder Joe lent you the horse; I'd 've done the same, even if I'd had to walk myself. I hope you won't miss the train. I'll ride down to the station with you, as some of the boys might want to string you up on account o' the horse—everybody knows him."

Overjoyed at this satisfactory turn of affairs, Waring touched Star with his spur and rode forward, with the repentant sheriff by his side, their horses in a rapid gallop. Mounting a rise, they saw the town before them, a mile distant. *The train was at the station!* Another touch of the spur, and Star stretched out into a run that gradually left the sheriff behind, well mounted though he was. A half mile yet to go! —A quarter!—The black smoke began to come in heavy puffs from the funnel of the engine, and the line of cars moved slowly away from the station. Then it was that Star showed the spirit that was in him. The quirt fell sharply on his flank for the first time that day, and he bounded forward and swept down upon the town like a whirlwind.

As the usual crowd of train-time loafers lounged around the corner of the station, their attention was attracted by the two swiftly approaching riders, and they paused to watch the race. Presently one cried:

"Hullo, that first horse is Coberly's black, an' he's sure movin' too. The other chap ain't in it. Why, it's the sheriff! An' he's after the other feller. Horse thief, by thunder! I'll fix him," and he reached for his hip.

The others took up the cry of "Horse Thief!" and as Waring flashed past the building at Star's top speed, a volley of shots greeted him, and the bullets sang around his head. Fortunately, the bullets went wild, and before any more could be fired, the sheriff tore into the crowd and roared:

"Stop shootin', you fools. The man's all right; he's only tryin' to catch the train!" At this there was a laugh, and then a rush to the track, where an unobstructed view of the race could be obtained.

The road ran for a mile beside the rails, as level as a floor. The train was gathering speed with every revolution of the wheels, but Star was traveling too, and gaining at every jump. The crowd at the station danced and howled in their excitement.

"Will he make it?"

"He's gainin'!"

"Look at that horse go!"

"Gee, he's movin'!"

"Hooray for the black!"

"He'll make it!!"

" He'll make it!!!"

Waring, with eyes fixed and jaw set, was riding desperately.

Thirty feet!—The spectators in the doorway of the last car gazed breathlessly. Twenty feet—and Star straining every nerve and muscle of his body. Ten feet—and still he gained. Only five feet now! Inch by inch, he crawled up. He was abreast of the platform!! Swerving his flying horse closer to the track, Waring leaned over, and grasping the railings with both hands, lifted himself from the saddle, kicked his feet from the stirrups, and swung himself over to the step of the car. The faint sound of a cheer reached him from the distant depot.

After calmly accepting the enthusiastic congratulations of the passengers who had witnessed his dramatic boarding of the train, Waring dropped into a seat with a sigh of relief, and was soon lost in thought. He was roused from his revery by a touch on the arm, and turned to find the conductor standing beside him. The sight of that official reminded him of the necessity of paying his fare, and he reached into his pocket for the required cash. His fingers encountered nothing more valuable than a knife and some matches. The other pockets were equally unproductive. Then he remembered, with a shock, that he had put his money in the little bundle, at that moment firmly attached to his saddle, some miles to the rear.

It was maddening. There was nothing to do but throw himself on the mercy of the man in the blue uniform. That person heard his excuses with an impassive face, and merely announced that he would have to get off at the next station. This was not at all in accordance with Waring's plans, and he endeavored to impress upon the conductor the importance of his being in Denver that evening. He might as well have addressed the Sphinx, so far as any effect his words had on the official, who said in answer to his entreaties:

"I'd lose my job if I let you ride free. You'll have to get off. It's only ten miles back to Empire, and if you left your money on your saddle, you can soon get it again, that is, if no one has swiped it before you get there."

Waring grew desperate. Was his ride after all to be fruitless? He remembered his reason for haste, and decided to take the conductor into his confidence. Leaning over, he whispered something quickly into his ear, and ended by showing him the postal card. At first the man looked incredulous, but a glance at Waring's earnest face reassured him. His expression softened, and he handed back the card with a sigh.

"I reckon I'll have to fix it for you, but the only way I can do it is to pay your fare out of my own pocket. I'll do that, and you can send me the money. It's three-sixty."

He took a slip from his pocket, upon which he wrote his name and address. This he gave to Waring, together with a cash receipt ticket, and, unheeding the latter's impulsive thanks, continued on his round of collection.

This occurrence reminded Waring of similar difficulties to be overcome in Denver, and he did some hard, rapid thinking as he was being whirled down through Clear Creek Canyon, but by the time the train shot past Table Mountain and out to the plain, his face bore a confident smile. The postal card had served him well thus far; perhaps its mission was not yet ended.

The car wheels were still turning when he strode through the big station, his heavy spurs ringing on the marble floor. Jumping into a carriage, he was driven to the nearest drugstore, where he consulted a directory.

"Number nine hundred South Seventeenth Street," he cried, as he reentered the vehicle. Arriving at his destination, he sprang out and, saying "Wait," ran up the steps of a palatial residence.

To the dignified butler who opened the door, he said, "I wish to see Mr. Foster. My name is Waring. I haven't a card with me."

Instinctively perceiving the gentleman beneath the rough flannel shirt and mud-covered chaps, the servant politely ushered him into the reception room, saying that he would see if Mr. Foster was in. Apparently he was, for he appeared almost immediately, the personification of keen-eyed, well-groomed finance.

"What can I do for you, Mr.—er—Waring?"

That young man took in every detail of his appearance, and he realized that he had a hard-headed man of business to deal with.

"Mr. Foster," he said, " you are the president of the Denver National Bank, which, I believe, handles the western interests of the Second National Bank of Boston?"

The other bowed, and Waring continued:

"I have an account at the Second, and I want you to cash a check for me. It is after banking hours, I know; and even if it were not, I have no immediate means of identification."

The banker's features stiffened perceptibly, but Waring went on: "It is of the greatest importance that I take the eastern express tonight, or I would not come to you in this irregular way—"

"One moment, Mr. Waring. Pardon me for interrupting you, but it will save your time as well as my own if I say that what you ask is impossible, as you should know. My advice to you is to wire your bank for the money."

Waring broke in impatiently:

"Of course I know I can do that, but it means a day's delay, and that is what I want to avoid. See here, Mr. Foster, I am willing to pay any amount within reason for the accommodation if you will oblige me."

The president began to look suspicious.

"It must be a very urgent matter that requires such haste," he said sarcastically. "Really, Mr. Waring, I must positively decline to do anything for you."

"It *is* an urgent matter," cried Waring. "I was about to explain it to you," and he went on and told of the postal card and its purport, adding a brief account of his efforts to get to the city in time to take the train that night.

"Let me see the card," said the banker. His voice had taken on a different inflection. Waring handed him the bit of pasteboard that had played such an important part in his adventures. Mr. Foster scrutinized it.

"From what is it taken, did you say?"

Upon hearing the answer, he left the room to return in a few minutes with a rather bulky musical score, which he laid upon the table, and turned the pages until he found what he sought. Carefully he compared the music on the card with that on the printed sheet. Then, turning to the younger man, he said in a kindly voice: "I will assist you, Mr. Waring. It will, of course, be a purely personal accommodation, as it is contrary to all my business methods, but I cannot resist such an appeal as this. Also, I consider myself a good judge of faces, and I feel safe in trusting yours. What amount do you require?"

Waring fairly beamed with joy. "A hundred dollars will be sufficient," he replied.

The banker motioned towards a desk. "Make your check out for a hundred and fifty. You will need that much, unless you care to travel in your present costume."

Waring made out the proper form, and handed it to the banker. The latter dropped into the vacated chair before the desk, and rapidly wrote a check for a like amount, which he passed over, saying: "You can cash this at the Brown Palace Hotel. I will phone the cashier, so you will have no trouble."

Waring tried to thank him, but he would not listen. "You are perfectly welcome, my boy. I am glad to be able to help you. I envy you, with all my heart. I would give half of all I own to be in your position," and his voice trembled a little. "You have my best wishes for a pleasant journey. Good-bye." A cordial hand grasp, and Waring ran down the steps with a light heart, his way at last clear before him.

"Telegraph office!" he shouted.

Ten minutes later, these words were speeding over the wire: "Postal received. Arrive Boston Friday night. See Luke 1:13—Jack."

When the Chicago Limited pulled out of Denver that evening, John Talbot Waring, clean-shaven, and attired in garments of the most approved cut, was standing on the rear platform of the last Pullman, softly humming a passage from the great oratorio, *The Messiah.* There was a tender light in his eyes as he gazed at the postal card he held in his hand.

And the words he sang were:

>*For unto us a child is born;*
>
>*Unto us a son is given.*

At the same moment, two thousand miles away in the East, a pale young wife was holding a telegram close to her lips. An open Bible lay on the bed beside her. Turning softly among her pillows, she glanced lovingly at the dainty cradle, and whispered:

"Thou shalt call his name John."

SEA ANCHOR

MARJORIE YOURD HILL

Coco was tired of following rules. And now to be stuck on a boring island all Christmas vacation with the family, well that was just too much!

She determined to escape.

If Father came at all, Coco was afraid, it would only be from a sense of duty. And that was hardly the spirit to start a winter holiday. You ought to feel enthusiastic, as the kids did. Coco watched the giggling capers of Janie and Tom—her sister, eleven, and brother, nine—and wished she could share their high spirits.

They were prancing around the wharf in constant danger of slipping into the icy sea, so excited about this winter visit to the island summer home (which they had not seen since before the war) that they had gone insane. The fact that Christmas was only four days away made them even crazier.

Mother had given up trying to calm them. She was sitting quietly inside the boat company's heated office, a gloved finger *tap-tap-tapping* on the arm of her chair, and her lovely gray eyes seeking the island road again and again. The boat was due to leave for Spruce Island in half an hour and Father was not here yet.

The three-man crew was loading mail and supplies for Spruce Village, with the help of Coco's fifteen-year-old brother, Peter. The northeast wind lashed the bay into steely waves. It was wild weather to be going out to the island. Greg, a year older than Coco, and a freshman at Harvard, pulled his coat collar up as he paced the wharf uneasily.

He stopped beside Coco now and said, "Looks as if quite a storm is blowing up. We might have such a bad spell that the boat would stop running, and I couldn't get back for the New Year's Eve party with Doug and the gang."

"I know." Coco nodded, thinking of her own secret plan. "I don't see why we couldn't have had this family reunion at some more accessible place."

She shivered and turned back into the grateful warmth of the office. Her mother flashed a nervous smile, and Coco felt a twinge of pity. Mother was always waiting. Maybe Father was never sure about the time and place because he was an artist. Maybe that's why their whole family life was odd.

Coco remembered family discussions last spring. They had been living at Grandmother Lawson's then, all except Greg and Peter, who were in prep school. In anticipation of Father's return to civilian life from the Army, Mother had achieved the miraculous: the promise of an apartment in New York City. Father, of course, would get back his old position with the McDuffy and Neal advertising agency.

Mother had not understood at first what Father meant when he said, "No," not "Of course."

"All right," she agreed reasonably, "there's Carmichael and Stratford. They're a bigger firm, anyway. Uncle Ned has connections there. He can get you in."

Father shook his head, his eyes tired. "That's just as bad. I mean I'd like to be through with all that for good."

"You mean give up your art work completely?" Mother cried, and everybody at the table stared.

Father explained, "No, but I'd like to retrieve what I gave up years ago. I'm not sure that I can do it, but I want to take time out to give it a try."

Coco remembered vaguely that long ago Father had had a studio as a struggling young artist, but with five children to feed, clothe, and educate, he had been persuaded to accept the financial security of a job as art director of McDuffy and Neal. Now, it seemed, he regretted having given up his portrait painting and wanted to return to it again.

So the family plans were rearranged. Father set out alone for Taos to paint; Greg and Peter got jobs on a farm for the summer; Mother found an opportunity to act as housemother and counselor at a school which ran a summer camp, just the thing for her and the younger two. And Coco was disposed of simply by staying on at Grandmother's. Everybody seemed to like the arrangements except Coco, who considered herself stuck in a deadly hole, and her life at a standstill.

Until she met Fizz Bates, that is. Fizz was in Mericassett visiting his married sister in his old home town. Grandmother shook her head when Coco first mentioned him, so after that Coco discreetly said little about the rides in his roadster and the drugstore meetings. She kept his wonderful letters secret, too, and her latest scheme for the New Year holiday. She'd bring that up at a propitious moment. If Greg had freedom to go and come as he pleased, she could, too. If everyone in the family was going his own way and leading his own life, she would, too. This idea of a family reunion in midwinter, on an island inhabited only by a score or so of fishing families, was preposterous.

Mother had insisted on it, though. Not Grandmother's horrified exhortations, nor the wagging of Mericassett tongues had stopped her. Only Father's refusal to come could have caused the plan to fall through. Mother had explained herself at Grandmother's only yesterday when she brought Janie and Tom down from boarding school.

Coco was stacking the luncheon dishes in the kitchen, but when she caught a queer note in Mother's voice she stopped scraping and piling.

Mother said with a little catch in her breath, "But, Mother, you don't understand! This family just has to be together again in our own home before it's too late. We've lived around so much with other people during the war and after, and been so separated, that I think—well, if we don't get together in a place of our own soon—" The rest of the sentence sounded as if stopped by a sob.

Coco silently slid a Haviland cup off its saucer and meticulously dumped out a few tea leaves. Her own throat felt tight, but she told herself it was already too late. Weren't they all set on lives of their own choosing—both she and Greg, as well as Father?

But she couldn't help wondering now, if it had been fear of just that which had made Mother so worried.

The captain barged in, scowling at a sheaf of papers.

"You the lady ordered the Franklin stove from Searles for your house out to the island?"

Mother nodded.

"It ain't here. Checked over everything settin' on the pier."

Coco's eyes widened at this complication. They needed the stove to supplement the fireplace and kitchen range. Otherwise the house would be uninhabitable.

"Oh, dear!" Mother murmured helplessly. "What shall I do?"

"Whyn't you just cancel the order? It's too late now to do you any good. Bert Mahoney said, when it weren't on the load Monday, he'd haul up his grandma's old stove—been settin' in his shed nineteen years—and warm your place up with it. He's had fires goin' two days now, and the house is snug. That old place o' Captain Wilcox' always did heat well."

Mother relaxed, and Coco took a deep breath. So the friendly Spruce Villagers were looking after them, as they had in former summers!

Suddenly the children began to scream. "He's here! He's come! Hi, Daddy, hi! Here we are!"

Father scrambled out of a taxi and braced himself for the onslaught of Janie and Tom, who hung on him so that he had to kiss Mother over their heads. He stretched out a hand to Coco and the older boys.

"Hi, everybody," he grinned. "My train was held up by snowstorms farther west, but here we are, all together at last."

The captain touched his visor. "It's a good thing you're makin' this sailin', because from the look of things we mayn't be makin' another trip for a while — maybe a week or ten days."

Coco and Greg exchanged uneasy looks. *That would ruin their plans.*

One thing stood out in Coco's mind in all the kaleidoscopic events of that homecoming day, and that was the moment she stood with her parents on the porch while Father fumbled with the keys. Janie and Tom were racing around the yard, exploring, while Greg and Peter lugged suitcases up the winding stone walk that led from the road.

"Seven years," Father said half under his breath, "I've carried this key all over the earth, and there were times I thought I'd never use it again. But thank God, Viv, I'm back here again at last. Are you glad, too?"

Coco had to turn away from the shining soft look on Mother's face. But she couldn't help hearing, though she pretended to be absorbed solely in Peter's struggle with three suitcases.

"Of course. It's going to be the answer to everything, Russ."

"It's your spirit that keeps me going, Viv, standing out against your critical family and the whole doubting world. It's all I've got to count on, really."

"Except yourself," Mother said firmly. "Here in this lovely spot, where we've all had such fun together, I know things will work out, Russ."

Arm in arm, Mother and Father stepped inside. Peter hurled the three suitcases on the porch and went back for the last. Janie and Tom pounded on them, squealing, and dragged them through the door. Coco stood alone on the porch, blinking a mist from her eyes.

It was silly, it was sentimental nonsense, that an old place where you had once spent your summers could do this to you. The house wasn't even very attractive, especially in the bleak, winter late-afternoon light. It needed paint, and a shutter was missing, and the front steps sagged ominously. But there were lights in all the windows, and gay voices inside, and its warm cheer evoked pleasant memories of the happy past.

But the past had vanished, and it was ridiculous to recall the sunset walks hand in hand with Father along the shore, when just to be with him made you feel so secure. It was foolish to tingle at the remembrance of the heavenly smell of the wild raspberry patch in the hot sun, where you all picked and laughed and joked together; or the delicious clambakes on the beach that ended after starlight; or the swims; or the sailboating.

I'm beyond all that, she argued with herself. *I have nothing in common with the rest of the family now. I must make my own life.*

This idea became an obsession which kept her from entering into the holiday preparations. Their stay would be snug, thanks to Bert Mahoney's grandma's stove. Father and the boys cut holes in the ceiling to let heat upstairs to the two bedrooms, one for the girls, and one for their parents.

The three boys pulled mattresses up close to the stove to sleep.

The family made quite a ceremony about cutting their own Christmas tree, and bringing in the Yule log. Mother had the oven always filled with spicy-smelling baking. On

Christmas Day, Coco kept telling herself that she was too old for that sort of thing, but she couldn't help enjoying the homemade presents, sticky candy, and childish decorations of crayoned Santa Clauses. When it was over, she resolved, she would speak about her plans. However, the right moment never seemed to come.

It kept on snowing, and the island took on the look of a Christmas card. The kids went coasting. Even Greg shed his dignity and seemed to enjoy himself, but when the Mahoney boy knocked at the door and shyly asked Coco if she cared to try out his new toboggan with him, she smiled regrets, and watched him plod away.

Let them all enjoy these childish pastimes—though how tall and good-looking that Bill Mahoney had grown since the last summer they had waded in tide pools, looking for starfish together! But let him go. Coco had other plans. When Greg took the boat to the mainland tomorrow, she was going, too. She had already put her best clothes in her suitcase.

Two weeks as a guest at Fizz's married sister's house, when he would be there for his college vacation—that was what she had planned. Surely her parents could not be unreasonable about that. Coco had had a letter from Sybil inviting her to stay there. Once away from home, she could begin to lead her own grown-up life, unhampered by family ideas that she was still a child. Fizz had written glowingly of the New Year's Eve ball at the country club, and other dances.

As Coco sat by the big picture window, dreaming of glamorous days and nights, her father wandered into the room, and stopped abruptly when his eyes fell on her, as if struck by something.

"Stay right where you are, Coco," he said intensely, "till I get my painting gear. That pose reminds me—"

What started as a quick sketch turned into a full painting. At last Father told Coco they'd better stop but he'd like to try it again tomorrow. "I'll call it *Portrait of a Girl Dreaming.*"

Coco told herself that this was the time to speak up and tell him what was on her mind. Tomorrow she wouldn't be here. But she said nothing aloud, except falteringly, "You said the pose reminded you of something, Father. I've been wondering what."

He looked at her for a long time before he spoke, and finally, with a softening light in his eyes he said, "You mother—the first time I painted her just after we were married. It was in Paris, and I was there on a fellowship, and we were terribly poor, but awfully happy, even though her family wasn't too keen about her marriage to a practically penniless artist.

"That picture was my first big success. It won a prize at an exhibition, and a South American millionaire bought it for what at that time was a fabulous sum."

He hesitated, then continued thoughtfully, "It had a quality I've never been able to catch again till now, seeing you. If I can get it down, Coco, I'll know I've not lost my ability. I'd like to make it larger, though, and the sea background more evocative."

"Won't that take a long time?" Coco's voice sounded extremely faint.

"Can't say," Father declared cheerfully. "Two or three weeks maybe." Then, her attitude penetrating his consciousness, he looked at her wonderingly. "You don't mind, Kitten, do you? I won't keep you sitting more than an hour or so a day."

Coco's tongue seemed to stick to the roof of her mouth. She said nothing, and her father picked up his things thinking her silence meant consent. She slipped away with an anguished heart. Father needed her, it was true, but just as a model, nothing more. Would she have to sacrifice her cherished scheme for a painter's whim? She could hardly sit quietly at dinner and listen to Greg talk about his plans for the trip tomorrow.

"The captain says it's calming, and he hopes to put out by nine A.M. Doug wants me to stay with him till classes begin, but I don't know. I may come back after the weekend and finish out the vacation with you."

Greg smiled engagingly, with a little-boy dimple in his cheek. "It's more fun than I expected here, and if I hadn't already promised the gang—"

Mother beamed at him "We'd like you with us, Greg, you know that. But you're the oldest, and branching out now, so if you want to be with your college friends, we'll understand."

Coco suddenly choked on a cinnamon bun. With everyone's attention focused on her, she wondered wildly why she didn't simply stand up and declare that she, too was old enough to branch out.

After Tom and Peter had thumped her on the back, she excused herself and went to her room.

Next morning she was too miserable to go down and say good-bye to Greg, but she heard it all.

Father sounded grave. "I don't like the look of the sea."

"I know, but the captain knows his stuff, and if he sails, I'll go along," declared Greg.

Mr. Mahoney honked, and Greg was off. By and by Coco pulled herself together and went down. Later in the morning she took the usual pose for her father, who worked in silent absorption squinting at his daughter as if she were a stranger.

What was growing on the canvas was strange to Coco. Her pictured self surprised her. *Portrait of a Girl Dreaming* was Coco as her father must see her, fresh and sweetly wistful. It was not the grown-up, sophisticated personality she had been trying to make of herself. *Could she*, Coco wondered gropingly, *have been mistaken about what sort of person she was?*

The other members of the family stopped to admire. Mother stood a long time before it. "It really has something, Russ. It will bring recognition again."

Father paused, brush in air. "It will be a canvas I can show the Institute Committee when they interview me next month for that teaching position."

Coco restrained a desire to bounce up and ask questions. If Father taught somewhere, they could all have a home together. It would mean security, without the sacrifice of Father's ambition.

"It took being here—all together in this old house—to put me in this mood again. I was beginning to be afraid that I'd lost it forever."

Coco's mother's face looked rosy and young, exactly like the portrait, as she laid her hands on her husband's shoulders. "We're all getting back something we feared we'd lost forever. Even the children. Isn't that so, Coco?" Her bright smile enfolded her daughter.

Coco could only smile back, a lump in her throat. *Grownups*, she thought, *talking like that! Why her parents were people struggling and learning, like herself. They weren't the fixed and solid demigods of her childhood, nor the disappointing idols with feet of clay of later years, but just people. Her father, who had been driven by circumstances out of his natural bent, was striving to get back again, without Coco's understanding or helping very much until now.*

At the sound of stomping feet on the porch she looked out. There was Greg back, and Bill Mahoney.

"Captain's not sailing! Seas still too heavy, though it's clearing. I may not even bother to make the trip tomorrow. It's a long way down to Boston just for a party. Think I'll spend New Year's Eve with the crowd here."

Bill stood just inside the door, looking red and eager, his eyes never leaving Coco's face. "We're planning a skating party at our pond, with cider to toast the New Year in around a bonfire. Will you come too, Coco?"

Coco looked at him, and at Greg, and a weight flew off her heart. She caught her breath. "I'd love it!"

Then, unexpectedly, she felt her lips tremble—with happiness, she supposed—and her eyes brimmed. It was silly of her, and she looked quickly out the window to hide her emotion.

The storm clouds were passing, rolling rapidly out to sea on a northwest wind. Half the sky was already blue, and sunlight shone upon the snow-covered island and the pounding sea. For a moment it was even more beautiful than in summer. It was like some of those quick flashes of insight you had sometimes when you thought about life.

You had to be where you could have vision, but you needed an anchor, too. Like this house—it was their sea anchor. It gave them both vision and security. Coco, her heart joyous, turned her eyes from the infinity of waves and sky, in toward the warm firelit room which held her family and friend.

"Hold that expression, Coco!" shouted Father, searching wildly among his tubes for some more white to squeeze on his palette. "That's the look I want. Now if I can only convey the light—"

A GIRL LIKE ME

NANCY N. RUE

Nothing was going right for Marijane in junior high. So where was God in all this? "I'd always been told that God had a purpose for each of us. Mine was obviously to take up space." And it would help a lot if that dweeb Jake Picard would stay away and mind his own business.

Even the nativity play was same ol' same ol'—

Or was it?

MONDAY, DECEMBER 17, 7:00 P.M.
IN OUR LIVING ROOM

O kay, we've got Jeremy picking up the tree—"

"Check!" Jeremy said—and knocked a plate of Christmas cookies off the coffee table.

"Mom planning Christmas dinner—"

"Check," Mom said, dimples going in and out at light speed.

"Sara taking care of decorations—"

Pause.

Jeremy looked hard at her. "Well?" he said.

Sara rolled her eyes but laughed. "Okay, okay—check," she said.

Dad looked back at the list. "Goodies for the shut-ins—that means everybody, whenever you have time to get in the kitchen and whip up a batch of something."

"Jeremy, please do not find time to get in the kitchen and whip up something," Sara said to our little brother. "We don't want these old people breaking their upper plates."

Jeremy stuck his tongue out at our older sister, but he still kept grinning. Nothing daunted the Christmas spirit of a ten-year-old. Now, a thirteen-year-old like me, nah, it didn't daunt mine either. I didn't have any to begin with.

"Mj," Dad said to me, dropping his eyes down the list, "we don't have you down for anything yet. What do you want to do?"

I shrugged. I'd been shrugging so much during the family meeting it was starting to look like a Jane Fonda shoulder exercise.

"You have to do *something*," Jeremy said.

"I do not!"

"Maybe Marijane hasn't thought of anything yet." Mom deepened a dimple at me, but I didn't smile back.

"Anyway," Dad said, "time's a-wasting for me to take each of you shopping for . . ." He shifted his eyes toward my mother and hissed loudly, "a present for You-Know-Who!"

Jeremy practically squirmed off the couch, and my mother grabbed the cookies before they took another dump.

"Dad, thanks," Sara said, "but I can go on my own this year."

Dad sighed. "I know when I've been usurped by a flock of giggling girls who take five hours to do one side of the mall." He looked at me. "You and me, Mj. Tomorrow night. We can do the *whole* mall in two hours."

Again I shrugged, but nobody noticed because Jeremy was launching into a ten-minute whine about how he wanted the first night's Mom-shopping. When the doorbell rang, I dashed for the foyer. Anything to get out of there.

Well, almost anything.

When I opened the door, all I saw were his eyes blinking from behind those over-sized glasses. The rest of his face was covered by the notepad he was holding.

"Collecting for your newspaper subscription," Jake said, and then he looked up. "Oh, it's you!"

"Of course it's me. I live here."

He lowered his pad to reveal the smile that was too big for his face. He sniffed and let it ramble all the way up to his earlobes. "I smell cookies."

"No, you don't," I said. "What do you want?"

"I told you. I'm collecting for your parents' newspaper subscription." He consulted his pad. "That's $6.80 for this month. But I'll gladly accept your science reports from last year as fair trade."

Jake Picard needed my old science reports about as much as Tom Cruise needs piano lessons. He was the smartest kid in the seventh grade. I wasn't the smartest kid in the eighth grade, but I knew enough not to give him an inch. He'd have me standing there at the door for the rest of my natural life.

"I'll get my dad," I said.

"Does he have old science reports?" Jake said.

While an all-out money search was staged—which produced four dollars and seventy-nine cents in change—Jake consumed a half dozen Christmas cookies and told Sara how to solve an algebra problem. I even searched under the couch cushions for money; I wanted him out of there that bad.

"Can you come by tomorrow afternoon?" Mom said. "I'll cash a check and have the money for you then."

"No prob," Jake said. "I won't even tack on a late charge."

I held the front door open for him while he ducked back to the coffee table and scooped up the last cookie. He stopped halfway out. "You going to that Christmas party at Roxanne Pfeiffer's?" he said to me.

I glared at him. "I don't even *know* Roxanne Pfeiffer," I said.

"Yes, you do. She's in our—"

"No, I'm not going."

"Don't beat around the bush, Mj," he said, smiling that obnoxious larger-than-life smile as he breezed out the door. "Just come right out and say what you think."

"Mj, is that the Christmas spirit?" my mother asked.

I just shrugged.

Tuesday, December 18, 8:00 a.m.
Aboard Bus #318-A

I haven't always been like this about Christmas, I thought as I looked out the bus window. I used to be as squirrelly as Jeremy when it came to dragging out the Christmas albums the day after Thanksgiving. But what was there to be excited about, even at Christmas, when you had this slowly-creeping-up feeling that you're destined to be a nobody?

Everybody had told me junior high was going to be a blast, and I'd spent all of seventh grade waiting for it to happen. I glanced around the bus. It seemed to have happened for everybody but me.

Chelsey Bennett in the front seat had made eighth-grade cheerleader. I had zits and no hips. I hadn't even tried out.

Mike Bach in the backseat was already student council sergeant at arms. I hadn't run for office. For Pete's sake, nobody knew me. At the end of seventh grade, exactly twelve people had signed my yearbook.

Across the aisle, Bonnie Sullivan was writing a note—to Blair Anthony, for sure. A lot of girls were getting into the boy thing. I was so nervous talking to boys my tongue turned into a Popsicle.

My eye caught on Jake, up front jacking his jaws to the bus driver. Even he had it all over me in one respect. The little dweeb made straight A's. I had to do twice as much homework as I had in elementary school, and I was doing "nice, average work."

I'd always been taught that God had a purpose for each of us. Mine was obviously to take up space.

I looked back out the window, in time to see some men setting up for the live creche at the Center Street Church. I used to get so excited about seeing the live animals and watching people from the community act out the nativity scene every night for the week before Christmas. This year I couldn't have cared any less if I'd been in a coma.

Tuesday, December 18, 1:30 p.m.
In the Junior High Auditorium

"All right, I want Christmas Past over here, Christmas Present here, Christmas Future right here and —" Mrs. Arnell looked over her glasses vaguely at the group I was standing in. "Crowd, just sort of scatter in this area and do some business."

The girl next to me stopped popping the rubber bands on her braces and headed excitedly for the nondescript "area" like it was Academy Award material. I followed, tail dragging, and stood with the rest of the Crowd. Our chorus/drama presentation of Dickens' *A Christmas Carol* was the biggie of the semester, and I should've been nursing a major case of goose bumps over it. But it was tough to get the giggles over being in the "Crowd," and it was a cinch a girl like me was never going to be anything more.

"Ps-s-s-t!"

I turned to meet a pair of mammoth glasses perched right at my shoulder.

"What do you want?" I whispered to Jake.

"*That's* Roxanne Pfeiffer," he said, and jerked his head to my right. I looked at the girl with the braces who was doing "Crowd" business like a Hollywood extra.

"So?" I said.

"She's the one having the party. You said you didn't know her."

"I still don't," I said. But I looked at her again. No wonder I'd never noticed her. She was just another girl like me.

Tuesday, December 18, 4:30 p.m.
In Our Kitchen

"Half a cup of brown sugar—" I muttered. It was like a rock. I banged the box on the counter.

If the shut-ins knew I was gritting my teeth the whole time I was making their oatmeal cookies, they probably would feed them to their dogs or something.

"Bah, humbug!" I said out loud.

The doorbell rang and I dropped the box on the counter. Saved.

Jake smiled at me over his notepad, the corners of his mouth dipping practically into his eardrums.

"Did your mom cash a check?" he asked.

"Yeah," I answered. "Wait here."

He didn't, of course. He followed me into the kitchen and plowed his finger through my cookie dough while I counted out the money.

"Gross," I said. "People are going to eat that."

"What? I'm not people?"

I shoved the money at him. "Here. Think you can find your way to the front door?"

"Just in case he can't, why don't I show him?"

My dad put his hand across my shoulder and patted Jake's. "Women these days, Jake," he said. "No manners, huh?"

They chatted like old cronies on the way to the front door. I picked up the wooden spoon and madly stirred the cookie dough. If I could just get these done before my dad came back—

"Marijane—"

He never called me anything except Mj unless I was in pretty deep.

"—as soon as you're finished with those, what say we make this shopping trip into an evening? Burgers. The mall. Maybe a frozen yogurt after?"

I gaped at him. He took that for a yes.

Tuesday, December 18, 8:00 p.m.
On Center Street

"I think your mother will like the slippers you picked out," Dad said. He turned the car onto Center Street and I plopped my yogurt cup into the litter bag without comment. I wanted to say, "Yeah, she'll think of me every time she wears them to take out the garbage," but I didn't. My dad hadn't lectured me yet about being rude to Jake that afternoon, and I wasn't going to do anything to jostle his memory.

"Mj, can I help you with anything?"

I looked at him sharply.

"You aren't having much fun this Christmas, and I just wondered if there's anything I can do."

"No," I said. "I'm fine."

"You're lying, my love," he said.

But he didn't say anymore, and neither did I—even when he pulled up to the Center Street Church and turned off the motor.

"Let's get out," he said.

It was the smell that got to me first, and with it the memories. How many years had I run from the car to the rope that separated the crowd from the creche so I could sniff big and get the animals up my nostrils—the sheep and sometimes a lamb or two, and the donkey.

And then there were the quiet sounds. The way the sheep chattered to each other. The way the donkey shifted his feet in the hay. The way Mary sighed.

I didn't run to the rope this time. But when Dad and I got there, it was all the same. It was the first thing about Christmas that was, and for a minute I forgot to be thirteen and bummed out.

"It's so real, isn't it?" Dad whispered to me.

I didn't answer, but it was. The shepherds were all huddled together, shifting their shoulders and grinning at the baby like proud uncles. Joseph was leaning over Mary and gazing out over the crowd to make sure none of us was going to make a move on his little family.

And Mary herself. She was small and young and she was looking down at the baby like she couldn't believe this was happening to her.

It was almost as if she could feel me watching her, because as I stared she looked up and smiled. The metal on her teeth shone in the lights, and I gasped.

It was Roxanne Pfeiffer—the girl with the rubber bands on her braces. The girl who knocked herself out being good "Crowd." The girl who was a lot like me.

And that wasn't even the half of it. I followed her gaze to the shepherds she was smiling at, and there he was, stroking the neck of a very smelly burro and gazing tenderly on the baby. I wouldn't have known it was Jake without the mondo-glasses—except nobody else had a smile that big.

And nobody else had a lump as big as the one I had in my throat, I know. And probably nobody else was thinking what I was thinking: *How Roxanne Pfeiffer was probably just like Mary, who was plain and average and couldn't believe God had picked her to give birth to the Saviour. How Jake Picard was probably a lot like the young shepherds who did the same old thing day after day, but knew when something amazing was happening to them, and were ready for it.*

How I was a lot like them, and didn't even realize how good that could be.

I put my cheek against the tweed of my dad's jacket. With a big sigh, he slipped his hand into mine.

WEDNESDAY, DECEMBER 19, 1:30 P.M.
JUNIOR HIGH AUDITORIUM

"Crowd," Mrs. Arnell said, "you're standing there like you're waiting in line at the express lane at the grocery store."

"Next!" Jake called out.

"Ebenezer Scrooge has just emerged from his house screaming 'Merry Christmas!' You're amazed. Let's show some spirit!"

There was a general groan from the Crowd.

"I want you to watch, uh—"

She pointed to Roxanne, who said her name so softly I'm sure only I heard it, but gave a grin that lit up the room.

"Roxanne and—" And then she pointed toward me. I looked over my shoulder.

"Mj," Jake said for me.

"Watch Roxanne and Mj," Mrs. Arnell said. "They're over here giving it everything they've got. I believe that they're *excited* townspeople on Christmas morning. I want the rest of you to be like them."

Mrs. Arnell strode back across the stage and Roxanne and I grinned at each other.

"Did you forget your name?" Jake asked.

"Who made you my interpreter?" I quizzed. But I dug into my pocket and pulled out a bulging Baggie. "Want some cookies?"

He stared at me.

"You had your fingers in the dough. You might as well eat your own germs," I instructed.

But as he took it from me, still stricken, I grinned.

"Merry Christmas," I said.

"You're so strange," he replied.

I shrugged. "What do you expect—from a girl like me?"

JOYFUL *AND* TRIUMPHANT

JOHN MCCAIN

How could he and his fellow prisoners of war in a hellhole of a North Vietnamese prisoner of war camp, victims of beatings, torture, solitary confinement in three-feet-by-five-feet cells, foul air, and malnutrition, even *think* of celebrating Christmas!

Yet—well, we'll let Senator McCain tell the story.

O come, all ye faithful, joyful and triumphant . . .

We sang little above a whisper, our eyes darting anxiously up to the barred windows for any sign of the guards.

"Joyful and triumphant"? Clad in tattered prisoner-of-war clothes, I looked around at the two dozen men huddled in a North Vietnamese prison cell. Lightbulbs hanging from the ceiling illuminated a gaunt and wretched group of men—grotesque caricatures of what had once been clean-shaven, superbly fit Air Force, Navy and Marine pilots and navigators.

We shivered from the damp night air and the fevers that plagued a number of us. Some men were permanently stooped from the effects of torture; others limped or leaned on makeshift crutches.

O come ye, o come ye to Bethlehem. Come and behold him, born the King of angels . . .

What a pathetic sight we were. Yet here, this Christmas Eve 1971, we were together for the first time, some after seven years of harrowing isolation and mistreatment at the hands of a cruel enemy.

We were keeping Christmas—the most special Christmas any of us ever would observe.

There had been Christmas services in North Vietnam in previous years, but they had been spiritless, ludicrous stage shows, orchestrated by the Vietnamese for propaganda purposes. This was *our* Christmas service, the only one we had ever been allowed to hold—though we feared that, at any moment, our captors might change their minds.

I had been designated chaplain by our senior-ranking P.O.W. officer, Col. George "Bud" Day, USAF. As we sang "O Come, All Ye Faithful," I looked down at the few sheets of paper upon which I had penciled the Bible verses that tell the story of Christ's birth.

I recalled how, a week earlier, Colonel Day had asked the camp commander for a Bible. No, he was told, there were no Bibles in North Vietnam. But four days later, the camp commander had come into our communal cell to announce, "We have found one Bible in Hanoi, and you can designate one person to copy from it for a few minutes."

Colonel Day had requested that I perform the task. Hastily I leafed through the worn book the Vietnamese had placed on a table just outside our cell door in the prison yard. I furiously copied the Christmas passages until a guard approached and took the Bible away.

The service was simple. After saying the Lord's Prayer, we sang Christmas carols, some of us mouthing the words until our pain-clouded memories caught up with our voices. Between each hymn I would read a portion of the story of Jesus' birth.

And the angel said unto them, Fear not: for, behold, I bring you good tidings of great joy, which shall be to all people. For unto you is born this day, in the city of David, a Savior, which is Christ the Lord.

Capt. Quincy Collins, a former choir director from the Air Force Academy, led the hymns. At first, we were nervous and stilted in our singing. Still burning in our memories was the time, almost a year before, when North Vietnamese guards had burst in on our church service, beaten the three men leading the prayers, and dragged them away to confinement. The rest of us were locked away for eleven months in three-by-five-foot cells. Indeed, this Christmas service was in part a defiant celebration of the return to our regular prison in Hanoi.

And as the service progressed, our boldness increased, the singing swelled. "O Little Town of Bethlehem," "Hark, the Herald Angels Sing," "It Came Upon the Midnight Clear." Our voices filled the cell, bound together as we shared the story of the Babe "away in a manger, no crib for a bed."

Finally it came time to sing perhaps the most beloved hymn:

Silent night, Holy night! All is calm, all is bright . . .

A half dozen of the men were too sick to stand. They sat on the raised concrete sleeping platform that ran down the middle of the cell. Our few blankets were placed around the shaking shoulders of the sickest men to protect them against the cold. Even these men looked up transfixed as we sang that hymn.

Round yon virgin mother and child. Holy infant so tender and mild . . .

Tears rolled down our unshaven faces. Suddenly we were two thousand years and half a world away in a village called Bethlehem. And neither war, nor torture, nor imprisonment, nor the centuries themselves had dimmed the hope born on that silent night so long before.

Sleep in heavenly peace, sleep in heavenly peace.

We had forgotten our wounds, our hunger, our pain. We raised prayers of thanks for the Christ child, for our families and homes, for our country. There was an absolutely exquisite feeling that all our burdens had been lifted. In a place designed to turn men into vicious animals, we clung to one another, sharing what comfort we had.

Some of us had managed to make crude gifts. One fellow had a precious commodity—a cotton washcloth. Somewhere he had found needle and thread and fashioned the cloth into a hat, which he gave to Bud Day. Some men exchanged dog tags. Others had used prison spoons to scratch out an IOU on bits of paper—some imaginary thing we wished another to have. We exchanged those chits with smiles and tearful thanks.

The Vietnamese guards did not disturb us. But as I looked up at the barred windows, I wished they had been looking in. I *wanted* them to see us—faithful, joyful and, yes, triumphant.

THE FIR TREE COUSINS

LUCRETIA D. CLAPP

Nancy Wells was aghast: "Why Ann, you don't give them the very same thing year after year, I hope?"

"Well, why not?" Ann demanded, a trifle sharply.

Nancy sighed. So it was to be Christmas as usual once again in the Brewster household.

Or was it?

Pretty Mrs. Brewster sat in the middle of her bedroom floor, surrounded by a billowy mass of tissue paper, layers of cotton batting, bits of ribbon, tinsel, and tags. She was tying up packages of various shapes and sizes, placing each one when finished in a heaped-up pile at one side. Her face was flushed; wisps of cotton clung to her dress and hair, and she glanced up anxiously now and then at the little clock on the desk as it ticked off the minutes of the short December afternoon.

"I'll never be through—*NEVER*!" she remarked disconsolately after one of these hurried glances. "And there's the box for cousin Henry's family that just *must* go tonight, and the home box. Oh, Nancy Wells!" she broke off suddenly as she caught sight of a slender little figure standing in the doorway, surveying her with merry brown eyes.

"Nancy Wells! Come right in here. You're as welcome as—as the day after Christmas!"

"So you've reached that stage, have you, Ann?" the visitor laughed as she picked her way carefully across the littered floor to an inviting wicker chair near the fire.

"Yes, I have. You know I always begin to feel that way just about this time, Nancy, only it seems to be a mite worse than usual this year."

Ann Brewster stretched out one cramped foot and groaned. "Here I am just slaving, while you—well, you look the very personification of elegant leisure. I suspect every single one of those forty-nine presents on your regular list is wrapped, and tied and labeled—and mailed, too, if mailed it has to be. Well, you can just take off your coat and hat, Nancy, fold yourself up Turklike on the floor here, and help me out. I've an appointment at four-thirty, and it's nearly that now. I'm not nearly through, but I just must finish today. If there's one thing I'm particular about, Nancy, it is that a gift shall reach the recipient on time. For my part, I don't want a Christmas present a week cold, so to speak, nor even a day And, somehow, I always manage to get mine off, even if I do half kill myself doing it."

"'Do your Christmas shopping early,'" quoted Nancy, mischievously, as she seated herself obediently on the floor.

"Yes; and 'only five more shopping days,'" Ann smiled ruefully. "Why don't you go on? Those well-meant little reminders I've had flaunted in my face every time I've stepped into a store or picked up a daily paper for the past six weeks. They have come to be as familiar as the street sign out there on that lamppost—and receive about the same amount of attention, too."

"Well, after all, Ann, it is a delightful sort of rush, now isn't it? I'm willing to admit that I'd miss it all dreadfully."

Nancy Wells looked about her appreciatively at the chintz-hung room glowing in the warmth of the open wood fire, and with its pleasant disarray of snowy paper and gay ribbons.

"My, but that's a lovely package!" she remarked, as Ann cut a square of tissue paper and measured a length of silver cord. "And what a clever idea that is! I should never have thought of using cotton batting and a sprinkling of diamond dust for the top layer."

"Well, you see, Nancy, this is for Cousin Harriet. She has everything anyone could possibly wish for, and she always sends me such beautiful things that I make a special effort to have my gift to her as dainty as possible and a little different."

Ann paused and glanced at the clock.

"My, look what time it is! I'll have to go. I wonder if you'd just as soon stay, Nancy, and finish up that little pile over there by the couch. They're for the fir tree cousins down on the farm."

"The *FIR* tree cousins! Whatever do you mean, Ann?"

Ann laughed gaily as she stood up and shook off the bits of tinsel and ribbon from her skirt.

"Oh, I always call them that in fun," she explained. "They're Tom's cousins that live down in Maine. The idea struck me, I suppose, because theirs is the 'Country of the Pointed Firs,' you know. I've never seen any of them, but I've always sent them a box at Christmas ever since I've been married."

"What fun!" Nancy exclaimed enthusiastically. "How many are there, and what do you send them?"

"I don't know that I should call it *fun* exactly," Ann answered dubiously. "This buying gifts for people you've never seen and only know by hearsay is—well—not unalloyed. Let's see—there are Cousin Henry and Cousin Lucy, then the boys, Alec and Joe and little Henry, and one girl, Louise, who is just between the two older boys. And, oh, yes, there's Grandma Lewis, Cousin Lucy's mother."

Ann ticked off the names on her fingers.

"Yes, there are just seven of them. Tom says they have a fine farm. He used to go there summers when he was a boy. He just adores Cousin Lucy, and actually wanted to take me down there on our wedding trip. You can't accuse me of procrastination as far as they are concerned, Nancy, for I always buy their things long before any of the others. You see, I usually know just about what I'm going to send each one. I hit upon a certain thing and stick to it as nearly as possible every year. It's easier."

"Why, Ann, you don't give them the very same thing year after year, I hope?" Nancy looked up in comical dismay.

"Well, why not?" Ann demanded a trifle sharply. "Take Cousin Henry, for instance. I usually get a nice warm muffler for him, because I'm sure he can—"

"But I should think—" Nancy interrupted.

"My dear, it's just *freezing* cold there! They have terrible winters, and one needs mufflers—and more mufflers! You can't have too many. Then I nearly always pick out an apron of some kind for Cousin Lucy. One can't have too many aprons, either, especially when she does all her own work. For Grandma Lewis, I choose a bag or something to put her knitting in. This year I found some sort of an affair for holding the yarn. I didn't understand it very well myself, although they told me it was perfectly simple; but I thought an experienced knitter like Grandma Lewis would know how to use it. Louise is just sixteen, so it's easy enough to select a pair of stockings or a handkerchief for her. As for the boys, Alec and Joe, I always get them neckties—they can't have too many, you know—and for little Henry a game or toy of some kind. Then Tom adds a box of candy. Promptly one week after Christmas I receive a perfectly proper, polite letter from Cousin Lucy, thanking me on behalf of every member of the fir tree household. It does sound a bit perfunctory, doesn't it, Nancy? Sort of a cut-and-dried performance all around. Somehow, Christmas is getting to be more and more like that every year; don't you think so? I must confess I'm glad, positively relieved, when it's over! I'm always a wreck, mentally as well as physically."

Nancy made no comment; instead she pointed with the scissors to a heap of large and small packages over at one side.

"What do you want done with those, Ann?"

"Oh, they go in the home box. That has to go tonight, too. I was just starting to tie them up. Do you suppose you'd have time to do them too, Nancy dear? I know I'm just imposing on you. Just put the two piles on my bed when you've finished wrapping, will you? Then Tom can pack them after dinner. Now I'm off. Good-bye, and thanks awfully."

A minute later Nancy Wells heard the front door slam, then the house settled down to an empty quiet, broken only by the rustling of tissue paper and the click of scissors as Nancy folded and cut and measured and snipped. The fire burned to a bed of dull embers; and beyond the small square window panes, the snow-lit landscape darkened to dusk.

"There!" said Nancy, as she gave a final pat to the last bow. "And how pretty they look, too," she added, leaning back to survey her handiwork. Then she carried them over to the bed and arranged them in two neat piles.

"Certainly looks like 'Merry Christmas,' all right." With which remark, she put on her coat and hat and went home.

It was several hours later that Ann Brewster surveyed with weariness, compounded with relief, the empty spaces on bed and floor. The last label had been pasted on while Tom stood by with hammer and nails, ready to perform the final offices. And the two boxes, the one for the fir tree cousins down on the Maine farm, the other for Ann's own family in Michigan, were now on their way to the downtown office.

"And now that's over for another year at least," she sighed. "And I'm too tired to care much whether those boxes reach their destination safely or not. Twelve months from tonight, in all probability, I shall be sitting in this same spot making that very same remark. And I used to just *love* Christmas, too."

Ann Brewster (she was Ann Martin then) had been brought up in a family where there had been little money to spare, even for necessities. Nevertheless, Mr. and Mrs. Martin had always contrived to make the day and the season itself one of happy memories for their four children. No elaborate celebration of later years ever held quite the same degree of delight and anticipation shared then by every member of the family. Ann recalled the weeks brimful of plans and mysterious secrets that preceded the day itself, with its simple gifts and its spirit of peace and good will toward all. Now it was so different!

"Tired, Ann?"

A masculine voice broke in on her reverie, and Tom's broad-shouldered figure filled the doorway.

"Cheer up! The boxes are on their way, or should be shortly, and a few days more will see the season's finish."

"That's just it, Tom. We're losing the spirit of Christmas—the simplicity and good wishes, I mean—that used to be the big thing about it."

Tom whistled thoughtfully, and when he spoke his voice had lost its merry banter. "I guess you're right there, Ann. We're certainly a long way off from the old days of five-cent horns and candy canes. A lot of that was youth, of course, but just the same this modern deal is all wrong. It's a selfish proposition, as I look at it. I don't believe I've ever told you, Ann, about a certain Christmas of mine, long ago. About the nicest I've ever known."

"Where was it? Do you mean at home?"

Ann looked up, interested.

"No." Tom's voice changed and a shadow crossed his face. "You know I never had much of a home, Ann. My parents both died when I was only a little chap, and I was sort of parceled out to various relatives for different seasons of the year. No, this Christmas I'm thinking of was with Cousin Henry and Cousin Lucy. Queer I haven't told you before."

"I knew you spent your summers there," Ann answered a little curiously, "but I've never heard of your being there for Christmas."

"Well, I was, and I've never forgotten it. It was my first glimpse of what a real homey Christmas can be. The tree was just a homemade affair—that is, the trimmings. We cut the tree ourselves, a beautiful slender fir, and hauled it down on a sled from the hill back of the house. We popped corn and made wreaths, strung cranberries, and cut stars out of colored paper. And I tell you that tree was pretty— it wasn't glittering with ornaments and blazing with candles or electric lights."

"Did you have presents?" asked Ann.

"Yes, I remember Cousin Henry gave me a pair of homemade snowshoes. Grandma Lewis had knit some red wristlets for me, and Cousin Lucy a cap to match. I was the happiest boy in the state of Maine!"

Tom paused a moment. "But somehow, Ann, what I remember most was the spirit of the day itself. Cousin Lucy had worked hard, I know, and in the evening had a lot of the neighbors in; but she was the life of the crowd. Ann, I'd like you to meet and really know Cousin Lucy. I wish she'd ask us to visit them sometime."

"Somehow, I never supposed—" Ann began hesitatingly.

"Supposed what?" Tom asked.

"Well, I guess I never gave your fir tree cousins much thought, Tom. I didn't think you cared particularly. You've never talked much about them nor made any effort to—"

"Yes, I know," Tom broke in, "and more's the shame to me, too. It's queer sometimes, that, no matter how much you may think of people, you just sort of drift apart. But you'd better get to bed now, Ann; you look tired to death."

The Thomas Brewsters faced each other across the breakfast table the morning after New Year's. There was a pile of letters beside Ann's plate.

"I know exactly what's in every one of these missives," she sighed.

Tom smiled as he opened his morning paper.

There was a silence for several minutes while Ann slowly slit the seals one by one. She picked up a square white envelope that bore her father's well-known handwriting, and a minute later a sudden exclamation made Tom look up.

"Why, Tom—Tom Brewster!"

Ann's eyes glanced down the single page; then she began to read aloud:

My dear Ann:

Perhaps you won't remember it, but you gave me a muffler for Christmas once long ago, when you were a very little girl. You picked it out yourself, and I'll say this—that you showed remarkable good taste. That muffler, or what's left of it, is tucked away somewhere in the attic now. The one you sent this year gives me almost as much pleasure as did that other one, although I suppose I'll have to concede that these new styles are really prettier (but not any warmer or more useful) than the old. Your mother thinks they must be coming back into favor again, but I don't care whether they are or not. They're warm and they help keep a clean collar clean. For my part, I'm glad we're getting away from the showy Christmases of the last few years and down to a simpler, saner giving and receiving.

Lots of love and thanks to you and Tom.
Father

Ann drew forth a small folded sheet that had been tucked inside the other one. It read:

Dear Ann,

I'm just going to add a line to put in with your father's, for we have a houseful of company and there's no time now for a real letter. Your box this year, although something of a surprise, was nonetheless welcome. I have thought for several years that we ought all of us to give simpler gifts. A remembrance, no matter how small, if carefully and thoughtfully chosen to meet the need or desire of the recipient, carries with it more of the real Christmas spirit than the costliest gift or one chosen at random. I don't know when I've had an apron given me before! I began to think they had gone out of fashion. I put yours right on, and your father said it made him think of when you children were little. The boys will write you themselves, but I'll just say that Ned and Harold both remarked that they were glad you sent them neckties. (You know we've always tried to think up something different, with the result that both are rather low on that article.) We've had lots of fun with Hugh's game. He confided to me that he'd been hoping somebody would give him one. So you see, Ann, dear, we are all pleased with our things and send you our grateful thanks.

Love to you both from
Mother

P.S. I was afraid my letter telling of your Aunt Cordelia's arrival had not reached you in time, but I need not have worried. She was much taken with that case for holding her yarn. She'd had one and lost it. And Katy was real pleased with that pretty handkerchief.

With a hand that trembled a little, and with burning cheeks, Ann drew forth the last letter in the pile. It was postmarked Maine, and contained two plain-lined sheets, tablet size.

"This is from Cousin Lucy," Ann began, a queer little note creeping into her voice:

My dear Ann:

When we opened your box on Christmas morning, I thought I had never seen anything so attractive. Seals and ribbons and greetings may not mean so much, perhaps, to you city people; but for us isolated ones, they add a great deal to our enjoyment and appreciation. Your gifts fulfilled certain long-felt desires, one or two of which I suspect are older than you are, Ann. Perhaps you cannot understand the joy of receiving something you've always wanted, yet did not really need. I am writing with my beautiful pin before me on the table. You see, it is the first one—the first really nice pin—I've ever owned. That is fulfilled desire number one. The second is the sight of your Cousin Henry enjoying a bit of leisure before the fire with his new book. I suppose Tom may have told you that once, as a young man, your Cousin Henry made this very trip to the headwaters of the Peace River. So few new and worthwhile books find their way to us. Louise and the boys will write later, so I'll only say that Alec actually takes his big flashlight to bed with him; Joe is inordinately proud of that safety razor; and as for little Henry—well, his father and I both feel that we ought to thank you on our own behalf, for all our efforts to make an out-of-door lad of him seem to have failed hitherto. He is the student of the family, but the new skates lure him outside and help to strike the proper balance. Louise loves her beaded bag, as, indeed, what girl wouldn't? And as for Grandma Lewis, she fairly flaunts that bit of rose point. She confided to me that at eighty years she had at last given up all hope of ever possessing a piece of real lace!

I have written a long letter, but I doubt if, after all, I've really succeeded in expressing even a small part of our appreciation to you and Tom for your carefully chosen gifts. To feel that a certain thing has been chosen especially for you—to fit your own individuality and particular desire, if not always need—this, it has always seemed to me, is the true spirit of Christmas. And I think you have found it, Ann. Before closing I want to ask if you and Tom can't arrange to make us a visit this summer?

> *Wishing you both a Happy New Year,*
> *Lovingly,*
> *Cousin Lucy*

Ann Brewster lay down the letter with something that was half a sob and half a laugh. "I'm just too ashamed to live!"

"Why, what's the matter, Ann?" Tom looked puzzled.

"Cousin Lucy speaks of my 'carefully chosen gifts.' And they weren't at all. They weren't even meant for any of them. You see," Ann swallowed the lump in her throat, "I've always just chosen their things at random. Yes, I have, Tom. One of those Christmas obligations you spoke of the other night, to be disposed of with as little time and effort as possible. And then last week, when I was hurrying to get everything off, Nancy Wells came over and I left a lot of things for her to finish wrapping while I dashed off to the dressmaker's. And I suppose, in some way, I got the fir tree cousins' and the home pile mixed."

Tom pushed back his chair from the table.

"Seems to me, Ann dear, that we've had the answer to our query, 'What's wrong with Christmas?' You've sort of stumbled upon the truth this year, but—"

Tom stopped, whistling thoughtfully as he drew on his overcoat. There was a misty light in Ann's eyes as she stood beside him.

When will you have your vacation, Tom?"

"August, probably."

"Well, we're going to spend it with our fir tree cousins! And, Tom, I can hardly wait!"

Christmas Memories

WHILE SHEPHERDS WATCHED

ADELINE SERGEANT

All by himself, the little boy slowly climbed the wide steps of the dark looming mansion. But then, rather than knocking on the great door, he drew his bow across the strings of his fiddle.

And began to play.

The setting is northern England in the 1890s.

A tall, spare, dark-eyed young man, with a violin case in his hand, came up the narrow stairs three steps at once, as though he were anxious to reach the little attic room which was his destination. There was a lamp in the hall below, but no light on the stairs or landings save the dim gleam which came through a skylight in the roof; and at six o'clock in the evening of the 24th of December, it is needless to remark that the top story was enveloped in total darkness. But Guy Fairfax seemed to know his way by instinct, and did not pause until he reached the scratched and shabby-looking door which formed the entrance to his abode. There he stopped short, waited, and listened for a moment, arrested by a sound that issued from the room.

It was the sound of a violin, faintly played, as though the instrument itself were small and the hand of the player weak. Presently there arose also a sweet little thread of a childish voice, singing to the tune picked out on the violin, the words of a well-known Christmas hymn:

"While shepherds watched their flocks by night,

All seated on the ground."

Guy's face contracted a little as if with pain; then he smoothed it resolutely, called up a smile, and opened the attic door.

It was a miserably bare room, not very clean nor very tidy, and the small fire that burned in the rusty grate did not avail to warm the atmosphere. On the bed, with an old fur cloak tucked round him for warmth, a little boy was curled up, his hands holding the tiny fiddle to the notes of which Guy had been listening. But he put it down at once and held out his hands with a crow of delight when Guy came in.

"Daddy! Daddy! Are you back so quick? I thought you wasn't coming till ever so long."

It was a sweet little voice, a sweet little face; but the lad's body was very frail and weak, and the dark eyes looked pathetically large for the delicate little face. It was with a sort of passionate yearning that Guy Fairfax pressed his child to his breast for a moment and then looked at him with a mournful foreboding which rendered his voice less cheerful than he meant it to be.

"I've run home for half an hour, Tony, to see that my boy is warm and comfortable," said the young man, folding the child close to him as he spoke.

"Oh, yes, I'm quite comfy," said Tony, contentedly. "I put on your old cloak and p'tended I was a bear; then I was a little choirboy singing carols in the street—Christmas carols, you know, Daddy, because Christmas is tomorrow, and it was tonight that the shepherds was watching their flocks—all seated on the ground."

His voice passed almost unconsciously from speech to song. Indeed, although Tony was only six years old, singing was as natural to him as speech. He came of a musical race: his father was a musician, first by choice, then by necessity, and his mother, who died when he was only two years old, had been a professional singer, belonging to a family who had lived half their lives upon the operatic stage. Tony inherited her tastes, just as he inherited her golden hair, but he had his father's brow and his father's eyes.

"You like carols, Tony!"

"At Christmas time, Daddy. Will the singers come down this street tonight, do you think?"

"Perhaps so. There used to be plenty of them when I was a boy."

"You lived here, when you were a little boy like me, didn't you, Daddy?"

"Not here in the town, Tony. A little way outside—at the big house I've told you about before."

Tony regarded his father with baby seriousness. "Won't you take me to see it while we're here? Or is the company going away tomorrow?"

Fairfax belonged to a traveling operatic company, and could not afford to do otherwise than the other members of the troupe; but he would have given a good deal to find himself in any other place rather than the big, northern manufacturing town, where, unfortunately, his family had been well known for many generations. He had broken with his relations long ago—but—well, it was trying to find himself so near the dear old Grange where his father was still living, two miles outside the town, and not be able to go near him nor even let him know that his son and grandson were so near.

"I can't take you to see it," he said, in a low voice to the little son. "There—there wouldn't be time."

He was ashamed of the subterfuge as he looked into Tony's innocent eyes; but Tony was only half attending after all.

"And Santa Claus?" he said. "Will he come down the chiminey to give me things as he did you when you were a little boy?"

"Really, Tony, we must look after your English. Chiminey indeed! You know better than that."

"It don't matter," said Tony, fearlessly. "Will he come down it, that's what I want to know?"

"Not down attic chimneys, I'm afraid," said the father, with a sigh.

"Oh–h! —But in at the door, maybe? Perhaps his sack would be too heavy for the chim–ney. He'll come all the way up the stairs, bump, bump, bumpity-bump, won't he?—and I shall stay awake and hear him."

"Better not," said Guy, rather sadly. "Santa Claus has forgotten us this year, mannie: he comes only to rich people."

"That's a shame," said Tony. "We aren't rich people, are we, Daddy?"

"Certainly not," answered the young man, thinking of the guinea a week which he was accustomed to receive on treasury day. "Not precisely rich, Tony; but not paupers—yet."

The bitter accent in his voice was caused by a vivid remembrance of some words that the angry old father had once addressed to him. "You need not darken my door again, sir; and when you and your wife are paupers, don't think that you'll get money out of me." The word 'paupers' always recalled the bitterness of that moment to his mind.

"What's paupers?" said Tony. Then, in an abstracted tone, "I suppose Santa Claus always came to the big house where you lived."

"I suppose he did."

"And does he come still?"

"If there were any children there, I daresay he would."

"Oh," said Tony, with a very solemn face. Then he said no more, but sat motionless, looking thoughtfully at the opposite wall, while his father rose from the bed and began to busy himself about various household matters, which might have seemed to an observer almost pathetic when done by the clumsy fingers of a man. Not that Guy's fingers were clumsy; they had all the delicacy of a born musician, and the gentleness of a woman; and it came quite naturally to him to build up the fire, hang Tony's flannel pajamas before it, warm some bread and milk for the child, and finally make and drink a cup of strong tea before he went back to the orchestra.

"Good night, Tony. Go to bed soon, there's a good boy. Shall I unfasten your clothes?"

"No, thank you, Daddy: I'se not a baby," said Tony, with dignity, and Guy went away laughing at this manifestation of infantile pride. He had little to laugh at, and it was a good thing for him that Tony's smiles and frowns and baby wiles, as well as the child's innate genius for music, kept his heart from growing hard. The amused light was still in his eyes when he reached the theater, but it would soon have died away had he known what Tony was doing while he was gone.

"It's a dreat pity," Tony soliloquized as he ate his bread and milk, when his father's steps had died away, "it's a dreat pity that Santa Claus doesn't come to poor little boys as well as rich ones. I s'pose he'll never think of coming here. But, if I lived in the house where Daddy used to live, he'd come, because Daddy said if there were any children there—oh I wish I could go to Daddy's old house and see Santa Claus for my own self! What a pity that Daddy doesn't live there now!"

He put away his empty bowl in a little wooden cupboard, and came slowly back to the fire. Then he yawned, and thought the room looked very lonely, and wondered what he could do to amuse himself. He was a self-reliant little lad, not often in want of occupation, but just now it seemed to him as though something had gone wrong with the world. He was vaguely dissatisfied, and knew not why.

Then a sudden idea occurred to him—one that sent the blood to his cheeks and the sparkle to his eyes. "Tony's ideas" were sometimes a trouble to his father. They were always original, but apt to be impracticable, and even dangerous. The idea that had come to him now was that he should go to the house where his father had lived, and ask to be allowed to wait for Santa Claus when he came down the chimney that night.

"It would be lovely," said Tony to himself. "I shouldn't be no trouble to nobody, and very likely I should be home again before Daddy got back from the theater. I should run all the way, and I should take my fiddle and play 'While shepherds watched,' and sing the words: and then the people of the house would say, 'Oh, there's the waits,' and they would open the front door wide and let me in."

The idea took complete possession of his little soul. As it happened, he knew the name of the house where his father had once lived, and had a general idea of its locality. It was two miles from the big town, but there was an omnibus which would take him almost all the way. And Tony, although kept as closely as possible to his father's side, had a good deal of experience concerning trams, omnibuses, trains, and other modes of transit; and he was not at all dismayed at the notion of making his way to a strange part of the town. He proceeded in haste to make preparations for his expedition. First, he found a piece of paper and scrawled upon it in enormous sprawling letters:

Plese, Daddy, I have gone to your old house to find Santerklawse, and I shall tell him to bring things to poor likkle boys as well as ricche ones.

—Tony

Tony's spelling was not his strong point. Then he put on his cap and his little overcoat, rather thin and very shabby, took his violin under his arm, and so set forth.

The sky was overcast, and the wind cold; but out in the streets the lamps were lighted, the shop windows were resplendent with holly, and a crowd of belated shoppers hustled each other on the pavements; so that Tony, in his delight at this novel and beautiful scene, didn't feel the cold and knew not the meaning of fatigue. At first he even forgot that he meant to go onto a tram and go to Stoneley, the suburb in which his father's home as a child was situated. The name of the house was Carston—as Tony knew; and in his ignorance of all difficulties, he intended to go by tramcar to Stoneley, and then ask the first passerby his way to Carston. That the place might be utterly changed from the time when his father was a boy never even entered Tony's head.

However, the innocent and ignorant sometimes seem guided towards right ways, right things, right people, in ways we do not know. Tony looked up straight into the face of the omnibus conductor at a street corner where several omnibuses were waiting, and said, "Are you going to Stoneley, please?"

And the man looked down at him kindly, and said:

"Ay, that I be. Do you want to go to Stoneley, little master?"

"Yes," said Tony, promptly scrambling up the steps, "and I want to go to a house at Stoneley—a house called Carston. Do you know where it is?"

"Why, yes," said the friendly conductor, in rather a doubtful voice. "I know Carston well enough, and we go almost past the gates, but what might you be wanting at Carston, I should like to know?"

"It's where my Daddy used to live," said Tony, settling himself into his seat.

"Oh, I see," said the man, feeling more satisfied. He supposed the boy must be the son of some coachman or gardener who lived at Carston; and Tony had so much self-possession and confidence that no more questions seemed necessary.

More passengers got in, the conductor shouted, the driver cracked his whip, and the omnibus moved on. It seemed a long time to Tony before it stopped to put him down in a dark road, where the conductor pointed encouragingly to a white gate at the end of a little lane, and told him that that was the way to Carston. "There'll be a bus back to town every quarter of an hour," he said; "but maybe you won't want one? You're going to spend Christmas with your father, I reckon?"

"Oh, yes," said Tony, not at all suspecting the drift of the question. And then the omnibus rolled away, leaving him all alone in the dark, with an unaccustomed sensation of fear and—an unusual thing for him—a strong disposition to cry.

But he mastered the weakness, and gripping the violin tighter, he turned towards the white gate at the end of the lane. It was unfastened, and when he had passed through it he found himself on a graveled walk, winding whitely between trees and plantations, towards a large, dark-looking mansion, which Tony divined to be Carston, his father's old home.

He followed the path until he came to the garden, and then he lost himself a little, but by and by he emerged from the shadows, and found that he was facing a wide flight of steps which led up to the terrace in front of the dining-room and drawing-room windows. Tony nodded quite joyfully when he saw the terrace and the steps. His father had told him about them many a time. He mounted them slowly and carefully, then, standing on the terrace, he looked about him a little while and then decided that it was time for him to begin to play. He felt rather cold now that he was not moving, and a snowflake or two melted upon his nose, and made him uncomfortable; nevertheless, it was with great resolution that he drew his bow across the strings of the fiddle, and began his favorite tune—

"While shepherds watched their flocks by night,

All seated on the ground."

"What's that caterwauling in the grounds, Norris?" said the master of the house to the butler, in his crustiest tones. He was at dinner, and the notes of a violin fell strangely upon his ear. "Did I not tell you that I would have no parties of carol singers this year? They only trample down the plants and destroy the young trees in the plantation. Go out and put a stop to that noise directly."

Norris went out with rather a grave face. It was a troubled one when he returned.

"It's not the carol singers at all, sir. It's—it's only a little boy."

"Send him away at once, then."

"If you please, sir, he says he wishes to speak to you. I—I think he's a gentleman's son, sir."

"What if he is? He can have no business here. Send him off. Some begging trick, I daresay."

But as the General—for that was the rank of the master of Carston—spoke, the music waxed louder and louder, and a sweet child's voice rang out like a bird's. To the vast surprise of the master and servant alike, the door of the dining room was pushed open, and there in the hall stood a child with shining hair and big brown eyes, playing and singing, as he had done at first:

"While shepherds watched their flocks by night,

All seated on the ground."

The General's white mustache bristled fiercely, and his voice was harsh and rasping when he spoke.

"Boy—you there! Stop that noise!"

Tony desisted, but turned a look of angelic reproach upon the speaker. "Don't you like it?" he said. "It's my greatest favorite. And you must know it quite well, because Daddy said he used to sing it to you when he was a little boy."

"When he—your father—what do you mean, child?"

"I ain't a child," said Tony, with dignity. "I'm a boy. It's quite a long time since I was a child."

"What's your name?" said the General, listening and smiling in spite of himself. But the answer banished all smile from his face.

"Anthony Liscard Fairfax," said Tony, triumphantly. "Isn't it a beautiful name? It's my grandfather's name, Daddy says. And I haven't never seen him in all my life." And his innocent, trustful eyes looked straight into the face of the very man who was his grandfather.

Norris gasped. He expected an explosion of anger: he almost feared violence. But for a minute or two the General stood perfectly silent. Then he said to the man, "You may go."

"Shall I go, too?" said Tony.

"No. Stand where you are. Now, tell me who told you to come here tonight?"

"Nobody told me. I thinked it for myself."

"Do you see these grapes and sweets?" persisted the General. "You shall have as many of them as you like if you'll let me know who suggested—who put it into your head—to come."

Tony's face grew red. He saw that he was not believed. But he answered gallantly:

"I told you—I thinked it for myself. Nobody said one word about coming, and I thinked of it only tonight when Daddy had gone to the theater. He's told me lots of things about this house, and how boo'ful it was."

"So you wanted to see it for yourself?"

"Yes. I wanted to see it, but that wasn't all. Santa Claus comes to this house, don't he?"

Tony pressed eagerly up to the General who seemed not to know how to answer him.

"I can't say. When the children were small—perhaps."

A vision came to him of himself and his wife, stealing from cot to cot to fill small stockings with toys and sweets in days long passed away. He could not finish his sentence.

"I know!" cried Tony. "Santa Claus always came here when Daddy was a little boy; and when I asked him why he never came to me, Daddy said that he only came to rich children and not to poor little boys like me."

"Are you poor?" said the General, hastily.

"We're not rich," replied Tony, quoting his father, "but we ain't paupers yet. Daddy says so. Who is paupers? I wanted Daddy to tell me, but he had to go to the theater."

"So he goes and amuses himself, and leaves you with nobody to care for you?"

"It ain't very amusing," said Tony. "It makes him awful tired to play such silly tunes every night in the or—kistra. But he has to do it, or else there wouldn't be no bread and milk for me, nor no baccy for Daddy."

"Where is your mother?" said the General.

The child's face grew grave. "God took her away," he answered, and the General suddenly felt that his old hatred of that singing woman who had beguiled his son into making her his wife was small-minded and despicable. But another notion made him frown.

"So you came here to see what you could get? You wanted Santa Claus's presents?"

"Oh, no, I didn't. I only thought I'd like to come—'cause Daddy says Santa Claus always came here at Christmas time, and it would be awful nice to see him; but I don't want anything myself. I just want to tell him that there are heaps of little boys much poorer than me, and that if he would go to the poor children it would be much better than going to the rich ones, don't you think so?"

"Well—sometimes," said the general.

"I thought, if you'd let me, I would stop here till quite, quite late," said Tony, confidentially. "I'd wait about till he came, and then I'd speak to him about the poor little boys. Then I'd go home to Daddy. But may I stop here, please, till Santa Claus comes?"

To his surprise, the old gentleman with the white mustache stooped down and took him into his arms. "My dear little boy," he said, "you may stop till Santa Claus comes—certainly; and you may stop forever, if you like."

When Guy Fairfax, half distracted by the note which he found on his table, arrived, panting with haste, at Carston that night, he was shown at once into the dining room, where the General sat in his armchair with a child's figure gently cradled on his knee. Tony was fast asleep, and the General would not move to disturb him. He only looked at his son for a moment, and then at the sleeping child.

"Forgive me, Guy," he said at last. "You—and this boy—are all that remain to me. Let him stay—and stay yourself, too, and cheer the last few years of my life. I was wrong—I know I was wrong, but you must come back to me."

And when Tony woke next morning, in a soft white bed and a cozy room, such as he had never seen before, he was a little bit grieved to find that Santa Claus had filled a stocking for him while he'd been fast asleep. But he was quite consoled when his father told him that the old gentleman with the white hair and mustache, who must henceforth be called Grandad, was the best Santa Claus that he had ever seen, and that Tony might go to him after breakfast and sit on his knee while he sang how shepherds "watched their flocks by night," as the Christ Child came with gifts of peace and joy and goodwill to men.

THE GOLD AND IVORY TABLECLOTH

HOWARD C. SCHADE

Late one December a big storm unleashed its deadly force on an old church. A huge chunk of rain-soaked plaster fell out of the wall just behind the altar. The dispirited young pastor and his wife almost wept. And Christmas was only two days away.

The true story of what followed has become one of the most treasured and oft-reread Christmas stories of our time.

At Christmastime men and women everywhere gather in their churches to wonder anew at the greatest miracle the world has ever known. But the story I like best to recall was not a miracle—not exactly.

It happened to a pastor who was very young. His church was very old. Once, long ago, it had flourished. Famous men had preached from its pulpit, prayed before its altar. Rich and poor alike had worshipped there and built it beautifully. Now the good days had passed from the section of town where it stood. But the pastor and his young wife believed in their run-down church. They felt that with paint, hammer and faith they could get it in shape. Together they went to work.

But late in December a severe storm whipped through the river valley, and the worst blow fell on the little church—a huge chunk of rain-soaked plaster fell out of the inside wall just behind the altar. Sorrowfully the pastor and his wife swept away the mess, but they couldn't hide the ragged hole.

The pastor looked at it and had to remind himself quickly, "Thy will be done!" But his wife wept, "Christmas is only two days away!"

That afternoon the dispirited couple attended the auction held for the benefit of a youth group. The auctioneer opened a box and shook out of its folds a handsome gold-and-ivory lace tablecloth. It was a magnificent item, nearly fifteen feet long. But it, too, dated from a long-vanished era. Who, today, had any use for such a thing? There were a few halfhearted bids. Then the pastor was seized with what he thought was a great idea. He bid it in for $6.50.

He carried the cloth back to the church and tacked it up on the wall behind the altar. It completely hid the hole! And the extraordinary beauty of its shimmering handwork cast a fine, holiday glow over the chancel. It was a great triumph. Happily he went back to preparing his Christmas sermon.

Just before noon on the day of Christmas Eve, as the pastor was opening the church, he noticed a woman standing in the cold at the bus stop.

"The bus won't be here for forty minutes!" he called, and invited her into the church to get warm.

She told him that she had come from the city that morning to be interviewed for a job as governess to the children of one of the wealthy families in town but she had been turned down. A war refugee, her English was imperfect.

The woman sat down in a pew and chafed her hands and rested. After a while she dropped her head and prayed. She looked up as the pastor began to adjust the great gold-and-ivory lace cloth across the hole. She rose suddenly and walked up the steps of the chancel. She looked at the tablecloth. The pastor smiled and started to tell her about the storm damage, but she didn't seem to listen. She took up a fold of the cloth and rubbed it between her fingers.

"It is mine!" she said. "It is my banquet cloth!" She lifted up a corner and showed the surprised pastor that there were initials monogrammed on it. "My husband had the cloth made especially for me in Brussels! There could not be another like it."

For the next few minutes the woman and the pastor talked excitedly together. She explained that she was Viennese; that she and her husband had opposed the Nazis and decided to leave the country. They were advised to go separately. Her husband put her on a train for Switzerland. They planned that he would join her as soon as he could arrange to ship their household goods across the border.

She never saw him again. Later she heard that he had died in a concentration camp.

"I have always felt that it was my fault—to leave without him," she said. "Perhaps these years of wandering have been my punishment!"

The pastor tried to comfort her, urged her to take the cloth with her. She refused. Then she went away.

As the church began to fill on Christmas Eve, it was clear that the cloth was going to be a great success. It had been skillfully designed to look its best by candlelight.

After the service, the pastor stood at the doorway; many people told him that the church looked beautiful. One gentle-faced, middle-aged man—he was the local clock-and-watch repairman—looked rather puzzled.

"It is strange," he said in his soft accent. "Many years ago my wife—God rest her—and I owned such a cloth. In our home in Vienna, my wife put it on the table"—and here he smiled—"only when the bishop came to dinner!"

The pastor suddenly became very excited. He told the jeweler about the woman who had been in church earlier in the day.

The startled jeweler clutched the pastor's arm. "Can it be? Does she live?"

Together the two got in touch with the family who had interviewed her. Then, in the pastor's car they started for the city. And as Christmas Day was born, this man and his wife—who had been separated through so many saddened Yuletides—were reunited.

To all who heard this story, the joyful purpose of the storm that had knocked a hole in the wall of the church was now quite clear. Of course, people said it was a miracle, but I think you will agree it was the season for it!

THE SOFT SPOT IN B606

AUTHOR UNKNOWN

In Portland Prison, no one was watched more closely than the dangerous convict known as B606. If he behaved, he'd finally be out in six months. But, since he had no hope, B606 didn't care if he *ever* got out.

Suddenly, the chief warden approached his cell, bringing a message: he was wanted by the governor of the prison.

Bells were pealing faintly, somewhere in the distance, when B606 was released from the punishment cells. Somewhere there was merriment and chiming of bells—but not in the great grim walls of the English prison; not in the grim, hardened heart of convict B606.

B606, for the five days just past, had been on bread and water in one of the punishment cells. He had been violent, and abusive to one of the wardens. B606 was a "tough 'un." In Portland Prison no one was more closely watched in the sullen gray-coat ranks.

"Merry Christmas," someone chanted in his ears as he shuffled into line with his mate on the parade ground. A loud laugh followed, as if it were a good joke to be merry at Christmas in Portland Prison. But the man—he was still a man—with the round badge marked with B606 on his gray jacket, started discernibly at the sound of the two words in his ear. Under the hard mask of his sullen face something like pain worked dimly. When had he heard those two words before? Who had said them in his ear years ago?

"Front rank, two paces to left—march!" The governor of the prison strode about, giving low-voiced orders to the guards. His keen, shaven face was softened a little by the Christmas "peace, good will" that had crept into it. He laughed out cheerily, now and then, and spoke a kind word to some numbered convicts in the lines. At the sight of B606 the stern lines tightened about his lips again. The Christmas look vanished. "Keep a lookout, Charlie," he muttered to the nearest warden. "He's a slippery one. There's blood in his eye today. No knowing how *he'll* celebrate Christmas."

"He's loony," growled the warden, surlily. "Twon't noways inconvenience me when he slings his hook. They ain't no soft spot in 'im."

"Well, keep a look-out a while longer, Charlie. Watch out sharp. He'll be out in a matter of six months now."

What's six months time to nine years and a half? But nevertheless, B606 felt no exultation. He had long since ceased to count off the months on his fingers. It did not matter one way or another that he was almost "out." The old despair and numbness in his heart had deadened hope long since.

The day lagged on inside the walls of Portland Prison. Outside it was Merry Christmas, and the people made merry among their own.

In the afternoon the chief warden approached the convict in the blue cap with the number B606 on his jacket, with a message from the governor. He was wanted at the receiving office. B606 strode along beside the warden indifferently. It did not occur to him to wonder at the unusual summons. It could only mean some fresh punishment—it didn't matter.

They had arrived at the receiving office. A little child was standing there beside a clam-faced Sister of Charity. The convict stared at them both in dull wonder. But at the sound of the child's voice he started violently.

"Merry Christmas, Daddy!" The slender little figure crossed to him and slipped a small brown hand into his hand. "Won't you say 'Merry Christmas' back, Daddy? It was such a piece of work to get here. I guess you'd never think how hard it was to get an order to come! It was the Sister who did it. You see, she promised Mother to bring me. Mother's dead."

For a moment it was silent in the dismal room. The governor turned away to gaze out the window, and the warden's rough face softened. The childish voice began again: "She tried to wait, Daddy—guess you'd never think how hard she tried! But when she knew she couldn't, she got everything ready for you, and told me to wait instead. I'm waiting now, Daddy—it's lonesome—you'd never think how lonesome it is!"

"But I keep counting the days off. Every night I cross one out. You can begin to expect when there's only a hundred an' eighty-six. When it's only one day left—my, think of that, Daddy! Mother used to. An' I know just what I'm going to do then— just exactly! Mother and I used to practice together. She told me just how I was to tidy up the kitchen, an' get the kettle all ready to boil, and be sure to remember the chair you always like to sit in—an' the g-ranium! O Daddy, Mother and I used to hope so it would be in bloom that day! She said for me to put on a new white apron an' stretch up tall, and smile. I guess you'd never think how much we practiced. The last time Mother cried a little, but that was because she was so tired—I cried, too. It was that night Mother died. I—it's very lonesome now, Daddy, but I'm waiting. You'll come right home, won't you, Daddy?"

The great hard fingers had closed around the small brown ones. The tears were trailing over the rough cheeks of B606. The Sister's calm face was broken into lines of weeping.

"I'm most twelve now, Daddy. You mustn't mind how little I am—I can stretch up tall! An' you'll laugh to see how I can keep house for you. There's a woman on the third floor helps me when I forget how Mother said to do. I've got a hundred and eighty-six days more to practice in, Daddy. Daddy, won't you say 'Merry Christmas'?"

The New Year came and grew on familiar terms with the world. Spring crept into the lanes and turned them green, and even the files of gray-coated convicts at their quarrying drew in the warm, sweet breaths and, in their way, rejoiced. The heart of one of them lightened within him as day followed day. On the walls of his cell he crossed off each one as it passed, and counted eagerly those that were left. They grew to be very few.

He practiced the home-going over and over, alone in his cell. It kept him happy and softened the fierce, angry light in his eyes. He grew peaceable and quiet among his mates. The wardens talked of it in amazement.

One summer day, B606 "went out." Across the strip of sea a child was waiting for him. The room was tidied and the kettle put on to boil, and in the sunny window the geranium was all in bloom. A new life had begun, and the prison shackles fell away from him. He was no longer B606. He was a man among men, and a child's love and faith strengthened him.

Christmas Memories

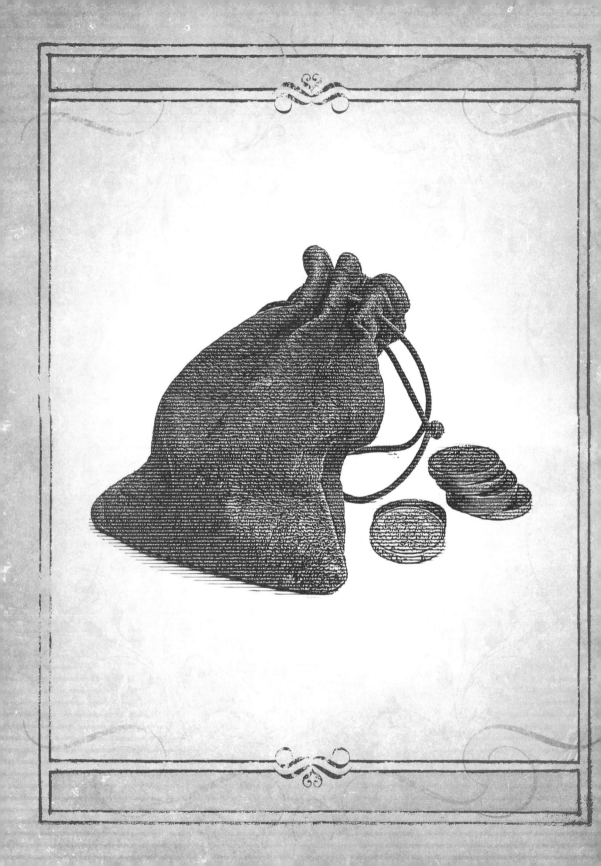

SANTA CLAUS IS KINDNESS

TEMPLE BAILEY

This isn't really a story about Santa Claus at all. But rather it's a story about a young woman named Nancy. Because her father and mother left each other, she no longer believed in goodness, constancy, enduring values—in marriage itself.

And that's the reason Simon decided not to marry her.

Christmas was only two days away when Nancy Spaulding discovered that she was in love with Simon Meriweather. The idea was not new to her, but hitherto she had fought it off. Simon was something of a prig, and she had known him all her life, a combination which does not always make for romance. Yet because she had known him throughout the years, Nancy forgave the priggishness. Or rather, she held that it had its origin in high-mindedness.

To Nancy's crowd, high-mindedness smacked of mid-Victorian ideals and all the stodgy virtues, but Nancy, defending him, declared that Simon's virtues set him apart.

"The rest of you are so standardized," she told Crane Mawson.

"If you mean me," Crane flung back at her, "you can stop right there. I am not standardized. My vices are my own, and Simon is welcome to his virtues."

"You would say that, of course, with all your money."

"Money has nothing to do with it."

"It has. You think I'll forgive your faults for the sake of your fortune."

Crane flushed. "Don't be brutal."

"Well, you shouldn't say such things of Simon."

It was in that moment of her defense of him that Nancy had come to know her heart. She wanted Simon, priggishness and all, for her husband. And she meant to have him.

He hadn't asked her yet, but that was a mere detail. He would if she wanted him to. He loved her. By every sign known to astute femininity she was certain of it. He didn't quite approve of her, but in spite of her faults he loved her.

The reason he didn't approve of her was that she was selfish and shallow. Only a few nights ago he had said:

"What's the matter with you, Nan? Life is something more than cakes and ale."

"Is it?"

"You know it is. You were a lovely little girl. You've lovely now, but you're slipping."

That was Simon—always telling you the truth about yourself. And, strange to say, Nancy found it refreshing. There were enough people to flatter you, but when Simon praised or blamed, it meant something. Now and then he admitted a mistake, but when he was right, he held to it.

"I had that crowd you're so keen about."

"Crane Mawson's?"

"Yes."

"But it's your crowd, too, Simon."

"In a way. But I don't fall for a lot of it. And you do. Snap out of it, darling."

"Out of what?"

"Well, you used to believe in things—"

He had stopped there, but she had known what he wanted to say. That the child Nancy had had faith and hope and courage. And now faith and hope and courage were dead words, for when she was fourteen, her life had changed. It was then that her father and mother had come to a parting of the ways. A divorce had followed, and after that Nancy had lived six months with one parent and six months with the other. Every other Christmas she spent with her father, who had married again and who gave wild parties. The alternate Christmas she spent with her mother, who had also married again and who also gave wild parties.

Nancy hated it all. Still, a mother was a mother, and a father, a father. She defended them savagely, saying things to Simon about love and marriage that she didn't mean, and saying them because of an exaggerated sense of loyalty which made her rush to the defense of that which was not defensible.

This Christmas she was to spend neither with her father, who was cruising in the Caribbean, nor her mother, who was cruising in the Mediterranean. As her Christmas celebration was therefore left to her own planning, Nancy thought a great deal about it. A lot of people had asked her to dine, but she had put them off. She had hoped Simon would ask her, but now it was too late. He lived alone with his father, and they were to spend the Christmas season with Simon's grandmother, who had an old-fashioned house in the hills of Vermont. That left Nancy definitely out. There was no reason why she should feel left out, but she did.

Feeling somewhat depressed, therefore, yet with something of hope in her heart, she decided to go downtown and do the last of her Christmas shopping. She took a bus part of the way, then walked to the shops. It was snowing, and she liked the snow. She liked, too, the hurrying crowds, the wreaths in the windows, the Santa Clauses on the corners. She dropped a dollar in the Christmas kettle of the Salvation Army lassie who teetered on her cold toes and smiled at Nancy from under her demure bonnet. Nancy smiled back.

It had been something of a wrench to give that dollar. She had a generous allowance from her father, but she had spent it all and had mortgaged future remittances. She had charge accounts everywhere, but cash was short, and she would have to conserve it until her Christmas gift checks came in.

Of course she might borrow from Simon. She had often done it, and there had never been any embarrassment about those borrowings.

"Be a good pal," she would say, "and lend me a few dollars."

And Simon would ask, "How much?" And sometimes it had been as much as a hundred dollars.

Simon had always been a dear about everything, and they had been such friends. When she was five and he was twelve, he had given her his first Christmas present. And he had taught her a song. Nancy, looking in the window as she passed, was seeing beyond them a rich and glowing room where she sat in a big chair by the fire, and Simon, a curly-headed lad of twelve, stood before her, beating time:

> *"A ship, a ship a-sailing,*
> *A-sailing on the sea,*
> *And it was deeply laden*
> *With pretty things for me . . ."*

It was not exactly a Christmas song, but they had sung it together every Christmas and called it their song. They would sing it together tonight, out under the stars if the snow stopped; and if the snow did not stop, they would sing it anyway.

She was to see him at Crane Mawson's. Crane had a big country place up the Hudson and was giving a party. They would skate on the pond and eat out of doors at midnight, with fires blazing and things cooking over the coals. Nancy was to go in Crane's car, for Simon, being more than usually busy before the holidays, would be late. Simon was twenty-seven and a member of his father's law firm. Nancy and a lot of the others would stay all night at Crane's, but Simon was motoring in. He asked Nancy if he could take her back with him, but she had said:

"Back to what? Aunt Edie?"

Aunt Edie was a great-aunt on Nancy's father's side. When Nancy was left high and dry on the shores of her parents' matrimonial differences, Aunt Edie came and played propriety. As she was over seventy and on a diet, her presence added little to the joy of Nancy's days.

Entering one of the big shops, Nancy made her way to the toy department. She had to buy something for Grace Marquis's twins. She could charge whatever she bought, and her sense of loneliness and depression dropped from her as she found herself in the midst of the crowds of children who, thrilled and excited, explored this modern fairyland.

She made her purchase and wandered to where the dolls were displayed in a section especially devoted to them. It was not the dolls which interested her as much as the faces of the little girls who were bunched in adoring groups about them. Here were the future mothers, drawn to these artificial babies by their potential maternity. With cheeks glowing, eyes shining, they hovered over the infants in bassinets, toddlers in rompers and short skirts, and the larger dolls grand as Cinderella at the famous ball.

One doll, lovelier than the rest, was enthroned on a pedestal. With blonde curls, blue eyes, and dimples, with rosy cheeks and a rosier frock, she was entrancing.

A little voice at Nancy's side said, "I want that one, Mother."

"I wish you might have it, Wendy, but we only came to look."

"Perhaps Santa Claus will bring it," she said hopefully.

"Oh, darling!" There was dismay in the mother's voice. "You mustn't be disappointed if he doesn't."

The little voice went on: "Well, maybe he will. He will know she would like me for a mother."

"I am sure she would, but—" The rest was lost in the babble of voices.

Turning a little, Nancy saw the mother and the child. Very shabby, the mother thin but smiling, the child enchanted by the peep into fairyland. Their presence in this great and fashionable place was undoubtedly an adventure into the unknown. The mother had brought her child to see, not to buy. Nancy liked the mother's voice. There was sweetness in it and a quality less tangible than sweetness. Courage, perhaps, or fortitude.

They were moving on.

"Do you think, Mother," the child was piping, "that Santa Claus might—?"

Nancy found herself following them. She had never bothered much about children. The sons and daughters of her friends were restless little creatures, a bit bored by life. Not like this child—hopeful, eager.

As they came out at last into the snowy street, the mother raised an umbrella. It was one of those with ribs poking through, but it sheltered the shabby pair from the snow, and the child hopped along by her mother's side like a happy robin.

With Nancy still following, they turned into a street which tapered off suddenly from elegance to squalor. Arriving at a grimy tenement, the mother and child ascended the steps and went in.

Nancy stood outside in the snow. She, too, carried an umbrella, but it was not one with ribs poking through. It was, indeed, particularly attractive, and Simon had given it to her. It had a jade ball on the handle, and the silk was a deeper shade. Nancy's hair was bright under her smart little hat, and the fur of her coat was as soft as a pussycat's. The coat had cost a fabulous sum. Nancy's father had given it to her because he was leaving her alone for Christmas while he cruised the Caribbean. Nancy felt that its richness was out of place in the squalor about her.

Looking up, she saw the child's face in the window on the second floor. Nancy waved, and the child waved back, and her eyes followed the lovely lady with interest.

Returning to the shop, Nancy bought the doll. She thought it better to deliver it herself than to send it. So back she went to the shabby street, her umbrella bobbing.

When she arrived at the grimy tenement, the child was not at the window. Nancy, ascending the stairs, set the box out of sight in the hall and knocked at a door on the second floor.

The mother of the child opened it.

Nancy said, "Could I speak to you a moment out here?"

The woman shut the door behind her, and Nancy found herself stammering: "I heard your little girl wish for the doll. I bought it. I want her to have it."

The woman faltered, "The doll in the shop?"

"Yes."

"Oh!" A flush came into the mother's cheeks. "A doll like that is too handsome for Wendy."

"But she wanted it."

"We want many things we can't have. Wendy needs other things." She stopped and forced a smile. "I'm afraid I must seem ungrateful. It is so good of you, but—" she stopped again.

There was a moment's awkward silence, then the woman said with a touch of wistfulness: "Perhaps I am wrong. Perhaps I should let her have it. Perhaps it will be worthwhile, if no other dreams come true for her, that this one will—" Her voice broke on that.

Nancy said impulsively, "Can't I help?"

The woman shook her head. "We're all right. And I'll let Wendy have the doll."

"I want her to think that Santa Claus brought it. It's such a darling thing to believe in Santa Claus and so dreadful when we don't."

"Yes," the woman said. "Santa Claus is kindness. I tell Wendy that, but she still clings to the idea of a saint with whiskers and sleigh bells. And if it makes her happier, why not?"

"Why not?" said Nancy, who didn't believe in anything.

The woman said, hesitating a little on the words: "Would you come in? I'd like to have you see my baby."

"I'd love to."

The room that they entered was very clean and bare. A well-scrubbed table was set with two plates and two cups. There was a basket of bread, a glass of milk for Wendy, and a little pot boiling on the stove gave out the savory odor of soup. Wendy, rising from her seat, was wide-eyed at the vision of loveliness in the pussycat coat.

Nancy held out her hands to her. "I'm Nancy Spaulding," she said, "and I've come to see the baby."

Wendy led the way pridefully to the bed where the baby lay. "His name," she said, "is Timothy."

"Timothy Bryan," the mother said. "I am Mrs. Bryan, and Wendy is Wendy Bryan."

With the introductions thus accomplished, the woman lifted the baby in her arms. Her eyes were happy as she looked at him. It seemed to Nancy incredible that with all the shabbiness, all the bareness of this poor home, the mother's eyes were happy.

She asked, "How old is he?"

"Six months. My husband died a year ago."

Nancy said, "Isn't it hard for you, having to take care of the two of them?"

"Hard? No. It's all that makes life worth living. I get sewing from one of the big shops, and I have milk for my babies and food enough for my strength. The hard thing was losing my husband. I loved him. But in my children he lives again. I think sometimes it is like the way I feel about our Lord at Christmas, that God lives in Him, in human form."

Tears were close to Nancy's eyes. She hadn't cried for years, not since that awful night when she had known that Daddy and Mother hated each other and that her home was wrecked. But here was something—something that she wanted. This woman was rich in love, and Nancy was poor. When, a little later, Nancy went away, she told herself that in spite of the woman's brave words, the need of the little family was great. Well, she'd see that they had a Christmas dinner, and she would tuck into an envelope a snug sum of money. She would have to borrow the money from Simon, darling Simon who never failed her; and who, that very night, if the gods were good, would ask her to marry him.

But Simon, as it happened, had no idea of asking Nancy to marry him. He loved her deeply, but she wasn't the kind of wife he wanted. A man had to be cautious in these days. The Meriweathers in the past had not been cautious—they had gone neck or nothing to their romantic enterprises, had plighted their troths at various Gretna Greens, or more conventionally at the altar, and had lived happily ever after—or unhappily, as the case might be.

But there had been this difference. The Meriweathers of previous generations had not had before them the menace of the divorce court. The wives of those earlier Simons had said solemnly at the altar. "Till death do us part." But the girls of Simon's set declared frankly and without shame that if they didn't like the men they married, they wouldn't live with them.

Nancy herself had said, "Do you think, if I made a mistake, I'd be tied for life to any man?"

And that wasn't Simon's idea of marriage. He wanted permanence. He wanted a wife who would help him to keep the green plant of their affection in full flower. He felt that he could love Nancy forever, but he feared that his love might not be enough to change her from a teasing sprite to a constant and contented spouse.

When Simon presented his matrimonial theories to Nancy for discussion, she held them up to scorn, calling him Simon Legree and Simple Simon and, now and then, wickedly, Simon Pure. Having no inferiority complex and only a normal amount of vanity, Simon had smiled through it all. But of late she had gone beyond teasing, beyond argument. She was playing around with Crane Mawson, and Simon's idea of a woman who would play around with Crane was not his idea of what he wanted in a wife.

He thought of these things as he stood uncertainly before a case in Tiffany's great shop trying to choose a gift for Nancy's Christmas. He had always given her a present and had found little difficulty in selecting it, but this year it was different. For the first time he was definitely placing her among the other women of his acquaintance. Hitherto she had been set apart in his mind as the woman he was going to marry. To the woman a man didn't intend to marry, in these modern days, one gave perfumes in crystal flasks, bits of jade set in dull gold, carved coral in silver bracelets, aquamarine earrings if her eyes matched them. Simon knew the litany of up-to-date feminine demands.

He drew the line only at jeweled lipsticks and cigarette holders. He had told Nancy on one occasion that he loved his love with an "N" because she was Neat and N-chanting, and Nancy had said,

"Well, I don't get lipstick on your hanky or cigarette ashes on your shirt front, but there are worse things, darling."

"What?"

"Getting on people's nerves."

"Do I? On yours?"

"On everybody's."

Well, if she meant people like Crane Mawson, Simon didn't care how much he got on their nerves. Crane's real name was Derwent, but he had a long figure and a long neck, and at school the somewhat ludicrous combination had incited his mates to call him "Crane." He was no longer ludicrous. He had gained pounds and muscle at college and prestige at football. His fresh coloring and his shock of fair curls were high notes in the good looks he had acquired. But the name still stuck.

Crane would, of course, give Nancy a present. But that was not Simon's worry. His worry was to choose one for her himself. He had thought of a Baxter print. Nancy was always hunting for a Josephine to match her Baxter Napoleon. Nobody seemed to know whether Baxter had ever really done a Josephine, but Nancy had not given up the hunt as hopeless. She had a desultory interest in collections. She acquired things because every one seemed to do it.

Simon, who did nothing because other people did it, collected objects that had to do with the art of fishing. He loved the out-of-doors, and, having traveled much, had brought home with him nets and creels and flies, ancient and modern, primitive and up to date. He spent much time in cataloguing his treasures, or, in right season, whipping the streams of the North or doing deep-sea fishing in warmer waters. He was, indeed, very much in earnest about it, and his preoccupation had given Nancy an opportunity to call him Simon the Fisherman.

"If you think you are teasing me," he had told her, "you are thinking wrong. Simon Peter was rather splendid."

Nancy's level gaze had studied him. "He was a fisher of men. And you are a fisher of women. They are all in love with you."

"All of them? Not you, Nancy?"

"Well, of course. I couldn't be."

"Why not?"

"I've known you too long and too well."

It sounded harsh, but it wasn't, for she had made a face at him to show she wasn't quite in earnest. She had a lovely little face, and her eyes were as wide and as candid as when she had stuck out her tongue the first time he had met her. And her red hair was as bright and beautiful as when he had pulled her long curls in return for her impishness.

It was when she was five that he had first given her a Christmas present—a pink china box filled with pink Jordan almonds and tied with pink ribbon. She had adored it and had kissed him. She had kissed him on Christmas Day every year until four years ago. Then she had said:

"I'm grown up. I'm not going to kiss any man now till I've promised to marry him."

It was old-fashioned, of course, but Simon liked it. He hoped she had not failed in her resolve, though at times he feared it. Crane had been rushing Nancy beyond anything. Perhaps he had already asked her to marry him. Perhaps she had said, "Yes." Perhaps he had kissed her. Simon didn't like to think about it.

He was hanging now over a tray of old brooches. There was one that he wanted for Nancy. It was not large and was of exquisitely painted porcelain set about with pearls. It was expensive, far beyond anything that Simon had expected to pay. But the head painted on it was the head of a Madonna, and the Madonna looked like Nancy. There was the same rich coloring of eyes and hair, and she wore a blue cloak about her shoulders. Nancy wore blue a lot, and Simon liked it.

But why should he buy a brooch like that? Nancy wasn't the Madonna type. He had an almost uncanny feeling that if the Madonna of the brooch lifted those modestly lowered lashes, she would show the impish, teasing eyes of Nancy.

Yet he wanted her to have it, and the extravagance would not break him. He wondered what Crane Mawson would give her. And as if the thought had brought him, he heard Crane's voice behind him.

"Only one day more to Christmas, Simon, and I've got a list as long as your arm. Ten cigarette holders for ten girls. Ten vanity cases, ditto. That settles the masses, as it were, but there's still the one girl. Look here, Simon, if you wanted to buy something for the Only Woman in your life, what would you get?"

Simon straightened up, and when Simon stood straight, his inches seemed to top those of Crane.

"What would I give her? I should give her precisely nothing."

Carrie laughed derisively. "You wouldn't get far with most women."

"Perhaps not with what you call the masses, but I might get farther with the one I wanted."

"Don't fool yourself, Simon. They can all be bought."

Simon did not answer. Why argue with Crane, who had millions and who could buy anything? Perhaps he could buy Nancy. Simon didn't want to buy a woman. He hadn't Crane's millions, and he was glad of it. And anyhow, why should he worry when he didn't want to marry Nancy?

Crane was saying, "Come over here and look at this."

He led the way to a case wherein were displayed certain gorgeous jewels. Crane had chosen from among the others a curled feather of diamonds tipped with emeralds. It could be worn, he explained eagerly, in a half dozen ways. "On her shoulder. In her hair—"

Nancy's shoulder! Nancy's hair!

"I've half a mind to get it for her," Crane told him. "Nancy, I mean. Think she'd object?"

"You'll have to decide that. It's you who are giving it."

"I'll toss a nickel . . . Heads she gets it, tails she doesn't."

He flipped the coin, and the head came up He was pleased and showed it. "The fates are with me," he said, and gave the clerk the order.

Simon said, "See you tonight," suddenly, and got out.

It was snowing, and with his hat pulled down and no umbrella, he made his way through the driving storm. Taxi men hailed him, but he would have none of them. He welcomed the pit-pat of soft flakes against his cheek. His mind whirled with the snow.

If Nancy married Crane, she would be unhappy. And he, Simon, might save her. By all the passion that was in him, he knew it. He knew that if tonight he took her in his arms and told her on a rushing tide of eloquence that she was his and nobody else should have her, he might win her.

But what then? What of this Nancy he would win? In the last analysis, what did she ask of life?

A good time? Money to spend? Freedom from care? She had told him a thousand times, "I want to dance through life, Simon."

But one couldn't dance through life. Simon knew that. He had lived through his mother's dreadful illness, had seen the pain that no drugs could ease. He had known his father's devotion. He had seen his mother cling and gain courage in the arms that loved her. He knew of those days of poverty when his mother was young and pretty and the dishonesty of his father's partner had brought failure in business. He knew the depth of tenderness with which the young couple had sustained each other. He had seen his tiny sister die and his mother's fortitude in the face of tragedy. The watchword of his home had been love. Not love that asks for things, but a sharing. If Nancy couldn't share, he couldn't make her happy. He couldn't make any woman happy who shirked life. She would lose his respect, his love. A man had to fight with his back to the wall in these days, and he needed a woman to buckle on his armor.

He went back to his office, worked late, and got home in time to dine with his father. Anticipating the late supper, he ate little.

His father queried, "Where's your appetite?"

"I'm saving up. Crane's having a late supper on the ice—sausages and scrambled eggs."

"Nancy going?"

"Yes, and dozens of others."

"Chaperones?"

"There aren't any such animals in these days. But Crane's parents will be somewhere about the house. It's a huge place, you know, and Crane has his own quarters. I'm glad the snow stopped. The wind will blow the ice clear."

Later, as they had their coffee in the living room, Simon's father said: "Your mother would be very happy if she knew you were going to marry Nancy. She loved her as a child and was sorry for her . . ."

"I'm not going to marry her."

"She's refused you?"

"I'm not going to ask her."

The older Simon Meriweather cleared his throat. "My dear boy, I thought it was settled."

"I thought so, too. But I can't do it."

"Can you tell me why?"

"Yes. I am not sure that if we married, things would last with her—permanent things, like you and Mother."

His father stared into the fire. His voice was husky when he spoke. "I never doubted your mother."

Simon's voice was eager. "That's what I mean. I've known Nancy for fifteen years, yet I feel that I don't know her. She was a lovely little girl. She's lovely now. But she makes light of things that I don't want made light of by my wife, by the—mother of my children . . ."

He stumbled over those last words, and his father said gently, "One never quite knows in the beginning."

"You knew with Mother."

"I loved her."

Simon's head went up. "You think I don't love Nancy?"

"I think, if you loved her, you might see beneath the surface."

Simon stood up, and there was a poignant note in his voice as he spoke: "Dad, they all think I'm a prig about such things, that I ask too much. Do you?"

And now his father stood beside him, his hand on his son's shoulder.

"No. In a way you are right. A woman must prove her worth before a man can marry her."

When Simon arrived at Crane's, Nancy and the others were on the ice. Nancy never looked more lovely than in her skating clothes. Tonight she wore white wool. There was no touch of color except the red of her hair and the red-gold of the scarf which blazed like a bright banner as she skated with Crane.

Simon spoke of the scarf when at last he had a chance at her. "It's a beautiful thing."

"Crane bought it in Switzerland when he was there for winter sports. He sent it to me last Christmas, but this is the first time I've worn it."

Simon said abruptly, "I'm not going to give you a Christmas present."

She was startled. "Why not?"

"Everybody gives you things."

They skated on for a few moments in silence. Then Nancy said,

"Of course you don't mean it."

"But I do."

She flashed a glance at him. "Have a heart, darling. I want something, if it's only a stick of candy."

"You'll get plenty of gifts. You won't miss mine."

Her laugh was low and provocative. "Jealous?"

"No." He could not tell her that it was something deeper than jealousy.

Their arms were linked, her hands in his, as they swayed in rhythmic motion. Simon was aware that Nancy's fingers had tightened on his, that her cheek was against his coat, that her face was lifted toward him.

"Be nice to me, Simon." Again the provocative note.

Simon, held by that note, his heart answering it, knew that in another moment, if he wasn't careful, Nancy would be in his arms. He would be saying the things it wasn't wise to be saying. He would be saying the things that would sweep them both away from reason. And marriage was a reasonable estate!

He said, therefore, with a lightness that hid the tumult in his heart, "If we don't get back in a hurry, we'll miss the eats."

The fingers that had tightened on his relaxed. She drew away from him. It was all he could do not to draw her back, but he did not.

In heavy silence they returned to where the crowd was gathered about a great fire that lighted the night, and where competent servants from Crane's huge house on the hill were doing expert things with gridirons and frying pans.

Nancy sat close to the fire, which, shining on her, showed her hair a mass of molten metal, and suddenly she said: "Let's play Consequences. I'll begin. I love my love with an 'S' because he is Stingy."

All eyes were turned on Simon.

"She means you," said several accusing voices.

He was cool. "Does she? Well, I love my love with an 'N' because she's Nonsensical."

Nancy came back with, "I love my love with a 'C' because he's Charming." She smiled at Crane.

Crane was standing beside her, his plate in his hand. His skating clothes were as blue as his eyes, and with his height and yellow hair he was like some young god of the old Norse legends. His laugh was strong and hearty as he flung his challenge back, "I love my love with an 'N,' because she's—Necessary."

Nancy flushed. "You're so obvious, Crane. And anyhow it's a stupid game." She stood up. "If you're all going to keep on eating, I'll sing for you. It's a song Simon taught me years ago."

She saw Simon's startled face. She knew he would hate having her sing before all these people the song which each Christmas they had sung alone together. Not that they had been sentimental about it, but each had felt that the silly little song meant something that was not on the surface. Yes, Simon would hate having her sing it. Well, let him. All the old things between them were dead. He had killed them when he had said,

"If we don't get back, we'll miss the eats."

Nothing could have been more revolting. That he could think of food when her head had been ready to tuck into the hollow of his shoulder, and when he had known, if he had any warmth in him, that she wanted him to take her in his arms. And he had not taken her. He had not wanted her.

She began to sing:

> *"A ship, a ship a-sailing,*
> *A-sailing on the sea,*
> *And it was pretty laden*
> *With pretty things for me.*

"There were raisins in the cabin
And almonds in the hold;
The sails were made of satin,
And the mast it was of gold . . ."

As the verse ended, there was a cry from the crowd: "Go on. Go on."

Nancy said, "Sing, everybody," and Crane joined in, and the others, stumbling over some of the words but getting the tune.

Simon was not singing. He sat staring at Nancy, and suddenly she stopped.

"Sing, Simon," she said.

He shook his head. "I've forgotten the words," he told her.

He saw her face grow white, but she finished the song bravely.

"The captain was a duck, a duck,
With a jacket on his back,
And when the fairy ship set sail,
The captain he said, 'Quack'."

An hour later, in Crane's big house, she was saying to Simon with sobbing breath:

"I'll never forgive you, never. You lied to me. You couldn't have forgotten the words—"

"Yes," he said sternly, "I have forgotten everything but that I love you, and that you could sing our song before all those grinning people."

He had not intended to say it, but, having said it, he turned on his heel and left her. They had been standing on the great stairway, and Nancy had peeled off her jacket and sweater. In her silk shirt and wool breeches she was like a handsome boy. And as she stood there alone when Simon had gone, Crane's eyes were on her Rosalind-like beauty.

He crossed the room. "Look here," he said, "I want to show you something."

"I'm dead for sleep. Wait till tomorrow."

"I don't want to wait, and you won't when I show you. Come on, darling."

She followed him upstairs to a small sitting room where he unlocked a cabinet, took out a box, and showed her, lying in a satin nest, the curled feather of diamonds tipped with emeralds. "You can wear it," he said, as he had said in the shop, "in a dozen ways. On your shoulder. In your hair—"

He stopped, for she was looking at him with eyes that were wide and stormy.

"You know I can't accept a thing like that from you, Crane."

"Why not? There are no strings tied to it."

"Aren't there?"

"Well, of course. I'm simply mad about you, and I want you for my wife. I can give you everything—"

She said sharply, "I'm not to be bought."

He laughed. "Simon said that this afternoon."

"Where?"

"In the shop I showed him this. I tossed a nickel to see whether I dared give it to you. I wasn't going to give it to you tonight, but when you were singing that song, you were like something out of a dream, and I knew I could never be happy without you."

She did not answer. She was looking down at the glittering feather. Oh, she didn't want to be a part of any one's dream but Simon's. Simon, who couldn't give her things like this. Simon, who had flung her love back in her face and had left her.

Crane was leaning down to her. "Darling—"

She gave him a little push. "Please—" she said in a breathless way, and ran madly up the stairs.

She found her room, locked the door, and flung herself on the bed sobbing. She had lost Simon. Why or how, she couldn't quite decide. Perhaps it was that silly song. Perhaps it was because he had seen Crane's present and had thought she might be bought.

Well, whatever it was, her Christmas was spoiled. There remained only to give to Wendy and the mother of Wendy something of Christmas joy. She thought of the mother's eyes as she had looked at her baby. And the things she had said of her husband. That in the children he still lived for the woman who loved him. Oh, if love had only been like that for her own father and mother. If only it might be like that for herself and Simon!

She slept at last and went away the next morning before any one was up. She left a note for Crane:

"I'm sorry, but I can't stay any longer. I think you will understand."

Arriving home, she made out the market list for the Christmas basket to be sent to Mrs. Bryan. There must be a chicken for roasting, and all the things to go with it; a tree and toys for Wendy and the baby; a loaf of bread to be delivered every day until the order was canceled; milk, too, must be sent daily.

All these things could be charged to her father's account, and certain warm garments and toys for the children could also be charged. Bob Spaulding never complained of bills, especially those of his daughter. In a way he loved her, but he had not loved her enough to live his life sanely and decently.

Her lists finished, she went to the cook with them. The chicken was to be roasted at home, and there would be gravy and mashed potatoes and other vegetables, all sent hot tomorrow. The tree Nancy would take over this afternoon and trim, and on her way to the toy shop she stopped and arranged with Mrs. Bryan that Wendy could be sent to a neighbor's so that the decorating might be done secretly.

There would be, she told herself with a flame of resentment sweeping her, no money to tuck in with the other things. For she couldn't borrow of Simon, not after the things that had happened. There was, of course, Aunt Edie, but Aunt Edie didn't believe in borrowing or lending.

At the lunch table Aunt Edie demanded: "Why aren't you eating, Nancy? Girls of today starve themselves. I wonder that they think of themselves as future mothers?"

Nancy did not answer. Her mind was not on food or on the future. She was thinking of Simon. By this time he was on his way to Vermont. In a few hours he would be dining with his grandmother, having those famous biscuits and maple syrup of which he had bragged. Men were like that. They would eat though the heavens fell!

But Simon was not on his way to Vermont. He was to leave town with his father at five-thirty. He was very busy, but all the morning, as he had worked over his papers, his mind had been distracted by thoughts of Nancy. He had a feeling that last night he had been brutal. But there was nothing to be done about it. He couldn't ask her to marry him. Not with his ideas of what marriage meant. And anyhow by this time she was probably engaged to Crane.

When the lunch hour arrived, he rushed to his club, had a glass of milk and not much with it, and was rushing out again when he met Crane Mawson. He would have rushed on, but Crane stopped him and said abruptly, "Well, I couldn't buy her . . ."

Simon stared at him. "Nancy?"

"Yes. I've taken that diamond feather back to Tiffany's. She wouldn't have it. She left my house before breakfast, and she left me flat. How's that for a merry Christmas?"

Simon, trying to be casual, said, "Perhaps better luck will come with the New Year."

"Better luck? Don't you believe it! If you had bet a thousand dollars yesterday that money couldn't buy a woman, you would have won it."

But Simon wasn't thinking of a thousand dollars. He was thinking that he must get back to Tiffany's and buy that brooch for Nancy. Even if he didn't approve of her, even if she was selfish and shallow and all the things that, God help him, he had said about her, she was still the little girl to whom he had once given the pink Jordan almonds in the pink box and who had kissed him and thanked him. He must think of that little girl Nancy, and of the Nancy who wouldn't be bought by Crane's jewels. Perhaps he could think of the two as one. Perhaps if he had thought of her in that way always, he wouldn't have been so smug and self-satisfied.

He looked at his watch. Time enough to run around to Tiffany's. Hailing a taxi, he rushed to the shop, bought the brooch, and, arriving at Nancy's, found her out.

"Do you know where she is?" he asked Aunt Edie.

Aunt Edie said, with some asperity: "She never tells me. You might ask Graham."

Graham was the butler. Miss Nancy had, he believed, some poor family on her mind. He thought cook might have the address. Cook had it, having noted it for the bread man. Simon rushed on. In the taxi he thought of what he would say to Nancy. He wasn't going to ask her to marry him, but he was going to tell her he was sorry.

And while he was thinking these things, Nancy, on her knees trimming the tree, said to Mrs. Bryan, "Do you think Wendy will like it?"

"She's never seen anything so pretty."

Nancy, sitting back on her heels, surveyed it—a thing of shining balls and silver snow, of tinsel. "It is rather nice. I'll finish it up and hide it in the closet while you go for Wendy."

The mother, pulling on her coat, said, "If you'll just keep an eye on the baby—"

But Nancy, tying balls and draping tinsel, did not think of the baby until a little cry roused her.

"Darling . ." She went to the basket and bent above it.

The baby stopped crying and smiled at her. She said almost shyly, "Hello, little Timothy."

Timothy. What a nice name! A Bible name. She liked Bible names. There was Simon, for instance. Simon, the Fisherman. Simon Peter. Rather a solemn name for a baby. She lifted the baby suddenly and hugged him. He was so adorable and warm and soft.

"Little Timothy," she said softly. "Little Timothy."

A knock sounded, and as she called, "Come in," the door opened, and Simon stood on the threshold.

He spoke with a touch of awkwardness, "Well, here I am."

"How did you find me?"

"They told me at the house," he answered, yet hardly knew what he was saying. For back of Nancy was a window, and the red-gold of the winter sunset lighted the blue of her dress and shone on her hair and on the head of the baby in her arms. "Oh, Madonna, Madonna," were the words in Simon's heart; but he could not speak them.

She held up the baby for him to see. "He's sweet, isn't he?"

"You're sweet." His voice wavered.

Their eyes met, and the look in Simon's made Nancy say hastily, "You see, I wanted to do something for somebody's Christmas." She told him about the meeting with Wendy and her mother. "They'll be coming back in a few minutes, and we'd better hide the tree."

She laid the baby in his basket. "I'm glad you came, Simon. I want to borrow some money."

"How much?"

"Could you let me have fifty?"

"More if you want it."

He took out his wallet and was counting the bills when he was suddenly aware of an incredible sound. Nancy was crying. He crammed the wallet in his pocket and drew her around so that she was within the circle of his arm.

"Dear girl, what is it?"

"Oh," she said, "I thought I was never going to borrow of you again. And I wanted to help Mrs. Bryan. I can't tell you how I feel about her, Simon. She loved her husband, and he's dead. Yet he lives for her and the children. Death hasn't parted them. Yet life parted my father and my mother. If only they had felt that way about me—that they lived in me—I might have been different. It was love I needed, Simon, and I didn't have it."

He could not speak. He held her close. Oh, what a fool he had been not to know that the hurt heart of a child had found a strange satisfaction in hurting others!

He said at last, his voice hoarse with emotion: "You're mine, Nancy. You know it, and I know it . . . And I want it to be forever."

"Not like Father and Mother?"

"Never like them, dearest."

They heard the voice of Wendy in the hall. When she opened the door, the tree was hidden. She was much excited.

"Santa Claus *is* coming. Mother says so. Perhaps he will bring me a doll."

Nancy bent and kissed her. "Perhaps."

"Mother says Santa Claus is kindness."

"He's more than that, darling. He's love, and everything—"

Simon at last got Nancy away.

"We're catching a five o'clock train," he told Mrs. Bryan, "and we'll have to make a run for it."

Whirling along in a taxi, he told Nancy, "We'll stop at the house for your bag."

"But, Simon—"

"You're going to Vermont with us. If my grandmother is going to be yours, she might as well give you a Christmas dinner."

The early darkness had come, and Nancy's head was on his shoulder. As they passed a street corner, a man in cheap Santa Claus clothes stood where the light shone on him. There were other cheap Santas on other corners. Too many of them, perhaps, but could there be too many? Santa Claus, the child had said, was kindness, and he, Simon, had not been kind. Well, he had the whole future in which to make up for it. To teach Nancy the love she had missed. And he would teach her in all humility. He who had misjudged her.

He said, "I've a present for you."

Her laugh was low. "A stick of candy, Simon?"

"Something better than that."

But he could not tell her. Tomorrow early, on Christmas morning, he would give her the Madonna, and she would know all that it meant to him.

A PRECIOUS MEMORY

D. T. DOIG

True, it was Christmas again, but not as it was when they still had Timmy. Now they could feel the very foundations of their home trembling because of the growing coldness between Mom and Dad.

And the family cake was the last straw, the last hope.

This contemporary Christmas story by David Doig of Scotland is, without question, one of the great ones.

I'm not sure who invented the Family Cake. My mother called it that, and for all I know it might have been her own idea. For as long as I can remember it has always been a part of Christmas.

Mom was a great one for making cakes and decorating them to suit the occasion—birthdays, anniversaries, weddings, Thanksgivings, even the Fourth of July.

But the Family Cake for Christmas was always the special one. It appeared in its full glory at supper on Christmas Eve, a prelude to all the surprises, mysteries, and excitement that were to come. The best thing about it was that Mom had carefully put all our names on it in different-colored icing.

There were five of us altogether, and each wedge of cake bore one name. Bob and Ruth were the names of Mom and Dad. Then there was Bess—that was I—the eldest. Then Matthew, five years younger; and finally little Timmy, who was the youngest. Each section had its candle, and a tiny Santa Claus stood in the middle, its feet stuck in the icing.

I had the honor, being the eldest child, of lighting the candles and carrying the cake in for dessert. There was always a loud cheer when I brought it in.

I can still see little Timmy in his high chair, his fingers clenched with excitement, his eyes glistening in the candlelight. He would gaze in wonder at the cake, the Christmas tree, the decorations. When Mom cut the cake, Timmy had to have his name pointed out so that he was sure his piece was the right one. Then he would clap his hands and laugh with joy.

My father would joke all through the meal and tell Mom how pretty she looked, and how lucky she was to have such a splendid family. It was a happy time.

Then one year Mom didn't make the Family Cake. That was the Christmas when Timmy wasn't there any more.

I was twelve when it happened. March was busy on the farm, with so many calves being born and all the lambing as well. Some of Dad's calves got scour, a difficult ailment to cure, and he seldom had a minute to himself.

One afternoon, Mom had to go into town for an appointment with the doctor, and Mrs. Harris, our part-time help, was ill. Matthew and I were in school so it fell to Dad to look after Timmy for two or three hours.

There was nothing special about that, for we were all used to taking turns caring for Timmy. Things seemed to be quiet on the farm that day, and Dad promised to take Timmy fishing for a couple of hours until Mom got back. The stream nearby flowed into an old mill pond, and it was often possible to find trout there.

They were just setting off when one of the farmhands came to report trouble with a newborn calf. Dad took Timmy with him to the shed where the calf and its mother were lying. Dad told Timmy to sit down on a bale of hay and wait.

While the business of working on the calf went on, it took the men a while to realize that Timmy was no longer there. Dad abandoned the calf at once and looked everywhere—in the house, in the tractor shed, and all over the barns. Soon everybody on the farm, as well as the neighbors, had joined in the search. Minutes dragged on into an hour and an hour into two hours.

It was Mrs. Harris's husband who found Timmy in the mill pond. He had wandered quietly down to the stream to look for fish. Nobody could tell how it had happened. We only knew when he was taken out it was too late.

After that, things could never be the same. All through that spring and summer we lived our lives and did the ordinary tasks. And we hid our grief as best we could when we weren't alone.

Dad was quieter now, and Mom went around with a brooding look on her face. She often spoke to Dad in a hard tone I hadn't heard before. Although I was only twelve, I knew something more than our loss was driving them apart.

I sensed that she blamed Dad for what had happened to Timmy. In her mind it had to be somebody's fault. Perhaps hers for not being there.

During all that time I never saw her cry, but there were times when she seemed like a statue or like somebody who was sleepwalking. Never once did she mention Timmy.

The months passed. Time began its work of healing, but the old, warm feeling of being a united family was no more. And yet my mother was even more attentive than before toward Matthew and me, anxiously watchful and protective. But between her and my father there remained a gulf—a distance which showed, not in silence, but in the lack of companionship and a certain wariness in their conversation.

Once, when they thought I had gone out of the house, I heard Dad say, "If that's how you feel, I could go and stay with Charles in Ontario."

I didn't think at the time that it meant anything more than a visit to an uncle, who was also a farmer, in Canada. Charles was Dad's brother, and I could barely remember the tall, wide-shouldered man who had once come here to see us.

But as the weeks passed and I sometimes caught the word "Canada" just before they broke off a conversation, I began to be afraid. Maybe Dad wasn't going there just for a visit.

Matthew, who was barely seven years old, wasn't aware of my fears or what caused them. He was the one who talked about Timmy, and he often talked to me about the things Timmy had said or done. He seemed to know I was the one who would really listen.

Harvest time came, and with it a golden spell of sun and ripeness. The early September days with their mellow plenty made me feel that the happy, close-knit days would come back again. My mother was busier than I had ever seen her. She never seemed to be still, and in October she and Mrs. Harris set about their usual task of brightening the house for the approach of Christmas.

They painted the kitchen and all the bedrooms. It was a bustling time, and any visitor would have thought that ours was a cheerful home that housed a happy family.

I knew, though, that it was all on the surface, and lurking beneath was a shadow that we couldn't chase away. Dad sometimes tried to bring back the old fun and banter. Matthew and I would always respond, but it would only be when Mom wasn't around.

Once, when the cleaning was going on, I saw Mrs. Harris stop outside the room that had been Timmy's. "Do you want me to start on this one?" she quietly asked my mother.

"No. We'll leave that for now," Mom replied very quickly.

In time, of course, December came around. There was no question that we wouldn't celebrate Christmas the way we always had.

A week before Christmas Day, Dad cut a spruce tree from the woods and soon all the baubles and lights were glittering in the corner of the living room. The other decorations went up one by one—festoons, the bright holly, and the sparkling tinsel. We wrapped our presents as usual and hid them until it was time to put them under the tree. The snow came in short, powdery showers, just enough to bring its extra magic to the bare trees and hedges.

It was just two days before Christmas Eve when I asked, "Have you made the Family Cake yet, Mom?"

She stopped what she was doing, and again I saw the sad, defeated look come into her eyes. "No, Bess. There's so much to do, and I don't think I'll have time. Maybe I'll make a special cake for New Year's Eve."

It was a bitter disappointment, like a broken promise, or as if something warm that had been a part of our lives no longer bound us all together.

I opened my mouth to protest, but then I realized she wasn't really telling me the truth. All the constraint between my mother and father, all the unnatural silences and the strange, secret discord suddenly swelled in my throat, and I could contain my fears no longer. "Mom—is Dad going away to live in Canada?"

That startled her, and she replied without looking directly at me. "We haven't decided anything yet. But your dad hasn't seen Uncle Charles for a very long time, and a change might do him good. It's been a hard year for him—and for us all."

Again, I was aware of hearing only half of the truth. I felt all the sure and safe things in our lives were slipping away. Tears filled my eyes, but I fought them back. "Why can't we all be happy again?" I cried, and turned away without waiting for an answer.

I didn't tell Matthew what I had found out about Canada. I suppose I still hoped it wouldn't happen. But I did tell him there was to be no Family Cake. He looked at me with round, disbelieving eyes.

"But, there's *always* been a Family Cake, Bess! It's the one where we all have our own special piece with our name and a candle on it. You know!"

I put my arm around him and made myself sound cheerful. "Never mind. Maybe I'll think up another surprise."

As I spoke, I suddenly knew what I was going to do. "I tell you what! If Mom can't make a Family Cake, we'll make it ourselves."

"Are you sure you know how?" he said, doubt in his voice "Suppose Mom won't let us?"

By now I was gripped with a firm resolve. "I've watched her making it before and I think I can do it. We'll keep it secret until Christmas Eve. Mrs. Harris will help us, and we can take all the things to her house and do it there."

That was how we spent the next two days, in conspiracy and excitement—Mrs. Harris enjoying the plot, covering up our absences from the house.

I'll admit that I needed more help with the preparation than I had thought, but I managed to do all the icing part myself, although it wasn't as neat and pretty as it would have been with Mom's expert touch.

Matthew watched me do it, leaning over Mrs. Harris's kitchen table with breathless concentration. "It's got to be like it always is," he said constantly. "Timmy's piece has got to be there too. It's his cake as well as ours, and his name has to be in blue."

Finally it was finished. We had bought the ingredients, and candles, and the funny little Santa Claus out of our allowances and put a pink and green ribbon around the cake.

Smuggling it into our house wasn't easy, but in the end the cake was brought home after dark on Christmas Eve and safely hidden in a cupboard on the porch.

Christmas Eve was the kind of day that happens in almost every home—friends bringing presents, Mom or Dad making hurried visits to the store for things that had almost been forgotten, and a general trend toward the kitchen, where my mother ruled with her usual grace. All that was missing was that mysterious something that had wielded its magic in other years. I could tell it was gone and I didn't know any way of bringing it back.

Dad tried to make Christmas seem as much fun as it ever was. He poured punch for us all and teased Matthew about hanging his stocking too low on the mantel. Even Mom smiled once or twice, and for a moment the family feeling came alive again.

It didn't last long. I caught Dad watching Mom with that lost look, knowing that he was wishing she would join in.

When supper was served, Matthew and I were so keyed up we could hardly eat a thing. We had agreed that as soon as the main course was over, I would make an excuse and go out to the porch cupboard for the cake. I had matches ready to light the candles. My heart was beating fast as I slipped out to the back.

It seemed to take ages to get the five candles lit, but at length I was ready. It was a smaller cake than the one Mom usually made, and the names on it were a bit blotchy, but it looked brave with its colors and candles. I was proud of it.

They were still sitting there when I carried it in and set it on the center of the table. Nobody spoke at first, but Matthew's face wore a triumphant grin.

Dad flashed a quick look at Mom, and said, "Well, where did that come from? I thought the Family Cake had gotten lost this year."

I put my arm around Matthew and laughed with the pleasure of seeing our plan succeed. "It's our surprise. Mom was so busy we thought we would do it ourselves—well, nearly by ourselves."

Mom said nothing. Her face had gone quite pale and she sat looking down at the cake with all the names on it. When she spoke her voice was hoarse and tight. "You shouldn't have done that. I told you there would be no cake. It doesn't mean the same anymore."

Matthew's smile vanished. I felt all the love and brightness fade into the hopeless feeling I knew so well. My despair was followed by a hot wave of anger.

"I don't understand!" I burst out. It's a *Family* Cake! We're still a family, aren't we?"

I was looking straight at my mother, and I couldn't stop the words tumbling out. "Is it because Timmy's name is on it? Do we have to leave him out of everything because he isn't here? Wherever he is, he would want it like this. He loved Christmas and the Family Cake. And he loved us, too. It's not fair to shut him out!"

I sat down, nervous and drained. It was Dad who spoke gently then to Mother. "Bess is right, Ruth. We have to accept things as they are, otherwise we'll destroy all we've got left."

Suddenly, it was like a dam breaking. Tears began to spill over my mother's cheeks—something I hadn't seen during all the long months since March. She pushed back her chair and hurried out of the room.

Dad followed her. Matthew and I were left alone, silent and shaken, looking at the festive table with the remains of the meal and the lopsided cake. Now it looked pathetic.

It seemed a long time, but after a bit they came back again, Mom and Dad. They stood very close, with Dad's arm around Mom's waist. Her tears were gone, her face flushed, and now she looked calm and somehow beautiful.

She came to me and kissed me. "I'm sorry, Bess," she said, simply.

After that Mom sat down and carefully cut the sections of the cake. Then she served each piece until there was only Timmy's portion, alone on the dish.

For me it was as if a storm had passed, leaving flowers limp but grateful for the rain. There was a new light in Dad's eyes, and I couldn't restrain myself from asking the question that was still in the front of my mind.

"Are you really going away to Canada, Dad?" I asked.

He smiled and shook his head. "Maybe next year when I find someone to look after the farm, we'll all go there for a vacation."

As we talked I heard a sound from outside, faint above the wailing wind.

"It's the carol singers!" Matthew shouted excitedly. "They're here!"

"Go and bring them in, Matthew," Dad said, "and we'll make some hot drinks for them."

There were seven singers, all young people we knew. They were glad to come inside out of the cold. After the cocoa was finished, they ranged themselves around our table and sang my favorite Christmas hymn.

It sounded especially beautiful because in spite of all the trouble we had passed through, we were a family again. I saw that Mom and Dad were holding hands and their eyes often met, something I hadn't seen in a long time.

And in the center of the table, on the untouched piece of cake, Timmy's little candle burned bravely on like a tiny beacon of faith. . . .

THE TINY FOOT

FREDERIC LOOMIS

Doctors hate to be forced into playing God in their practice of medicine. Yet that was exactly the issue facing Dr. Loomis in the operating room. Should he or should he not enable the deformed fetus to be born?

This moving true story has become in recent years, one of the most cherished Christmas stories in the world.

Doctor, just a moment, please, before you go into the delivery room." The man was about thirty-five, well-dressed and intelligent, an executive of a large oil company. His first baby was to arrive within the hour. He had spent the preceding hours by his wife's bedside, miserable with the feeling of helplessness and anxiety common to all prospective fathers at such a time, but nevertheless standing by to comfort her by his presence.

"I must tell you one thing before the baby gets here, doctor," he said. "I want that baby and so does Irene, more than we ever wanted anything else, I think—but not if it isn't all right. I want you to promise me right now that if it is defective—and I know you can usually tell—you will not let it live. No one need ever know it, but *it must not live*. I am depending on you.

Few doctors have escaped that problem. I had not been in California long before I encountered it there, just as I had encountered it elsewhere. Fortunately, it is a problem that usually solves itself. Babies that are defective, either mentally or physically, after all are infrequent. Yet the possibility of having one hounds almost every waiting mother. Her first question on opening her eyes after a baby is born is always either "What is it?" or "Is it all right?" Whichever question comes first, the other invariably follows, and the one as to its condition is always the more important. . . .

However they may feel about it in individual instances, doctors rightly resent and resist the rather persistent effort to make them the judges of life and death. Our load of responsibility is enough without that. "Judgment is difficult," as Hippocrates said, "when the preservation of life is the only question." If the added burden of deciding whether or not life *should* be preserved were placed upon us, it would be entirely too much. Moreover, the entire morale of medicine would be immediately threatened or destroyed. . . .

Two years after I came to California, there came to my office one day a fragile young woman, expecting her first baby. Her history was not good from an emotional standpoint, though she came from a fine family.

I built her up as well as I could and found her increasingly wholesome and interesting as time went on, partly because of the effort she was making to be calm and patient and to keep her emotional and nervous reactions under control.

One month before her baby was due, her routine examination showed that her baby was in a breech position. As a rule, the baby's head is in the lower part of the uterus for months before delivery, not because it is heavier and "sinks" in the surrounding fluid, but simply because it fits more comfortably in that position. There is no routine spontaneous "turning" of all babies at the seventh or eighth month, as is so generally supposed, but the occasional baby found in a breech position in the last month not infrequently changes to the normal vertex position with the head down by the time it is ready to be born, so that only about one baby in twenty-five is born in the breech position.

This is fortunate, as the death-rate of breech babies is comparatively high because of the difficulty in delivering the after-coming head, and the imperative need of delivering it rather quickly after the body is born. At that moment the cord becomes compressed between the baby's hard little head and the mother's bony pelvis. When no oxygen reaches the baby's blood stream, it inevitably dies in a few short minutes. Everyone in the delivery room is tense, except the mother herself, in a breech delivery, especially if it is a first baby, when the difficulty is greater. The mother is usually quietly asleep or almost so.

The case I was speaking of was a "complete" breech—the baby's legs and feet being folded under it, tailor-fashion—in contrast to the "frank" breech, in which the thighs and legs are folded back on a baby's body like a jackknife, the little rear end backing its way into the world first of all.

The hardest thing for the attending doctor to do with any breech delivery is to keep his hands away from it until the natural forces of expulsion have thoroughly dilated the firm maternal structures which delay its progress. I waited as patiently as I could, sending frequent messages to the excited family in the corridor outside.

At last the time had come, and I gently drew down one little foot. I grasped the other but, for some reason I could not understand, it would not come down beside the first one. I pulled again, gently enough but with a little force, with light pressure on the abdomen from above by my assisting nurse, and the baby's body moved down just enough for me to see that it was a little girl—and then, to my consternation, I saw that the other foot would *never* be beside the first one. The entire thigh from the hip to the knee was missing and that one foot never could reach below the opposite knee. And a baby girl was to suffer this, a curious defect that I had never seen before, nor have I since!

There followed the hardest struggle I have ever had with myself. I knew what a dreadful effect it would have upon the unstable nervous system of the mother. I felt sure that the family would almost certainly impoverish itself in taking the child to every famous orthopedist in the world whose achievements might offer a ray of hope.

Most of all, I saw this little girl sitting sadly by herself while other girls laughed and danced and ran and played—and then I suddenly realized that there was something that would save every pang but one, and that one thing was in my power.

One breech baby in ten dies in delivery because it is not delivered rapidly enough, and now—if only I did not hurry! If I could slow my hand, if I could make myself delay those few short moments. It would not be an easy delivery, anyway. No one in all this world would ever know. The mother, after the first shock of grief, would probably be glad she had lost a child so sadly handicapped. In a year or two she would try again and this tragic fate would never be repeated.

"*Don't bring this suffering upon them*," the small voice within me said. "This baby has never taken a breath—don't let her ever take one . . . you probably can't get it out in time anyway . . . *don't hurry* . . . don't be a damn fool and bring this terrible thing upon them. . . . Suppose your conscience does hurt a little; can't you stand it better than they can? Maybe your conscience will hurt worse if you *do* get it out in time. . . ."

I motioned to the nurse for the warm sterile towel which is always ready for me in a breech delivery to wrap around the baby's body so that the stimulation of the cold air of the outside world may not induce a sudden expansion of the baby's chest, causing the aspiration of fluid or mucus which might bring death.

But this time the towel was only to conceal from the attending nurses that which my eyes alone had seen. With the touch of that pitiful little foot in my hand, a pang of sorrow for the baby's future swept through me, and my decision was made.

I glanced at the clock. Three of the allotted seven or eight minutes had already gone. Every eye in the room was upon me and I could feel the tension in their eagerness to do instantly what I asked, totally unaware of what I was feeling. I hoped they could not possibly detect the tension of my own struggle at that moment.

These nurses had seen me deliver dozens of breech babies successfully—yes, and they had seen me fail, too. Now they were going to see me fail again. For the first time in my medical life I was deliberately discarding what I had been taught was right for something that I felt sure was better.

I slipped my hand beneath the towel to feel the pulsations of the baby's cord, a certain index of its condition. Two or three minutes more would be enough. So that

I might seem to be doing something, I drew the baby down a little lower to "split out" the arms, the usual next step, and as I did so the little pink foot on the good side bobbed out from its protecting towel and pressed firmly against my slowly moving hand, the hand into whose keeping the safety of the mother and the baby had been entrusted. There was a sudden convulsive movement of the baby's body, an actual feeling of strength and life and vigor.

It was too much. I couldn't do it. I delivered the baby with her pitiful little leg. I told the family and the next day, with a catch in my voice, I told the mother.

Every foreboding came true. The mother was in a hospital for several months. I saw her once or twice and she looked like a wraith of her former self. I heard of them indirectly from time to time. They had been to Rochester, Minnesota. They had been to Chicago and to Boston. Finally I lost track of them altogether.

As the years went on, I blamed myself bitterly for not having had the strength to yield to my temptation.

Through the many years that I have been here, there has developed in our hospital a pretty custom of staging an elaborate Christmas party each year for the employees, the nurses, and the doctors of the staff.

There is always a beautifully decorated tree on the stage of our little auditorium. The girls spend weeks in preparation. We have so many difficult things to do during the year, so much discipline, and so many of the stern realities of life, that we have set aside this one day to touch upon the emotional and spiritual side. It is almost like going to an impressive church service, as each year we dedicate ourselves anew to the year ahead.

This past year the arrangement was somewhat changed. The tree, on one side of the stage, had been sprayed with silver paint and was hung with scores of gleaming silver and tinsel ornaments, without a trace of color anywhere and with no lights hung upon the tree itself. It shown but faintly in the dimly lighted auditorium.

Every doctor of the staff who could possibly be there was in his seat. The first rows were reserved for the nurses and in a moment the procession entered, each girl in uniform, each one crowned by her nurse's cap, her badge of office. Around their shoulders were their blue Red Cross capes, one end tossed back to show the deep red lining.

We rose as one man to do them honor, and as the last one reached her seat and we settled in our places again, the organ began the opening notes of one of the oldest of our carols.

Slowly down the middle aisle, marching from the back of the auditorium, came twenty other girls singing softly, our own nurses, in full uniform, each holding high a lighted candle, while through the auditorium floated the familiar strains of *Silent Night*. We were on our feet again instantly. I could have killed anyone who spoke to me then, because I couldn't have answered, and by the time they reached their seats I couldn't see.

And then a great blue floodlight at the back was turned on very slowly, gradually covering the tree with increasing splendor: brighter and brighter until every ornament was almost a flame. On the opposite side of the stage a curtain was slowly drawn and we saw three lovely young musicians, all in shimmering white evening gowns. They played very softly in unison with the organ—a harp, a cello, and a violin. I am quite sure I was not the only old sissy there whose eyes were filled with tears.

I have always like the harp and I love to watch the grace of a skillful player. I was especially fascinated by this young harpist. She played extraordinarily well, as if she loved it. Her slender fingers flickered across the strings, and as the nurses sang, her face, made beautiful by a mass of auburn hair, was upturned as if the world that moment were a wonderful and holy place.

I waited, when the short program was over, to congratulate the chief nurse on the unusual effects she had arranged. And as I sat alone, there came running down the aisle a woman whom I did not know. She came to me with arms outstretched.

"Oh, you *saw* her," she cried. "You must have recognized your baby. That was my daughter who played the harp—and I saw you watching her. Don't you remember the little girl who was born with only one good leg seventeen years ago? We tried everything else first, but now she has a whole artificial leg on that side— but you would never know it, would you? She can walk, she can swim, and she can almost dance.

"But, best of all, through all those years when she couldn't do those things, she learned to use her hands so wonderfully. She is going to be one of the world's great harpists. She enters the university this year at seventeen. She is my whole life and now she is so happy. . . . And here she is!"

As we spoke, this sweet young girl had quietly approached us, her eyes glowing, and now she stood beside me.

"This is your first doctor, my dear—our doctor," her mother said. Her voice trembled. I could see her literally swept back, as I was, through all the years of heartache to the day when I told her what she had to face. "He was the first one to tell me about you. He brought you to me."

Impulsively I took the child in my arms. Across her warm young shoulder I saw the creeping clock of the delivery room of seventeen years before. I lived again those awful moments when her life was in my hand, when I had decided on deliberate infanticide.

I held her away from me and looked at her.

"You never will know, my dear," I said, "you never will know, nor will anyone else in all the world, just what tonight has meant to me. Go back to your harp for a moment, please—and play *Silent Night* for me alone. I have a load on my shoulders that no one has ever seen, a load that only you can take away."

Her mother sat beside me and quietly took my hand as her daughter played. Perhaps she knew what was in my mind. And as the last strains of *Silent Night, Holy Night* faded again, I think I found the answer, and the comfort, I had waited for so long.

LIKE A CANDLE IN THE WINDOW

MARGARET E. SANGSTER, JR.

Joan Carter had had enough. She'd married Greg, not a church-full of people who apparently felt they owned every minute of the young pastor's life. Grimly, she decided on a showdown: if he didn't take her side, then it was all over.

Greg lifted her tenderly across the threshold of the little gray stone house, and held her tightly in his arms. Her clear blue eyes looked up into his, and then suddenly she buried her head in the fold of his arm and sobbed out—

"Oh, Gregory Carter, I love you—love you with all my heart, but I wish I didn't."

"Well, Mrs. Carter, for a bride of two weeks—that is quite a statement. Would you mind telling me why you wish you didn't love your husband?"

"All my life I've told myself, *Joan, don't ever marry a preacher—marry a lawyer, a farmer, a tailor, a baker, but don't ever marry a preacher.* And here I am—married to you, the pastor of a church in a little mountain town a thousand miles from nowhere—and I want a husband—a husband all my own!"

"Any complaints so far?" smiled Gregory. "You have had my entire and undivided attention for the past two weeks. I thought we had quite a honeymoon."

Joan snuggled her head into the spot between Greg's ear and his collarbone.

"I've loved every minute of the past two weeks, but that is just it. For two weeks I have had a wonderful husband who gave me his undivided love and attention, but for the rest of my life I must share you with everybody—your whole congregation and anyone else who needs you. I'm tired of your people! They met us at the station and drove us from one end of the town to the other. My hand aches from being squeezed, I'm gummy from being kissed by women I've never seen before. Probably they're looking at us right now—staring through the windows, three or four of them in my kitchen—watching! I feel as if we would live in a glass house for the rest of our lives!"

There was a creak somewhere in the back of the house and involuntarily Greg glanced back over his shoulder. Joan's sobs stopped abruptly, she dabbed at her eyes with a handkerchief and called, "Come on out—come out wherever you are."

The hall door opened and they streamed in, laughing and calling, "Welcome home!"

The senior deacon, the junior deacon, and their wives and children, the Dorcas and the choir. They were all there, and they had food—pies, cakes and sandwiches. Greg went forward to greet them and they gathered around him.

They love Greg, thought Joan. *He's their pastor. Oh, make me strong enough to accept them!* and then suddenly she was angry. *Greg's my husband! He belongs to me. It's our life and we are going to live it.*

They left finally, and Joan sank down on the living room sofa. The room was a mess. Dirty cups and plates sticky with cake frosting—half eaten sandwiches curling up at the edges.

Greg said gently, "The women will come back tomorrow—they'll clean everything up."

"But, I don't want them to come back! I want to wash my own dishes and clean my own house."

Greg laughed. "You were an only child, darling—you've never learned to share."

"But, Greg, you'll never belong entirely to me. I want a husband who goes to work at eight and comes home at five, and between five and eight will belong to me."

"I'll always belong to you, dear. We both belong to our Heavenly Father and because we do, we belong to each other. You will find that love is like the widow's meal: the more you give, the more you have for yourself. Life in this secluded little community is hard and dull, and oh, my dear, we have so much to give. Our lives must be like a guiding star—like a candle in a window—to show those who pass by the way home."

And so they settled down—the young Carters—Gregory Carter and his wife Joan—living indeed in a gold fish bowl in a small mountain village. Living in a stone house, separated from a stone church by twenty paces of snowy lawn.

Greg preached fervently and honestly from the pulpit. He drove out into the country to call on the sick parishioners, to perform marriage services and pray above open graves. And Joan, at home, did her best to keep the parsonage shining, to cook meals that were nourishing and edible, to think according to the pattern of her new life She had a ceaseless stream of callers—somebody every day. Mrs. Judson, across the street— "You say you were born in New York City? My, my, how you must miss the bright lights and all the goin's on. Nothin' but God's mountains to look at here, and Main Street." And Joan would murmur, "It's a charming little town."

"That coat you wore to church last Sunday, honey, was it real mink or muskrat?"

"Mink," Joan would nod. "Daddy gave it to me when I was eighteen."

Or Mrs. Tenney from around the corner would drop in to help her dry the dishes and exclaim, "Land sakes, dearie! You don't use these fancy dishes every day, I hope!"

And Joan would answer, "Yes, they were wedding gifts, and I like to use them."

When Joan protested to her husband that she was tired of all the women giving her advice and prying into her own personal affairs, Greg answered, "Darling, the city you came from is made up of many little islands, and on each island people live by and to themselves. But it's different when you live in a small town. It's all one island, and you're common property."

When they had been married for one month, Joan thought it called for a celebration and baked a pie, her very first. It was lemon meringue, and it was beautiful. That evening she set the table with their best china and silver. She gathered flowers and placed them in the center of the table with a tall candle at either end. The table was beautiful and the dinner was delicious. Joan was thinking, *How wonderful to have an evening all to ourselves.*

She had just cleared the plates away and was going for her triumph, the lemon meringue pie, to set before her husband, when there was a knock at the door. Answering, Greg heard, "Gooda evening—you are ze meenister, please? I am Tony and this is Maria —we like to get married please."

"Get married?" asked Greg. "Are you alone? Where are your families?"

"Oh, please, we have no families. You see, I come five year ago from Italy. All ze time I maka ze shoes, every day I maka shoes, maka shoes, and sava my money. Till at last I have enough to bring Maria. She is all ze time waiting in ze old country. And now, today, she comes. I gotta ze house ready. Oh, we are very happy, and now we lika get married please. We have no family in this country —no mamma, no papa, no brother, no sister, just Maria and Tony, thasa all. And now, we lika get married. Too bad no family, but with flowers on the table and candles, justa like nice wedding."

Greg hesitated. "But if Maria has just come, she does not speak English. She will not understand the ceremony."

"Oh, no matter," answered Tony. "You tella me, I tella Maria. We do okay."

And so with Joan as witness, the service proceeded with Tony translating each vow carefully. And when at last Greg had pronounced them man and wife, Tony smiled at Joan and said hopefully, "Maybe you be like a sister to Maria. She has only me, Tony. No mamma, no sister, in this country." And suddenly Joan remembered the lemon meringue pie. Four of the very best plates were placed on the table and the china cups were filled with steaming chocolate, and the pie that was baked just for two became a wedding feast for four.

Joan did try to be like a sister to Maria. Maria was a beautiful girl, gracious and charming, and Joan enjoyed taking her to the village market and helping her a bit to master the new language. She made it a point to see that she met the other young women in the congregation, and several times Tony and Maria were dinner guests at the parsonage.

But Joan still found it very hard to accept "Greg's people." "Why can't we ever have a little time to ourselves? Why must the house always be filled with your people?" she demanded of Greg.

"They aren't my people, darling," he answered. "They are God's people, the sheep of His pasture, and it was God who sent us here to be the shepherd of His flock."

And Joan had choked back the tears as she answered, "Maybe He sent you. Oh, if we only had a home—a real home that was all ours. Why must we share everything with your people?"

"Because, dear, I'm their pastor, and you're their pastor's wife. Whatever is ours must be theirs, too."

The day Greg had promised to take Joan shopping in the city—sixty miles away —just as they were ready to leave, Nash Simpson had come in and said his oldest boy was determined to leave home—that with the summer planting and all they needed him desperately, and besides, what would a boy his age do in the big city—wouldn't Greg come over and talk to him? And Greg had gone and talked until it was too late to make the shopping trip. But he had persuaded the boy to stay and help his father until the harvest was over, and had promised that he would go with him in the fall and help him find work and a place to live in the city, if he still wanted to go.

The night Joan's sister and her husband had stopped to visit them on their way home from a business trip—they were just sitting down to dinner when the doctor called—Silas Wathers was badly hurt, nearly cut his leg off with a scythe. Wouldn't the pastor drive out with the doctor? And Greg had gone, and the sister had wondered how Joan managed, never being able to depend on having her husband at home. Joan had lifted her chin a bit and said, "Oh, that is part of being a pastor's wife," but she had wondered herself how she stood it.

When Mr. Carlton, the only wealthy member of the congregation, gave the church a new organ, Joan was the only one who could play it; so it was Joan who played for the choir—and this brought responsibilities and more people making demands of her, though she loved the music and devoted much time to planning the numbers for each service.

Sarah Bradley had finished high school and was to go in to the State College for the fall term. She appeared at Joan's door one morning with the catalog under her arm. "Oh, Mrs. Carter, won't you help me choose my clothes? I want to look as nice as the other girls at school. If you would just help me—you always look so nice." And Joan had spent the morning with her until the order was made out—a dress for parties, a neat suit for church, skirts and blouses and sweaters for school. And Joan had contributed some gay little scarves and a dainty handkerchief. Sarah went home with a light heart though Joan's ironing was still undone.

"Mrs. Carlton was here today," Joan announced at dinner a week before Thanksgiving. "She says we must have Thanksgiving with them, we must go there directly after the service." She paused, and then, "But we're not going, Greg. I want to have this Thanksgiving alone, with you. It will be our first Thanksgiving together, our last as bride and groom, and I want to cook our dinner. I want to serve it on my own dishes to my husband."

"Mr. Carlton is our greatest benefactor," said Greg. "He's also our best friend. It was he, you know, who had the oil burner put in this parsonage. He gave the money for the organ. We'll *have* to go to his house for Thanksgiving, darling. They have extended the invitation to show their friendship and love for us."

"All right, Greg Carter, you may go and eat Thanksgiving dinner with the Carltons, but *I* am staying home. I married you, not your congregation. It's you I love, not all your people." And so Greg told his senior deacon that Joan was not feeling well, that they would have to decline their invitation. But somehow the dinner was not the success Joan had anticipated.

And then suddenly it was the morning of Christmas Eve, and the sky was a leaden gray. By noon it was snowing, and by late afternoon a blizzard was howling. And Mr. Carlton's gift, the oil burner, wasn't working the way it should. But in spite of the cold, Joan had decorated the room with the evergreen and holly berries Greg had brought in, and a gay little Christmas tree stood in the corner near the window. "Oh, Greg," Joan said, "Christmas is a wonderful time!" And then the telephone rang.

"Darling," said Greg as he returned from the telephone, "you remember old Mr. Murray? He's taken a turn for the worse; he may not live the night out. I must go to him."

"Through this blizzard?" Joan asked. Greg nodded.

"And leave me alone on Christmas Eve?"

"You'll be all right, darling. Remember we have a lifetime ahead of us to spend Christmas together, and this is perhaps the last one on this earth for Mr. Murray. I must do what I can for him, dear."

"All right! But this is the last Christmas I'm spending here. I'm going home to my family in New York. How can anybody be happy, married to an impersonal minister who belongs to everybody but his wife?"

So Greg kissed her, held her tightly for a moment, and then started out in his small elderly car; and as the white pencils of snow broke against his windshield, he prayed—for a safe journey, that he might bring strength and courage and faith to Mr. Murray; for Joan's protection and for their happiness. And Joan pressed her nose to the window pane and tried to see across a white world.

"Oh, Greg, Greg, you are so fine and good, but I want you all to myself."

And as she looked, she saw a light coming toward her through the storm. She watched until a knock sounded at the door. "Come in," she called and turned to see Mrs. Tenney. She had come with a loaf of freshly baked bread, warm and fragrant.

"Oh, Mrs. Tenney, you came through the storm to bring this to us!"

"My dear, I had to come. It's Christmas Eve, and I had to come and tell you how much you have done for me during the year. I hope you haven't minded me coming in so often, just in time to dry your dishes. Somehow as I have touched those sparkling glasses and dainty cups it has made me want to keep my hands and heart clean and shining like them. It's made me realize that life isn't all just work and hardship. There is beauty all around us if we just look for it. You can't know what it has meant to come to the parsonage here, so spotless and pretty. This isn't much but I hope you'll enjoy it and know how much we love you."

As Joan stood holding the warm loaf of bread, tears filled her eyes, but she wiped them quickly as a voice called out, "Anybody home?" It was Mrs. Judson from across the street.

"All alone? I thought as much. I knew about old Mr. Murray, and I figured the pastor'd be out there with him. 'Tain't exactly nice to spend Christmas Eve alone, so I just thought I'd run over for a few minutes. My! Your house looks right Christmasy. But then, this house always looks just the way a pastor's home should look. Neat as a pin, flowers here and there for a bit of cheer, and comfortable chairs just where they're needed most. I hope I haven't been a bother to you, but it always just starts my day out right to run over for just a minute or two. And I've said more'n once, it's no wonder our pastor is such a success, always full of courage and cheer. With such a home to come to when his work is over. And your clothes, seemed a mite extravagant at first, but more men'd come home if their wives kept themselves prettied up and looked like something worth comin' home to! Oh yes, I've said many a time, says I, 'Our pastor's wife does her part and does it well.' My! I might near forgot, here's a pint of my strawberry preserves. I hope you'll like them."

Sarah Bradley stopped by to show Joan how well her suit fit and to tell her how well she was getting on at college. "Oh, Mrs. Carter, I don't know what I'd ever have done without your help. The girls all like my clothes, and they like me! Oh, I just love you, Mrs. Carter, and I hope I can be just like you someday. I think it would be just wonderful being a minister's wife, everybody loves you so."

Tony and Maria came through the snow to bring a beautiful scarf of dainty handwork. "To say thank you for your kindness," said Maria in her broken English.

"You've been like my sister," and she stooped to kiss Joan's hand. And Tony added, "In the spring comes a little bambino, and if it is a girl, we call her Joan. You think the name is good?"

It was Mr. Carlton who stopped next. He came in stamping the snow from his boots. "Well, just stopped in to wish you a Merry Christmas. We won't ask you to spend Christmas with us. Figured maybe you'd like to be alone bein's this is your first Christmas together in your own home. I just had the oil tank filled and left a bushel of apples on the back step. I don't know what we'd do without you and the pastor, Mrs. Carter. You've done a lot for this community. Why, it seems like you've been like a guiding star, like a candle set in a window, to show us poor folks the way. I reckon the pastor is out with old Mr. Murray, figured he'd be there. Well, give him my greetings and don't forget to count on us for anything we can do."

It was almost midnight when Joan heard the car turn in the driveway. She rushed to the door and opened it to light the way for Greg.

"Well, darling, I'm home in time for Christmas. Has it been dreadfully lonely? Has it been a terribly long evening for you?"

"I've missed you, dear; but our people have seen to it that it was not long nor lonely. The house has been filled with them, and who could be lonely when you are surrounded by love and kindness? When you belong to the whole community?"

Greg gathered her into his arms and carried her into the house.

"Oh, Greg, wouldn't it have been terrible if I had married some stuffed shirt of a polo player, or some rising young executive? I love you, Greg Carter, love you with all my heart, and I'm glad, glad, glad that I do. I wouldn't change places with anyone in this whole wide world. I'm going to write to my cousin Rosalie and thank her again for bringing us together."

"It was God who brought us together, dear. He had His eye on you all the time because He knew you'd make the perfect wife for the pastor of a little church, in a little town, a thousand miles from nowhere."

THE BELLS DIDN'T RING

ISABEL T. DINGMAN

The alarm clock—the alarm clock! It had failed to ring! The train had already left, and the roads were impassable because of a snowstorm. Yet, to miss Christmas was unthinkable!

There remained only one option—but in the Manitoba of the 1920's, it wasn't much of one. Should she dare to try it?

Milk bottles rattled outside the apartment door, and Molly stirred sleepily. The covers were slipping off; it must be nearly time to get up—school again—no, that was over for a while, she was in Regina at Anne's place. And the alarm had been set for six because the train left at seven.

She groaned softly. What an unearthly hour for a train to leave! And why did girls have to talk half the night when they slept in the same room? Would there be time for another forty winks? There was a shaft of gray light coming through the window; she might as well look at her watch and see.

The room was cold. She shivered as her feet touched the bare floor, and hunched her shoulders together under the thin nightgown. It was hard to see the watch face in the light . . .

"No, no!" she cried, startled, when her sleep-dimmed eyes made out the figures.

"What's 'at?" murmured Anne drowsily from her bed.

"My watch says seven thirty, but it must be wrong—where's that alarm?"

With one bound Anne was out of bed, reached for the clock, turned on the light.

"Yes, it says seven thirty too—oh, my dear, whatever could have happened?" she moaned. "It's set for six—the pointer is at 'alarm,' the clock is going, the winder is —Molly, I'll never forgive myself —the alarm spring isn't wound!"

Molly flung herself on the bed and burst into tears.

"Oh, my lands, and I thought I was so careful," Anne went on mournfully. "But listen, dear—there must be some other way of getting home. Can't you take a train tomorrow?"

"The train to my home town goes only on Tuesdays, Thursdays, and Saturdays," Molly said shakily. "By the time I get there Christmas will be all over —the dinner—the presents—and we've never been separated before—" She buried her face in the pillows.

"Well, could you get a train to some nearby point and drive over—say to Granton?" Anne suggested.

A gleam of hope lit up Molly's doleful face. "Phone the station and see," she begged. "It's just thirty miles from home."

Anne turned from the phone discouraged. "It left at seven twenty-five, and is a Daily except Sunday," she reported. "Not another till Monday. But how about driving all the way? It's only two hundred several miles, and if you can get a car to go I'll pay the difference between the cost and your train fare, I feel so guilty."

"Have you forgotten the blizzard last night?" Molly sobbed. "I thought my train would never get in. There will be drifts several feet deep over the road, a car couldn't possibly get through, and anyhow it would cost a fortune. Too bad I can't sprout wings and fly," she added bitterly.

"A sail, a sail," Anne cried, slipping into her dressing gown. "Your words, my dear, have given me a bright idea. I'll phone Jimmy."

"It's me," she said a minute later. "Old dear, can planes fly in weather like this? Well, listen. My friend Molly Marstone's here—that teacher from Poplar Creek I told you about—and she's missed her train home because I made a mess of setting the alarm. Her home's at Pike—some little place in Manitoba with the most awful train service, and there won't be another till Tuesday. It's tragedy, I tell you—family of twelve, always together on Christmas, and she has a whole suitcase full of presents tied up in tissue paper, and it'll just about kill her if she doesn't get there. Would one of the airmen take her over and what does it cost?—Fifty dollars? Oh, man, remember she's just a poor schoolteacher and I'm a working girl myself —What's that? Publicity? Well, I'll say she wouldn't mind! There's not much she wouldn't do to get home. I'll ask her."

Molly was sitting up on the bed, wide-eyed. "What are you talking about?" she asked, twisting her hands nervously.

"It's like this," Anne explained. "Jimmy's a reporter, but on the side he does publicity for the airplane company. They're having a hard time making people believe that flying in winter is safe and pleasant. Now it would cost $50 to charter a plane, but Jimmy says if you'll let your picture go in the papers, with a story about teacher from frontier flying home to family reunion and all that, he's sure one of the boys will take you over for nothing! Could anything be more gorgeous?"

"Fly—picture in the paper—Oh, Anne, I couldn't—" Molly began.

"All right, then, if you'd rather miss going home," Anne said, turning to the phone.

"Oh yes, I'll do anything—tell him I will—ask him to let us know about arrangements—Anne, this is terrible," she cried incoherently. This was more like a nightmare than any day before Christmas she had ever known!

She sank back against the pillows, trembling. Fly home to Pike—all that way? Why, she had been scared even to go up at the Exhibition when so many of the girls had taken ten minute flights which supplied them with conversation for weeks. And in winter too—it was terrifying. But if she didn't, there was a dreary week-end, the awful anticlimax of arriving after the great day was over—she might as well risk her life, she'd want to die anyway if she couldn't be home for Christmas. And having her picture in the paper—the trustees and all the people in the school district would talk, and the girls she had been to Normal with—but after all, it was nothing to be ashamed of, to fly. Wouldn't the old town be excited, though—they'd arrive before the train, so she wouldn't need to wire the folks. With a sudden upward tilt of her chin Molly began to dress.

Jimmy arrived at nine o'clock.

"It's O.K." he announced. "Dutch Baker will take her over, and the papers are willing to use the story, with cuts. News is always dead the day before Christmas. They should be pretty snappy pictures too," he added, looking at Molly approvingly. "You're to go to the photographers now and have some shots, then we'll take more at the landing field. Come right along—Dutch is in the car downstairs. You won't get away till nearly noon, as the plane has to be overhauled a bit, but we've got to rush to get those cuts in.

"You're a lucky girl," Molly whispered to Anne as they put on hats and coats. "I'd give my eyeteeth for a beau like him. You should see my swains at Poplar Creek!"

A tall man in aviator's uniform was standing beside Jimmy at the curb. When he turned towards them Molly's heart missed several beats. Those were the bluest eyes she had ever seen. She seemed to be drowned in their blueness—his face was so bronzed, that was why—and he was very erect and held his head like a prince. It could never be true that she was to ride two hundred miles in an airplane with him. Pretty soon the alarm would go off—but Jimmy was going through the motions of making introductions.

"So this is the little girl who nearly missed Santa Claus," the godlike person said, in warm, rich tones which sent a series of little shivers up and down her spine. "Well, our bus is guaranteed to overtake any team of reindeer that ever set out from the North Pole. Your worries are over now; sit back and have a good time."

Molly tried to speak, but somehow the words wouldn't come. *He'll think me the dumbest thing that ever came out of the backwoods*, she thought miserably. Unfortunately she could not see how big and bright her eyes were, or what a wild-rose flush had spread over her cheeks.

At the studio, pictures were taken of Molly alone, and Molly beside the airman, and Molly with her arms full of the parcels which would not have had a chance of being Christmas presents but for his aid. Then came instructions about what to wear, a quick change, and more shots beside the plane, with Molly in leather coat, helmet, goggles, and fur-lined boots. A hurried luncheon—and she was climbing, trembling, into her seat, and Dutch was fastening a leather belt around her waist. Anne kissed her hastily, whispered, "He's single, dear—Merry Christmas"; Jimmy shook hands and assured her there was nothing to be afraid of; and with a loud roar the plane left the snow-covered field and soared gracefully into the air.

Oh, such a din! Surely something must be wrong with the engine. Molly clutched the leather strap, and looked anxiously at the pilot. But he seemed perfectly calm. Goodness, she felt queer already—wouldn't it be dreadful if she was airsick. They had stopped going up now, and were heading northeast, towards the obscure little corner of the woods where Pike lay. She plucked up courage to look over the edge, and smiled in spite of her fears to see how absurdly small the streets and houses and people looked. Nobody was paying any attention to them, either —planes were as common as cars now, not like the time she had first seen one at Brandon Fair.

After the first exciting moments, Molly sat back and snuggled down inside the high fur collar, fur robe, and other wrappings. It was comfy—she could almost go to sleep, with that monotonous humming in her ears—but it would be a great waste of time to sleep now. Even if she lived to be a grizzled old maid teacher retiring on her pension she could always get a thrill out of remembering this Christmas Eve ride through the clouds. It wasn't only the new sights and sounds and sensations. It was more being close to the most wonderful man she had ever seen in her life. If only she hadn't been so tongue-tied when she met him or there was some chance now to show him how nice she could be. But it was no use trying to talk above that roar, and as for coquettish glances—Molly chuckled at the idea of a swathed mummy trying to send languishing looks through goggles. If only he would stay and spend Christmas with them! But he intended to start right back after they landed, and make Regina again before dark.

It was one of those perfect winter days which often come on the prairies around Christmas time. Heavy snow had fallen the night before, covering the ugly fields and bare woods with a thick blanket of dazzling whiteness. There was no wind, the sky was a kindly gray, and the air was like wine. The whole country seemed hushed, waiting for the magic of Christmas to spread its sway.

As the miles sped past, however, the sky became darker, a breeze sprang up, and occasionally flakes of snow floated past. Molly noticed that Dutch was intent on his controls, and no longer turned back to wave reassuringly from time to time. Terror gripped her heart. If a blizzard came up, they'd have to stop—there wouldn't be any danger, of course, but they might be stuck in some little dump on the prairie for days before it would be safe to go on. He'd hate her for having got him into it. But oh, if the snow kept away for another half hour they'd be there. Already she recognized the Assiniboine river, and the hills to the south.

Ten miles from Pike, the storm came up in earnest, and the roar of the wind mingled with the roar of the north wind in a duet horrible to hear. But the snow was not too thick yet—the spires of the little town could be seen, and she had explained to Dutch about the fields nearby where it would be safe to land. Just a few minutes would get them there.

She signaled wildly to him, pointing downward to Brady's pasture field. That was one of the best spots of all, and just half a mile from home. He nodded assent, the nose of the plane turned earthwards, and with a slow, gliding motion the machine started down. They couldn't be more than five feet from the ground now —all danger was over—but what on earth was that crashing sound? One wing of the plane had caught on a barbed wire fence, and while the body landed smoothly on the snow, there was a sickening droop to the canvas spread out so proudly a moment before.

Dutch jumped out and helped Molly to alight. She was so stiff and frightened that she could hardly stand, and had to steady herself by clinging to his arm. "Oh, I'm sorry! Is it really serious?" she asked, pushing back her goggles and looking at him with tear-filled eyes.

"Serious enough, I'm afraid," he answered. "But in any case I couldn't start back till the storm was over. Don't let it spoil your Christmas. Where do we go from here? Will you trust me with that precious suitcase?" And they trudged side by side through the whirling snow.

It was all so different from what she had expected! The town didn't even know they were here—and she felt so badly about this accident—but it had its points, too; he'd have to stay overnight anyway, even if he did fly back next day. Still, he likely had a date with some girl in Regina, and would be sore.

"I suppose this is going to upset all your plans for Christmas?" she said sadly.

"Not a bit of it—there ain't no such thing," he said. "I was asked to go to a party tonight, which would likely have lasted till tomorrow afternoon, but I hadn't decided to be there. That kind of a party doesn't seem right for Christmas Eve, somehow—it's one time when I remember the old days at home."

"Haven't you a home now?" the girl asked softly.

"Been alone in the world for the last five years," he said. She did not answer, but her sympathy made the silence warm and vibrant as they walked on through the barrage of snowflakes.

Molly turned in at the gate of a big, rambling house with wreaths of holly in every glowing window. Racing up the steps she threw the door open, and rushed into the living room with a joyous "Yoohoo!" Brothers and sisters of assorted sizes sprang up like Jacks in the box from chairs and sofas, her mother stretched out eager arms, and half-laughing, half-crying, the girl rushed into them, while shrieks and questions and greetings made a deafening noise.

For a moment she forgot all about Dutch—but only for a moment. Then she turned and saw him standing in the background, looking shy, almost wistful! Remorsefully she darted towards him, caught him by the arm, and drew him into the circle, where she introduced him to her family, ranging from wee David, aged four, to married sister Mary who had two babies. Then they sat in front of a roaring fireplace, while the little sisters pulled off Molly's boots, the little brothers took charge of Dutch's helmet and overcoat, and everybody from David up asked questions and tried to tell bits of news. Oh, she was happy! And she'd have missed it all if it hadn't been for him!

When Dutch got up and said he had better be going to the hotel, there was a storm of protest. In the first place, there was no hotel; and even if there had been, they wouldn't allow him to go there, when he had been so wonderfully kind. The boys especially made it clear that he would depart only over their dead bodies. The aviator had replaced the cowboy, fireman, and engineer as youthful idols, and to have one as a Christmas guest was the heighth of bliss.

Molly was afraid that he might be bored. But he seemed to be having a good time that evening, with two or three youngsters on his knee and older boys trying to talk to him seriously. He appeared to enjoy the carols, which were a family tradition on Christmas Eve, and joined in lustily. Christmas Day he went to church in the morning and ate enormously at dinner time. And on Monday it took a lot of persuasion from air-minded youths to go to Brady's pasture and see just what was wrong with the plane. Molly was very glad that he hadn't got it fixed before dark. Now he could go with her to the dance in the town hall. Really, her family had been so devoted that she herself had hardly seen anything of him!

It was the same at the dance—all the girls wanted to be introduced, and they were with a party both going to the hall and coming home. But on the morning of December 27th, he found her alone in the little upstairs den.

"Busy?" he asked, coming in and sitting down beside her. "I've come to say good-bye—those repairs can't be stretched out any further with all those sharp-eyed boys looking on."

"Why— What—" she began, with a puzzled frown.

"I couldn't help it," he said. "It would have been very easy to go back Sunday morning, but I had to see more of you. I didn't know there were any girls like you left, or any families like yours. Gee, Molly, what have you done to me? I—"

The door opened and four young brothers came in and gathered around Dutch. He looked at the girl in dismay.

"Listen—we'll never have a minute alone here," he whispered. "Will you come to Regina a day ahead of time when you go back to your school? I've a lot to tell you —and something very important to ask you."

"Meet the train on Friday," she said softly.

"I will," he answered. "And young woman, if you miss this one—"

"I'll go and set the alarm myself, right now," she replied.

BETHANY'S CHRISTMAS CAROL

BY MABEL MCKEE

All too often, wealth, rather than enhancing or deepening marital love, drives a wedge into it instead. This is the tragedy the young nurse faced, this lovely nurse named Carol because she was born on Christmas Day!

Was there anything she could do to help heal the inner wounds of her sad-faced patient?

For three quarters of a century now, this has been considered to be Mabel McKee's greatest Christmas story.

They called her Carol Meloney eleven months of the year at Bethany Hospital. But during the twelfth, which was December, they termed her "Christmas Carol," and she was so merry and happy that most of the patients there thought that was the sole reason the dusky-eyed, auburn-haired little nurse was called a Christmas name.

But the head of the nurses and all the others down to the newest probationer could have told you that the reason was because Carol was born on Christmas Day just twenty-one years before! Also that her frail little mother, who had seen five little brothers and sisters come into the parsonage home before Carol, declared that her newest baby sang instead of cried on that Christmas Day she was born, and had said to her minister husband, "Let's call her Carol, dear."

Always in that parsonage home, from which the mother soon slipped away, they called her "Carol, dear," and she was as fragrant and sweet and lovely as a Christmas Carol.

But this Christmas week, Carol wasn't happy; didn't want to sing. Down in the baby ward lay her wee namesake, until a week ago snuggled beside its little mother. But that little mother had, without warning, slipped away, leaving her precious baby to the happy nurse of Bethany whose name she had given it because she wanted the baby to be merry and cheerful and lovable too—had slipped away without breaking her silence or letting anybody there know who were her relatives, if she had any, or if there were some other persons with a claim on the child. Carol lifted the little one in her arms and said, "I'm going to keep her in my own family. The mother really gave her to me, you know. There is my oldest sister, Marie, both of whose babies died a year ago. I'm going to ask Marie to keep her because she is another Christmas Carol."

Standing there close beside the tiny basket bed, Carol had made all her plans. She would go home to Marie on Christmas Day, and she would lay the baby in her arms and say, "I've brought you another Christmas Carol, dear, whose mother has slipped away just as mine did while I was still tiny."

Marie couldn't refuse to keep the baby, and the child would take the lonely ache out of Marie's heart. Oh, this Christmas promised to be the very happiest one she had known, just because she had such a wonderful gift to give. But "best-laid schemes o' mice and men gang aft a-gley." Young Dr. Greig assigned her to the peritonitis case in Room 26 when the regular nurse came down with the measles. The patient refused to change nurses again, and since she was really quite ill, no one dared offend her. Carol looked down at the white toes of her Oxfords when the superintendent told her that she would have to change her plans about going home for Christmas, and then the tears came in spite of her best efforts.

"Oh, I'm not thinking of myself," the girl sobbed, "but if Marie doesn't get my blessed baby as a Christmas present, I'm afraid she'll not have such a happy holiday."

The head nurse patted Carol's red-brown curls. "Patient in 26 is sick at heart as well as in body," she confided. "We assigned you to the case because we thought that you could cheer her up. She and her husband have been drawing apart for a long time. She is grieving, and it's your duty to try to coax bitterness from her heart and smiles back to her lips."

Carol found Mrs. Joseph Cartwright an ideal patient, in spite of what people said about her being a bit queer. When her friends sent her great boxes of flowers, she always divided them with some patients who had none. She introduced the young nurse to the club-women who came to see her, and in every way treated her with such consideration that at times she felt like a sister to the rich woman.

But when everybody was gone, Mrs. Cartwright just turned her face toward the wall and lay very still, only speaking to Carol when she wanted something. She even protested when the girl brought in two holly wreaths for the windows. "I do not celebrate Christmas any more, my dear," she explained. "Take the wreaths to someone who can share the Christmas Spirit."

On this morning before Christmas Day she seemed more nervous than usual, and the doctor took Carol outside of the room. "Don't let her have visitors today," he warned. "They will only make her remember other holidays which have been happier. We must keep her from doing much of that, or she will have a relapse."

Carol was almost ready to go shopping then. Her eyes held a glint of happy anticipation. All her presents for her own people had been sent home, but she had to get an array of gifts for tiny Carol. The other nurses at Bethany wanted to help make the orphan baby's first Christmas a real one.

She found the best substitute in the hospital for her patient, and then started on her way upstairs, to her own room. She heard the choir next door practicing Christmas carols. They would sing them that evening in the hospital, winding through the corridors and stopping at the doors of patients who were convalescing.

Carol listened. "Away in a manger," they began, and immediately she thought of the tiny baby which was now hers, lying in its plain little basket in the baby ward, and though she had a dozen things to do, the girl ran through the garlanded halls, down the stairs to the floor below, and into the baby's room, where she lifted her wee namesake and held her close in her arms.

"Marie's darling baby!" she whispered. "You're going to make our Marie happy again and drive away the sad shadows from her eyes. You little precious."

The tiny baby was beautiful, with tiny petal-like hands, cupid's bow mouth, and hair that was going to be golden. She was dressed in a little white slip of the regulation hospital style. Carol was to get her a beautiful nainsook dress, delicately embroidered, with the money the other nurses had given. Oh, how hard it was for her to wait until she could get to town and select it!

Back into the gay corridors she skipped, and down the stairs just in time to meet a messenger boy with a package for her patient. It bore the seal of the city's most expensive jewelry shop. When the boy seemed bewildered, Carol offered to take it to Mrs. Cartwright.

Perhaps that is all she would have known about the jeweler's box had not the substitute asked her to stay a moment while she made a telephone call, and Carol stayed, straightening a magazine here or a bottle there as she waited.

The gleam of platinum caught her attention. The package had been unwrapped and disclosed a beautiful white satin box in which was an expensive wrist watch, a wreath with diamonds surrounding the face. Mrs. Cartwright's hand held the white card on which were the words, "Christmas Greetings," and the gray one under it which bore, in engraved letters, "Joseph Cartwright."

One long minute she studied the cards and the gift, then snapped the white velvet box shut and laid it on the table beside her bed. Tears trickled from between her closed eyelids.

Carol had seen it all through the big mirror, even the two cards which carried no hint of the affection that changes gifts from cold, inanimate things to love tokens.

"Oh, the poor dear!" she sighed, "why couldn't he have just said, 'with love'?"

The substitute nurse came back, and Carol hurried out into the spicy cold—hurried by all the late shoppers with their odd-shaped parcels, passed people who smiled and called "Merry Christmas" to each other through the falling snow, and as she hurried she sang softly to herself.

At the corner she decided to carry a great bowl of holly into Mrs. Cartwright's room that evening. At the next one she decided to carry tiny Carol into that room the next morning and see if the little Christmas visitor couldn't change that tired, heartbroken look into a tender smile. At the third corner she decided to buy Mrs. Cartwright a gift and write on the card, "With love—Carol."

At the big store where she bought tiny Carol's Christmas dress, little wool shirts and stockings, and a pink-and-white-wooly baby blanket, she went on the quest for a gift for the sick lady. She didn't have much to spend. All the brothers and sisters and nieces and nephews had sadly depleted her purse. And wee Carol had almost finished it. She never dreamed that babies were such expensive bits of joy.

She wandered to the book counter. She thought of a gift book, full of sentiment, and with a beautiful binding. The head of the department came to wait on her. Carol liked the "head" for she loved books as she did people, and talked of them as if they were alive.

"I'm buying a little book for Mrs. Joseph Cartwright," she confided. "Do you know her?"

"Know her? I should said I do. Why, she used to bring her little son in here for me to help her choose his nursery rhyme books. She was the most adorable mother I ever knew."

"Oh," Carol's eyes opened wide. "I didn't know she had a little boy. She never mentions him. She's ill at Bethany Hospital, and I am her nurse."

The other woman's hands clasped Carol's. "Didn't you know she had a little boy? He died about three years ago? Haven't you ever heard what a bitter tragedy her home life has become?"

Then Carol felt more than pity for her patient—felt understanding and real love. Meanwhile the girl was talking—telling of Mrs. Cartwright's generous gifts to orphanages, to charity institutions, to every place that held a needy child.

Swayed by a new feeling, Carol bought the most beautiful book in the department and a dainty Christmas card, which read:

"I'm giving myself instead of wealth,

And all I have to you."

She knew, somehow, that Mrs. Cartwright would really know she meant it. Hugging the bundles in her arms, she went out into the snow, to be pelted on the way home by two little boys with snowballs, to race down the avenue with other belated Christmas shoppers, and tell everybody who passed her, "Merry Christmas."

She had forgotten the disappointment she had felt because she couldn't be with her family. She was thinking of Christmas now as a day to especially love and be especially interested in the whole wide, weary world.

As she passed the tiny chapel on the corner, she slipped in to see the beautiful decorations. Just above the chancel hung a painting of the Christ as a tiny babe in the rude Bethlehem manger, and underneath it was the inscription:

"He gave the world's greatest Gift to all."

It was right then the beautiful Christmas idea was born in her heart. It came with a cruel twist, though it was beautiful. She *couldn't* do it, she told herself. She would be robbing not only herself, but Marie, whom she loved so dearly. For she knew the little baby would bring joy to Marie through all the years that followed.

"But Marie can love another baby," the voice said. "Hasn't she often talked of adopting one?" All you need to do is to encourage her, and she'll go right to an orphanage and get one."

Carol clasped her hands in front of her and knelt and prayed. Was it right for her to give away the wee baby, to whom the mother had given her name? Would it bring joy to Mrs. Cartwright's heart? Would she accept the gift, even if it were offered?

"You can offer it," the voice whispered. You can *try* to bring her great joy." Carol bowed her head still lower. Lovingly she held close to her heart the miniature nainsook dress she had bought for her tiny namesake. And as she held it, there came to her mind the message her mother had left for her when she slipped away a few weeks after her birth: "I'm giving you to your sisters, dear baby, so they will not miss me so much. Babies heal heartaches better than anything else can. You were my Christmas gift, so I know you will be a love baby and love girl and then a love woman, who will love others all through your life."

Marie had told her that many, many times when she had been naughty and selfish in her childhood—told her that she must never cause anything except happiness, because she was a Christmas Carol to sing through the years.

Carol held the tiny dress closer and looked at the picture. "I'll give it for your sake, Jesus." Back in her room again she unpacked the little bundles, laid the nainsook dress and Christmas card close together, then slipped up to Mrs. Cartwright's room. The patient had had her supper, the substitute said, and did not wish to be disturbed.

Carol went to the baby ward next, took tiny Carol back to her room, dressed her in the nainsook dress, and wrapped her in the pink-and-white blanket. Then she carried her to Mrs. Cartwright's room, entered softly on tiptoe, laid the tiny mite in the curve of her patient's arm, put the card in her hand, then slipped out before the sick woman could turn her head.

Carol's bell rang sharply half an hour later. Breathlessly she answered the call. Mrs. Cartwright's curved arm still held the baby. Her mouth was smiling though her eyes were misty.

"Oh, my dear, my dear," she began, "How could you be so generous as to give the tiny Christmas Carol you had planned to take to your sister? Oh, the wonder of your gift!" (The substitute only that afternoon had told Mrs. Cartwright the story of the tiny baby which Carol loved so dearly.) She was going to keep the baby. She wanted to adopt it, and wished a message sent asking Mr. Cartwright to come at once.

He always wanted me to take a baby into our home," she whispered to Carol, "but until you gave me little Carol, I felt I couldn't hold one in my arms after Billy died."

Half an hour later Carol heard a rush outside the door, and saw a big man, whom she instantly knew as Mr. Cartwright, coming into the room. This time she fairly ran out into the hall, where she felt herself the most lonely person in the whole world. She wandered on until she reached the corridor where the choir from the nearby church and nurses off duty were forming in line, ready for their march through the hospital. She heard the "specials" gently opening doors so their patients would not miss the singing.

She slipped into the line, right after the probationer whose mother had died a few weeks before, and patted the girl's shoulder comfortingly and held her hand as they began to march. Her other hand held one of the open songbooks, and her sweet, girlish soprano sang with the others.

They passed the men's ward and the old veteran, whose Grand Army button shone as did his eyes, waved his hand at them; passed the woman's ward where there was a little lame girl keeping time to the music with her crutch, passed many other rooms, and entered the corridor off of which opened the room Carol had just left.

She glanced through the door ajar. Mrs. Cartwright still held the baby close to her heart, and her hand was resting on the bowed head of her husband. Her eyes were so beautiful and brilliant that Carol knew the spirit of Christmas was in her heart at last.

THE GIFT OF THE MAGI

O. HENRY (WILLIAM SYDNEY PORTER)

Only one dollar and eighty-seven cents with which to buy a present for her Jim. Times were hard: so many had lost their jobs, and those who hadn't had seen their wages slashed. So, clearly, there was no hope at all.

Or was there?

This is one of the most famous, and most beloved, Christmas stories ever written.

One dollar and eighty-seven cents. That was all. And sixty cents of it was in pennies. Pennies saved one and two at a time by bulldozing the grocer and the vegetable man and the butcher until one's cheeks burned with the silent imputation of parsimony that such close dealing implied. Three times Della counted it. One dollar and eighty-seven cents. And the next day would be Christmas.

There was clearly nothing to do but flop down on the shabby little couch and howl. So Della did it. Which instigates the moral reflection that life is made up of sobs, sniffles, and smiles, with sniffles predominating.

While the mistress of the home is gradually subsiding from the first stage to the second, take a look at the home. A furnished flat at $8 per week. It did not exactly beggar description, but it certainly had that word on the lookout for the mendicancy squad.

In the vestibule below was a letterbox into which no letter would go, and an electric button from which no mortal finger could coax a ring. Also appertaining thereunto was a card bearing the name "Mr. James Dillingham Young."

The "Dillingham" had been flung to the breeze during a former period of prosperity when its possessor was being paid $30 per week. Now, when the income was shrunk to $20, the letters of "Dillingham" looked blurred, as though they were thinking seriously of contracting to a modest and unassuming D. But whenever Mr. James Dillingham Young came home and reached his flat above he was called "Jim" and greatly hugged by Mrs. James Dillingham Young, already introduced to you as Della. Which is all very good.

Della finished her cry and attended to her cheeks with the powder rag. She stood by the window and looked out dully at a gray cat walking a gray fence in a gray backyard. Tomorrow would be Christmas Day, and she had only $1.87 with which to buy Jim a present. She had been saving every penny she could for months, with this result. Twenty dollars a week doesn't go far. Expenses had been greater than she had calculated. They always are. Only $1.87 to buy a present for Jim. Her Jim. Many a happy hour she had spent planning for something nice for him. Something fine and rare and sterling—something just a little bit near to being worthy of the honor of being owned by Jim.

There was a pier-glass between the windows of the room. Perhaps you have seen a pier-glass in an $8 flat. A very thin and very agile person may, by observing his reflection in a rapid sequence of longitudinal strips, obtain a fairly accurate conception of his looks. Della, being slender, had mastered the art.

Suddenly she whirled from the window and stood before the glass. Her eyes were shining brilliantly, but her face had lost its color within twenty seconds. Rapidly she pulled down her hair and let it fall to its full length.

Now, there were two possessions of the James Dillingham Youngs in which they both took a mighty pride. One was Jim's gold watch that had been his father's and his grandfather's. The other was Della's hair. Had the Queen of Sheba lived in the flat across the airshaft, Della would have let her hair hang out the window some day to dry just to depreciate Her Majesty's jewels and gifts. Had King Solomon been the janitor, with all his treasures piled up in the basement, Jim would have pulled out his watch every time he passed, just to see him pluck at his beard from envy.

So now Della's beautiful hair fell about her rippling and shining like a cascade of brown waters. It reached below her knee and made itself almost a garment for her. And then she did it up again nervously and quickly. Once she faltered for a minute and stood still while a tear or two splashed on the worn red carpet.

On went her old brown jacket; on went her old brown hat. With a whirl of skirts and with the brilliant sparkle still in her eyes, she fluttered out the door and down the stairs to the street.

Where she stopped the sign read: "Mme. Sofronie. Hair Goods of All Kinds." One flight up Della ran, and collected herself, panting. Madame, large, too white, chilly, hardly looked the "Sofronie."

"Will you buy my hair?" asked Della.

"I buy hair," said Madame. "Take yer hat off and let's have a sight at the looks of it."

Down rippled the brown cascade.

"Twenty dollars," said Madame, lifting the mass with a practiced hand.

"Give it to me quick," said Della.

Oh, and the next two hours tripped by on rosy wings. Forget the hashed metaphor. She was ransacking the stores for Jim's present.

She found it at last. It surely had been made for Jim and no one else. There was no other like it in any of the stores, and she had turned all of them inside out. It was a platinum fob chain simple and chaste in design, properly proclaiming its value by substance alone and not by meretricious ornamentation—as all good things should do. It was even worthy of The Watch. As soon as she saw it she knew that it must be Jim's. It was like him. Quietness and value—the description applied to both. Twenty-one dollars they took from her for it, and she hurried home with the 87 cents. With that chain on his watch Jim might be properly anxious about the time in any company. Grand as the watch was, he sometimes looked at it on the sly on account of the old leather strap that he used in place of a chain.

When Della reached home her intoxication gave way a little to prudence and reason. She got out her curling irons and lighted the gas and went to work repairing the ravages made by generosity added to love. Which is always a tremendous task, dear friends—a mammoth task.

Within forty minutes her head was covered with tiny, close-lying curls that made her look wonderfully like a truant schoolboy. She looked at her reflection in the mirror long, carefully, and critically.

"If Jim doesn't kill me," she said to herself, "before he takes a second look at me, he'll say I look like a Coney Island chorus girl. But what could I do—oh! what could I do with a dollar and eighty-seven cents?"

At seven o'clock the coffee was made and the frying pan was on the back of the stove hot and ready to cook the chops.

Jim was never late. Della doubled the fob chain in her hand and sat on the corner of the table near the door that he always entered. Then she heard his step on the stair away down on the first flight, and she turned white for just a moment. She had a habit of saying little silent prayers about the simplest everyday things, and now she whispered: "Please God, make him think I am still pretty."

The door opened and Jim stepped in and closed it. He looked thin and very serious. Poor fellow, he was only twenty-two—and to be burdened with a family! He needed a new overcoat and he was without gloves.

Jim stopped inside the door, as immovable as a setter at the scent of quail. His eyes were fixed upon Della, and there was an expression in them that she could not read, and it terrified her. It was not anger, nor surprise, nor disapproval, nor horror, nor any of the sentiments that she had been prepared for He simply stared at her fixedly with that peculiar expression on his face.

Della wriggled off the table and went for him.

"Jim, darling," she cried, "don't look at me that way. I had my hair cut off and sold it because I couldn't have lived through Christmas without giving you a present. It'll grow out again—you won't mind, will you? I just had to do it. My hair grows awfully fast. Say 'Merry Christmas!' Jim, and let's be happy. You don't know what a nice—what a beautiful nice gift I've got for you."

"You've cut off your hair?" asked Jim, laboriously, as if he had not arrived at that patent fact yet even after the hardest mental labor.

"Cut it off and sold it," said Della. "Don't you like me just as well, anyhow? I'm me without my hair, ain't I?"

Jim looked about the room curiously.

"You say your hair is gone?" he said, with an air almost of idiocy.

"You needn't look for it," said Della. "It's sold, I tell you—sold and gone, too. It's Christmas Eve, boy. Be good to me, for it went for you. Maybe the hairs of my head were numbered," she went on with a sudden serious sweetness, "but nobody could ever count my love for you. Shall I put the chops on, Jim?"

Out of his trance Jim seemed quickly to wake. He enfolded his Della. For ten seconds let us regard with discreet scrutiny some inconsequential object in the other direction. Eight dollars a week or a million a year—what is the difference? A mathematician or a wit would give you the wrong answer. The magi brought valuable gifts, but that was not among them. This dark assertion will be illuminated later on.

Jim drew a package from his overcoat pocket and threw it upon the table.

"Don't make any mistake, Dell," he said, "about me. I don't think there's anything in the way of a haircut or a shave or a shampoo that could make me like my girl any less. But if you'll unwrap that package you may see why you had me going a while at first."

White fingers and nimble tore at the string and paper. And then an ecstatic scream of joy; and then, alas! a quick feminine change to hysterical tears and wails, necessitating the immediate employment of all the comforting powers of the lord of the flat.

For there lay The Combs—the set of combs, side and back, that Della had worshipped for long in a Broadway window. Beautiful combs, pure tortoise shell, with jewelled rims—just the shade to wear in the beautiful vanished hair. They were expensive combs, she knew, and her heart had simply craved and yearned over them without the least hope of possession. And now, they were hers, but the tresses that should have adorned the coveted adornments were gone.

But she hugged them to her bosom, and at length she was able to look up with dim eyes and a smile and say: "My hair grows so fast, Jim!"

And then Della leaped up like a little singed cat and cried, "Oh, oh!"

Jim had not yet seen his beautiful present. She held it out to him eagerly upon her open palm. The dull precious metal seemed to flash with a reflection of her bright and ardent spirit.

"Isn't it a dandy, Jim? I hunted all over town to find it. You'll have to look at the time a hundred times a day now. Give me your watch. I want to see how it looks on it."

Instead of obeying, Jim tumbled down on the couch and put his hands under the back of his head and smiled.

"Dell," he said, "let's put our Christmas presents away and keep 'em a while. They're too nice to use just at present. I sold the watch to get the money to buy your combs. And now suppose you put the chops on."

The magi, as you know, were wise men—wonderfully wise men—who brought gifts to the Babe in the manger. They invented the art of giving Christmas presents. Being wise, their gifts were no doubt wise ones, possibly bearing the privilege of exchange in case of duplication. And here I have lamely related to you the uneventful chronicle of two foolish children in a flat who most unwisely sacrificed for each other the greatest treasures of their house. But in a last word to the wise of these days let it be said that of all who give gifts these two were the wisest. Everywhere they are wisest. They are the magi.

Christmas Memories

SECRETS OF THE HEART

PEARL S. BUCK

There are lots of stories depicting young love, and many about young married love—but what about great love cut short by the untimely death of a husband and father? What happens then to the brokenhearted woman left behind?

This is just such a story, and it may very well be one of Pearl Buck's greatest.

Mrs. Allenby listened to her daughter's plans for the holiday, and then it was time for her to make her announcement. "I won't be here for Christmas," Mrs. Allenby said, keeping her voice as casual as she could.

Her daughter Margaret stared at her. "What *do* you mean?" Margaret demanded. "It's impossible! Not here for Christmas? Where are you going?"

"I haven't decided," Mrs. Allenby said. She carefully tied a silver bow on a small package. Inside was a brooch for Margaret, a circle of pearls set in gold that she had found only yesterday in an antique shop. When the package was tied to her satisfaction she handed it to her daughter.

"For you—not to be opened until. . . . I'll deliver the other gifts for all of you, parents and children, to each of your houses before I go."

Margaret, about to leave after an hour of lively talk, sat down again in the blue velvet chair by the fire. They were in her mother's living room. The December sun was blazing through the windows, paling the flames that were crackling in the low grate.

"But, Mother, you've never been away at Christmastime!' Margaret cried.

"So this year I shall be," Mrs. Allenby said, her voice pleasant but firm.

She leaned back in her own blue velvet chair opposite and gazed at her daughter affectionately. "You're putting on a little weight, aren't you, dear?"

"Don't try to change the subject," Margaret said. "No, I'm not putting on weight and I'm *not* pregnant, if that's what you mean. Four children are enough— though I'd rather enjoy a baby again! Benjie will be starting school next year and the house will be empty. But back to you now—when are you going?"

"I haven't decided," Mrs. Allenby said. Perhaps tomorrow but perhaps not until Christmas Eve. I'll see when I get ready."

"I shan't enjoy Christmas, at all," Margaret said rather shortly.

"You will," Mrs. Allenby said. "And I suggest that you take the opportunity of my absence and not have the other families with you. Four of you, with your accumulated children, adorable as they are—well, it's simply too much, even of those adorable grandchildren."

"Mother, if I didn't know you love us—"

Mrs. Allenby interrupted. "Indeed, I love you all, but I think you should be alone for Christmas, each pair of parents with their own children, the children alone with only their own parents and brothers and sisters. You've no idea—" She stopped.

"Idea of what?" Margaret demanded, her eyes very blue under her dark hair. She was a small creature, but possessed of a mighty spirit. Hot or cold, she was all extremes.

"How peaceful it would be," Mrs. Allenby said rather lamely.

Her daughter looked at her critically. "You aren't being noble or something, are you? Thinking we don't want you or something stupid like that?"

"Oh no, indeed," Mrs. Allenby said. "Nothing like that."

Margaret was silent for a full half-minute, regarding her mother with suspicious eyes. "You aren't carrying on some sort of secret romance?"

Mrs. Allenby blushed. "Margaret, how *can* you—"

"You *are*!" Margaret cried.

"I am *not*," Mrs. Allenby said flatly. "At my age," she added.

"You're still pretty," Margaret said.

"Oh, nonsense," Mrs. Allenby said.

Margaret looked at her mother fondly and then rose. "Well, keep your secrets, but I still tell you I shan't enjoy Christmas for a minute, wondering where you are." She put her arms about her mother and kissed her. "And this present—the package is so small I know it's expensive and you shouldn't have. . . ."

"It's my money, darling," Mrs. Allenby said, laughing.

Margaret kissed her mother again, ran to the door and stopped to look back. "Tell me where you're going," she asked again, her voice coaxing.

Mrs. Allenby laughed. "Go home and tend your children," she said gaily and waved good-bye.

Alone with the fire, the winter sun streaming across the Abusson carpet, the bowl of holly on the table, the book-lined walls, Mrs. Allenby was suddenly aware of a deep relief. She loved her house, she loved her children and their children, but—but what? She did not know what came after this *but*. Simply that she longed not to be here on Christmas. She would leave early in the morning of Christmas Eve. That would see her at the cabin in Vermont by nightfall. Now she rose, gathered some bits of silver cord and wrapping paper which she threw into the fire, and went upstairs to pack.

By eight the morning of Christmas Eve she was in her car and headed north. Snow threatened from a smooth gray sky, and in Vermont, the radio told her, it was already snowing. They had often gone skiing in Vermont in the old days, she and Leonard, before they were married. And it was to Vermont that they had gone for they honeymoon, but in October, and too early for skiing. How glorious it had been, nevertheless, the mountains glittering in scarlet and gold!

"In celebration of our wedding," Leonard had said.

It was because of him, of course, that she wanted to have Christmas alone, and in Vermont. They had always come here alone. It had been his demand.

"Let's never go to Vermont with the children—always alone," he had said.

"Selfish, aren't you," she had teased, with love.

"Plenty of other places to ski with them," he had retorted.

"Of course we mustn't let them know—they'd be hurt," she had said.

"No reason why they should know this place even exists," he had agreed.

That was just after they had built the cabin and now it was the place essential to her, for there she could refresh, revitalize, her memory of Leonard. She was frightened because she was forgetting him, losing him—not the sum total of him, of course, but the clarity of detail of his looks, the dark eyes and the sandy hair. He had died so heartbreakingly young, the children still small, and their own children never to see their grandfather—see the way he walked, his tall spare frame moving in his own half-awkward, curiously graceful fashion. The memory came strong at Christmas, especially—he had loved sprawling on the floor with his children, showing them how to play with the toys he chose for them with such care.

The snow was beginning to fall now, a few flakes, growing heavier as she drove out of the traffic and toward the mountains. She would reach the cabin late this evening. Leonard had designed the cabin before any of the children were born so it had only three rooms. He had not wanted children too soon.

"Let's be solid with each other first," he had said.

They had come to the cabin often during the first years of their life together, as often as he could get away from the laboratories where he worked as a research scientist. After the children came, it was less often and at last, when he was dead, not at all—that is, she had never come back alone. Yet she had not thought of selling it. Gradually she had not thought of it at all, though she knew now she had not forgotten it.

The hours sped past. She was a fast driver but steady, Leonard always said, and it was she who usually did the driving when they went to the cabin, the quiet hours giving him time to think. He had said gratefully, "What it means to a man like me not to have to talk—"

Yet, some laboratory problem solved, he would be suddenly gay with lively talk. They had good talk together, and it was not until his voice was stilled in death that she realized how good the talk was, and that there always had been something to talk about.

The day slipped past noon, and the snow continued to fall. Before darkness fell she reached the village and there she stopped to buy food for a day or two. The old storekeeper was gone, and a young man, a stranger, had taken his place. He looked at her curiously but asked no questions as he carried the box of groceries to her car. She drove on then in the dusk, up the winding graveled road to the tip of the snow-covered hill. The road narrowed, and within a few yards she saw the cabin. The trees had grown enormous, but the cabin was still there, as enduring as Leonard had planned it to be.

She got out of the car and lifted a flat stone. Yes, the key was still there, too, the big brass key.

"I hate little keys," Leonard had said. "They lose themselves on purpose."

So they had found the huge, old brass lock, a heavy and substantial one. She fitted the key into the hole, and the door creaked open. *Dear God, it couldn't be the same after all these years*—but it *was* the same.

"We must always leave it as though we were coming back tomorrow," Leonard had said.

It was dusty, of course, and it smelled of the forest and dead leaves. But it had been built so solidly that bird and beast had found no entrance. The logs in the great fireplace were ready to light, and in the bedroom the bed was made—damp and musty, doubtless, but there it was, and the fire would soon drive out the dampness. She would hang the bedclothes before the chimney piece.

She lit the fire and the big oil lamp, then she unpacked the car, and sat down in the old rocking chair to rest a few minutes before preparing food. So here she was, unexpectedly really, for she had made no long-standing plans to come here. It had come over her suddenly, the need to find Leonard somehow, even to remember him. And this had happened when she was buying the brooch for Margaret. It had taken a little time to find it.

"Are you looking for something for yourself?" the young woman in the antique shop had asked.

"No," she had replied, "I'm just looking."

"A tie pin for your husband, perhaps?" the young woman had persisted.

"I have no husband," she had replied, shortly. Then she had corrected herself. "I mean—he died many years ago."

But her instinctive reply had frightened her. No husband—was she forgetting Leonard? Impossible—but perhaps true? And here it was Christmas again, and if ever he was not to be forgotten it was at Christmas, the time he loved best. And suddenly all her heart had cried out for him. Yet where was he to be found, if not in memory? And suddenly she needed to be alone this Christmas. The children, grown into men and women, and their children, whom he had never seen, were strangers to him; and living in their midst, she had almost allowed herself to become a stranger to him, too.

She got up to open a can of soup and put it on the stove. Then she found the dust cloths in a drawer where she had folded them, freshly washed, and she dusted the furniture before she ate. The fire was roaring up the chimney and the room had lost its chill. The snow was falling more heavily now and by morning it would be piled against the door. The main road would be plowed, however, since there were many new houses for skiers who had started coming here in increasing numbers— she had read of that. And Leonard always saw to it that the snow shovel hung inside the shed at the end of the cabin.

She pulled the small drop-leaf table before the fire and set out her supper, a bowl of bean soup, bread and cheese and fruit, and she ate with appetite. When she had eaten she folded the table away against the wall. Then she heated water and took her bath in a primitive tin tub. It was all so easy, so natural, to do what they had done, she and Leonard, here alone in the forest. Clean and warm in her flannel nightgown she went into the bed, now warm and dry, but still smelling of autumn leaves, and fell into dreamless sleep.

She woke the next morning to sunshine glittering upon new-fallen snow. For a moment she didn't know where she was. Here, where she had always been with Leonard, her right hand reached for him instinctively. Then she remembered. It was Christmas Day and she was alone. No, not alone, for her first thought summoned Leonard to her mind. She lay for a moment in the warm bed. Then she spoke.

"I can talk out loud here—there is no one to hear me and wonder."

She heard her own voice and was comforted by its calm. "I can talk all I want to out loud," she went on.

A pleasant peace crept into her heart and body, as gentle as a perfume, and she smiled.

"We spent our first Christmas here," she reminded herself.

They had driven up through snow flurries that year, and, as she had done, only together, they had waked to another day of sun upon snow. Then Leonard had got up to light the fire and heat the water.

"Lie still, sweetheart," he had commanded. "There's no one here to hurry us—a glorious Christmas Day."

He had come back to bed, shivering, and they had begun the day with love.

Later they had breakfasted on the small table before the fire, and while she washed the dishes, he had gone out and cut a little tree and had brought it in, glistening with ice, and they had decorated it. They had remembered to bring tinsel and a few silver ornaments, and they had tied their gifts to the branches.

"I've planned every moment of this day," he had said. When they had admired the tree, they opened their presents. She had given him a gold band for his wristwatch and he had given her a necklace that was a delicate silver chain.

"To bind you to me forever," he had said, slipping it over her head.

She had loved the chain through all the years and wore it often. She had even brought it with her, to wear with her red wool dress today. Remembering, she got up from the bed and ran into the other room to build the fire.

She laid bits of bark and slivers of dry wood on the lingering coals. She had made such a mighty fire last night that under the ashes there were still live coals. In a few minutes the blaze sprang up in sharp flickering points. Leonard had taught her how to make a proper fire that first year, and she had never forgotten.

She filled the big kettle now with water from the kitchen pump and hung it on the crane above the fire. When the water was hot she washed and dressed, putting on her red dress, and sat down at the table for breakfast. And when she finished eating and washed the dishes, she put on Leonard's lumber jacket, which hung as usual behind the door, and went out to cut a tree—a very tiny one, just to set on the table. The tree ornaments were where Leonard had put them, years ago, in the wall drawer under the window, and she tied them on the tree. Then she found the gift she brought for herself in her bag, and she tied it to the tree.

"A year or two and perhaps there'll be more than the two of us," Leonard had said, on their third Christmas. "We've had over two years alone. Now let's have our children— four of them—close together while we're still young. They can enjoy each other and us, and there'll be years for us alone after they've grown up and don't need us any more."

"We can't bring a baby to this cabin in the middle of winter," she had said.

"We'll take Christmas where we find it," he had told her.

And sharing his desire, as she loved to do because she loved him, by the next Christmas they had a son, named for his father but called Lennie. He was three months old that Christmas and they spent it, the three of them, in their first house, a modest one on a quiet street in the small Connecticut town where she still lived.

"I'm sure he sees the tree," Leonard had insisted.

Lennie, lying on the rug, had stared steadily at the glittering tree, still not a very big tree but one loaded with gifts. Then he had smiled, and both she and Leonard had laughed and reached for each other's hand.

"I'm glad we're alone, the three of us," Leonard had said. "It's selfish of me not to want to go to either of our parents, but we have our own home now, you and I and our child. That's the trinity of love, my love."

In less than two years they had their daughter, Margaret.

"Another one and we'll need a bigger house," Leonard had said on Christmas Day.

Lennie, an accomplished walker by then, had been pulling things off the tree. Margaret had been propped on pillows on the couch.

"Oh Leonard, the payments on this one—" she had cried.

Before she could finish he had stopped her with a kiss: "A present for you, darling—I'm being promoted."

She had reproached him in her joy. "And you didn't tell me!"

"Christmas gift," he had said.

They had started to build their new house that next spring. By November it was still not quite finished but they moved in anyway to celebrate Dickie's birth.

"It was such an occasion," she said aloud now, smiling.

She noticed then that the fire was burning low, the logs mere coals and the ashes falling. She rose and got a new log from the stack, though it took all her strength to lift it.

"I wish you would realize you aren't a giant," Leonard had said so many times. "You're too impulsive—you see something you want done and you rush to do it yourself, forgetting that you have an able-bodied man around."

The log fell crookedly and she had to kneel to straighten it. Flames sprang from the coals and she dusted her hands and sat down again in the rocking chair.

That first Christmas in their new house had been a blessed one. Two little children ran about the room, shouting with delight, and Dickie sat propped on the couch. Lennie had his first tricycle and Margaret her first real doll. She loved dolls from that day on, and from them learned to love babies—nowadays her own. But little Dickie. . . .

The tears were hot against her eyelids now and she bit her lip. There was more than joy to remember. There was also sorrow. Dickie had died before the next Christmas. Death had come suddenly, stealing into the house. She had put him to bed one night a few days before Christmas, and in the morning had gone to wake him and had found him dead. The beautiful body was there, white as the snow outside the window, and the blue eyes were still closed as if in sleep. Unpredicted, unexplained, and she still wept when she thought of it. She wept now as if she had lost him only yesterday. Back then she had known she must try to comfort Leonard, although in weeks upon weeks, he would not be comforted. But for his sake she had been compelled not to weep, compelled to seem brave when she was not brave.

"Don't even speak of Christmas," he had said that dreadful year. And against every beat of her own aching heart she had persuaded him.

"Dearest, there are the others. They've been looking forward to Christmas Day. We must go on as usual—as best we can."

"You are right, I know," he had said at last. "But don't expect too much of me."

They had both been glad when Christmas Day was over, that heartbreaking day.

"Oh, how did we ever. . . ." she whispered now and sobbed.

It was still unendurable and she got up from the rocking chair.

"I shall make myself a cup of tea," she said aloud.

While the tea was steeping, she made herself a turkey sandwich from the sliced meat she had bought the day before. The sun was already past zenith and the room had lost its glow. When she had eaten the sandwich and had drunk her tea she felt better. She put another log on the fire and then she went to the window seat and sat looking out on the wintry landscape, the field covered with snow, the spruce forest tipped with snow, the white birch trees, and the peak of the mountain beyond, all drenched in the pure light of afternoon.

She and Leonard had endured that terrible Christmas, and in the spring she was pregnant again.

By the next Christmas Day, Ronald was born, and two years later Ellen.

"Enough," Leonard had told her, laughing. "You produce wonderful babies, my pet, but enough is enough."

So there had been no more and thereafter her Christmas Days became a blur of happiness, the kinds of celebration varying only with the ages of the children, gifts changing from toys to adolescent treasures and at last to young adult possessions.

"I wish, Leonard darling, that you could have seen the first grandchild," she said now, her gaze fixed on the peak of the mountain, glowing in early sunset.

That would have been their happiest Christmas, the year Margaret's first child, Jimmy, was born, a little bundle of joy and mischief. Impossible to believe that now he was in college!

"You would have laughed all day, my darling, at his antics," she said aloud and laughed to herself at the very thought of what had never been.

When the children were almost grown came the years when Leonard took her with him on business trips. He was the head of his own company by then and they had traveled to Europe and sometimes even to Asia. It had seemed to her that everyone treated her as though she were a queen, and that was because he was the king. But they had always managed to be home for Christmas, what with the children growing up and getting married and she had talked of the grandchildren coming along, though Leonard had laughed at the idea of her being a grandmother.

"Didn't I tell you it was right for us to have the children when we were young? Now we can enjoy ourselves, doing whatever we like, for years to come."

Not so many years, at that, for nineteen years and thirteen days ago Leonard had come home at midday saying that he felt ill. His heart, so robust an organ all his life, had developed its own secret weakness, had suddenly stopped, beyond recall.

She stared out the window now, as the shadows of evening crept over the landscape. There was nothing more to say, for long ago all questions had been asked and answered, in some fashion or other. Only the eternal *why* remained and to that there was no answer. She sat in silence but strangely comforted. She had wanted to remember him clearly, and in remembering, he had come back to her.

At this moment she heard a knock on the door. With no sense of alarm she opened it and saw a man standing there, a man with a graying beard.

"I'm Andrew Bond, ma'am, a neighbor. My wife says she saw smoke here and I thought I'd better come over."

She put out her hand. "Why, Andrew Bond, your father used to look after the cabin for us. You've forgotten."

He stared at her. "No, I haven't forgotten—but are you here alone, ma'am?"

"Yes, for the day, that is. I came just to—well, I just came."

"Yes, ma'am. So you aren't staying?"

"No, if you'll dig me out tomorrow morning?"

"Yes, ma'am, I'll be glad to."

"Will you come in?"

"No, thanks. Wife's got supper on and she doesn't like to wait!"

"Well, thank you for coming, Andrew. And I hope you had a merry Christmas."

"Well, my wife and me, we've had a happy Christmas, anyway. Our son come home from Vietnam—wounded, but alive."

"I'm glad he's alive," she said fervently, as though he were someone she knew. But she was really glad.

"Thank you, ma'am," he said. "I'll see you in the morning, ma'am."

"I'll see you in the morning," she echoed.

She closed the door and lit the lamp and heaved another log on the fire. She decided she would eat something and then go to bed early. Tomorrow she would be home again, ready to see them all, the children and their children. She had had her day, her Christmas Day. She went to the window and stood looking out into the gathering darkness. . . . Happy? Who knows what that is?

No, wounded—but alive!

Christmas Memories

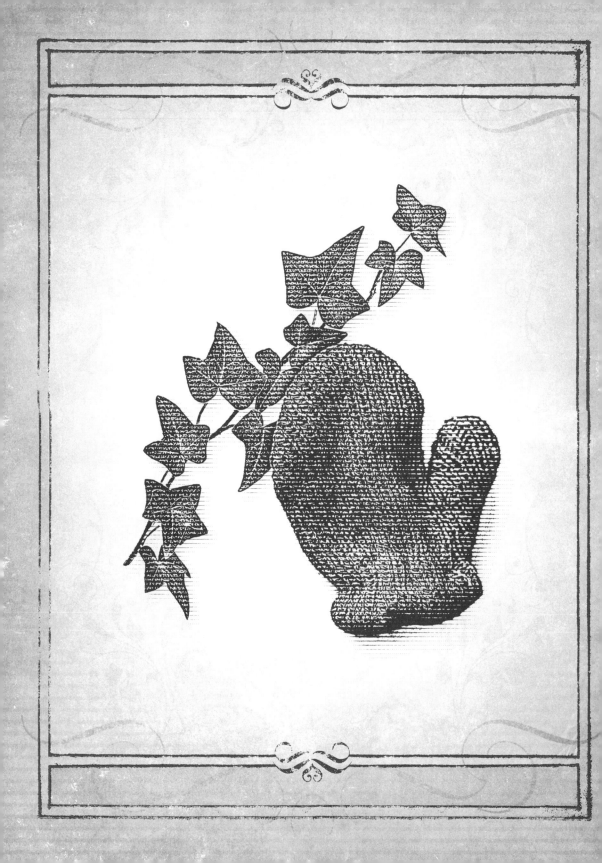

THERE'S A SONG IN THE AIR

KATHERINE REEVES

Thomas and Amy Martin had once had it all: each other, a lovely home, and Carol. Then Carol was taken from them, and there was no longer much to live for. As for adopting a child, not even Vinnie could persuade them to consider such a thing.

Then came a strange little face in the ivy.

Amy Martin took the second-best broom from its corner on the back porch and went out to sweep the walk under the grape arbor.

The bricks here were uneven, and some of them were mossy and held the moisture. If ice collected Thomas might slip and fall when he took the trash out to the alley. At least that was the excuse she gave herself. But she really wanted to see if the child was there again this morning.

She didn't like to admit it to herself, but something about the whole affair gave her a slightly uncomfortable feeling. For three weeks, ever since she had first been aware of the face staring at her through the December tangle of vines on the back fence—the fence that shut her property off from the alley—she had not quite felt that she belonged to herself. Her privacy was crumbling, and all because a strange child insisted on watching her whenever she came out the back door.

It was a mysterious kind of thing. There was no young child, that she knew of, in any of the homes whose back gates opened on the alley. And this child was a silent, shabby little thing, acting as though she knew she shouldn't be here. The one time when Amy had spoken to her and said, "Where's your home, little one?" the child had stared at her, then had run down the alley and disappeared. She had dropped one faded, dirty mitten in her flight. The mitten, washed and mended, now lay on the shelf on the back porch. Amy had planned to give it to her this morning.

The bricks of the wide old walk under the arbor were laid in herringbone style, and even in winter fine green lines of moss outlined the pattern. In a way the arbor was like Thomas and Amy Martin. It clung a little to the past, as though, if it waited, it might recapture what had gone.

In this respect, too, it was like the quiet, polished house that also seemed forever to be waiting; like the attic where the dollhouse stood in its dust cover of unbleached muslin; where the little beaver muff lay in the holly red box, swathed in tissue and moth balls; where the bright music box waited to play its tinkling tune of Christmas:

> *There's a song in the air!*
> *There's a star in the sky! . . .*

Amy swept carefully, working her way to the very end of the arbor and the alley gate before she allowed herself to look. But there was no small face, framed in an old blue woolen scarf, peering through the palings. Amy was aware of a sharp sense of—something—in her breast, relief, no doubt.

"Well," she said half aloud, knocking the broom against the fence to clear it of leaves and twigs. "Maybe the visitation is over. Maybe every move I make won't be watched now." And just to be sure she was at last completely free of the black eyes she unlatched the back gate and looked searchingly up and down the alley.

It was empty, except for the neat row of trash cans set out beside each householder's gate in readiness for the weekly collection. As she stood there the Warrens' cat, pursued by the Adams' dog, streaked past her and up one post of the arbor. From the security of the top her sharp, indignant hiss was loud in the silence of the alley. But there was no child. Amy latched the gate the went slowly back up the walk to the house.

"What kind of child is it?" Thomas asked her at supper. Of all the silly questions a husband could ask this was about the silliest.

"What kind of child? Why, just a plain child. You know what a child is, Tom."

He ignored her heavily ironic tone. "How old, Amy? Girl or boy?"

"Girl—I'd say she's five or six years old . . ." She watched him narrowly but there was no change in the expression on his face. "Mostly eyes. She just stands there and watches me with those big, black eyes. Never speaks."

"Wonder why she isn't in school in the daytime. But I can't see anything to get upset about, dear. Probably just thinks you're a funny old woman. And how right she is . . ." He laughed and passed his plate for more peach pie. But the words and the laugh didn't sound gay and impertinent, as she knew he meant them to.

She tried to match his effort. "I don't mind being called funny, but *old*— Thomas Martin, if you begin calling me an old woman now, when I'm thirty-seven, what will you be calling me when I'm sixty? Anyway, you're two years older than I am, don't forget." But the words sounded hollow to her. And when she looked across the table into Tom's face she saw the old wound there, the shadow that was somehow deeper at Christmas than at other times, or harder to mask, perhaps.

She put an extra spoonful of peaches on his plate and passed it back to him.

"Want to go to a movie? Dickens' *A Christmas Carol* is playing downtown somewhere. The lights might be pretty tonight, too."

"No, thank you, dear. I feel a little tired tonight. Let's just sit by our own fire."

"Suits me." He got up and went around the table and bent down, putting his lips against her cheek. She reached up and held his face against hers for just an instant.

"If we could just stop the clock—or better yet, set it up into the New Year."

"Amy—have you thought maybe we're alone too much these days? I mean—maybe we've—"

The doorbell chimed musically through the house, and there was a sound of quick footsteps in the hallway. Then the footsteps paused, and in a moment a voice called, "Where is everybody? Any coffee left? I could use a cup."

"Vinnie!"

The middle-aged woman who came through the doorway into the dining room was peeling off her driving gloves. Her head was bare, and her dark, graying hair was windblown. In the heavy gabardine car coat with its pushed-back hood she seemed shapeless, sturdy, and plain. But her cheeks were as red as those of a child who has been playing in the sun. And her eyes of deep, clear blue were so candid and beautiful they caught the eye of the beholder, immediately. It was a lived-in face, strong, vital.

Thomas took her gloves and coat. "Sit here, dear. I'll get you a napkin and some silver." He pulled out a chair for her.

"Have you had any supper?" Amy lifted her face for Vinnie's kiss. "I imagine that's a foolish question."

"Hamburger at the diner, between calls. But their coffee isn't any good. Do I see peach pie?"

Amy poured coffee and served a plate of dessert for her.

"Ummm—good. No one in the world but you and my grandma ever made dried peach pie as good as this." She savored the food.

"You look tired, Vinnie. And we haven't seen you for days. When did we last see her, Tom?

"When she came for Sunday breakfast and had an emergency call before she got in the door. Two weeks ago, that was."

"That was old Mr. Willoughby's hip. He's doing fine now. His daughter's coming to take him home with her as soon as he can be moved. The children want Gramp home for Christmas, and I'm going to let him go."

"Will things let up a bit, do you think, with the holidays so close?"

"I don't know, Tom. I don't understand why it is, but the nearer Christmas gets the worse life is for a doctor. People seem to confuse me with a social worker, or a pastor. I've been called for as many sick hearts today as I have sick bodies."

"Sometimes it's hard to tell the difference," said Tom.

"Why do people have to break up their homes at Christmas? Anytime—for that matter. But why must children have to take it on the chin at Christmas? Why do people who aren't going to stick together ever have children, anyway? I'm getting pretty sick of this casual attitude toward children, especially at Christmas."

"I suppose," said Tom, "if a home is going to break up the fact that it's Christmas isn't of any special significance. It's the breakup that matters, regardless of when it comes, if there isn't any love to hold things together."

"Why is there such a dearth of that basic commodity?" She laughed. "Somebody ought to study the economics of love supply and demand . . ."

There was silence for a moment. Then Vinnie reached out and put a hand on Amy's. "I haven't forgotten what tonight is. Thank God, you've had love to pull you through."

"It's a hard day," said Amy. "It's just that her birthday's tomorrow—Christmas Eve. We always celebrated it then, you remember."

"That makes it harder, and in a way easier, to ask you what I came to ask you," said Vinnie.

There was stillness so deep it could almost be heard in the room. The grandfather clock in the library ticked in its steady, relentless way, giving each second its full and proper place in the passing parade of time. A gust of wind blew a branch against the side of the house with a soft, sweeping sound. The kettle over its low flame in the kitchen snored gently. Each sound was round and whole in the intense stillness of the dining room.

"I've been trying to make up my mind all day to come to you," said Vinnie. "It's about a child . . ."

Thomas put his fork down, and it clattered sharply on the edge of his plate. "No," he said, his voice coming out harsh and strained. "No, Vinnie, don't try to do us good. We can't stand it. We don't want a child. We don't want anyone here in Carol's place. Carol is dead. No child can take her place. We have forgotten how to be parents. Don't ask us, Vinnie, because we'll have to say no, and it will hurt all of us."

Amy looked first at her husband, then at Vinnie, whose blue eyes were full of love and compassion.

"Vinnie . . . dear Vinnie . . . we know you love us." Amy spoke gently, but her voice was tired and old. "For three long years you've tried all the ways you know to help us. But a child isn't the answer." She put her face in her hands. "Can't you understand this simple thing, Vinnie? When you've lost so much of what your hope and love were built on there's nothing that can be a substitute."

"Yes," said Vinnie quietly. "I can understand that. It was that very thing that brought me to you. I felt that you two, of all the people I know, would understand that."

"Stop it," said Thomas. "I know what you're trying to do, Vinnie. But Amy and I have come to some kind of equilibrium, and we're not going to have it undone, for anyone or anything."

"Listen to me, you two." Vinnie's voice was warm and very gentle, but there was an insistent quality in it that drew the eyes of the other two to her face. "Just listen a minute, without talking, without resisting me." The urgency in her tone cut through the gentleness.

"I am not conniving in any way to get you involved emotionally with any child. I've always tried to be straightforward with you, and I shall be now. I know—no one better—how you've struggled to accept the fact that one snowy December afternoon, three years ago, your six-year-old child steered her sled into the path of a truck and was killed. Maybe you remember that I was with you that night." She looked from one face to the other.

The faces she looked into were bleak, remembering.

"But maybe you've forgotten something else. For a whole year after Carol's death her friends trooped through this house and yard, using her roller skates, swinging in her swing, playing with her dolls, reading her books. And why?"

The clock struck a deep, mellow tone for the half hour.

"Because you wanted it that way. You wanted to keep that kind of love alive." The blue eyes were very bright. "It was one of the loveliest things I ever knew—one of the most truly beautiful. I'd seen it once before, with a mother and father who'd lost their only son. But the difference is they were able to go on giving to children. What happened to you?"

"Lots of things." Thomas' voice was low. "The children began to forget Carol. New children came into the neighborhood. The house was just a big cooky jar inhabited by two funny people. You know what happened as well as we do."

"So you began to close the door." Vinnie sighed. "Well, I came to ask you to take a child in for a few weeks, as a humane act, to me and to her. There's literally no place for her to go."

"Where are her parents?"

"That's a long story, Tom. She's one of the casualties. She's one of those who are taking it on the chin, not only at Christmas—it's been three years now since she knew any kind of stability, and before that I can guess that there wasn't much love."

Amy refilled Vinnie's cup. There was a stillness on her face, and she did not speak.

"She's been riding around with me all day while I made my calls. It was one notch better than spending the day in the county welfare worker's office, which was the alternative. The worker and I have been trying to find a place for her. No one wants her." Vinnie's voice was bitter. "The family where she was temporarily placed simply refused to keep her another day. They said she ran away, whenever they let her out of their sight, and they never knew where she was."

"Did she?" Amy's voice was very quiet. It seemed on the surface disinterested. But Vinnie sensed something indefinable in it.

"Yes, I think she did. She says she wasn't running away. She was just visiting her lady. That's all we can get out of her."

"Her lady . . ." Thomas and Amy said the words together.

"Yes. When we ask her where her lady is she says, 'Sweeping the walk,' or, 'In the backyard,' or something that doesn't make sense, to us, anyway."

Amy's gaze was locked with Thomas.' But if there was anything unusual in this Vinnie didn't seem to notice.

"She cried once, today—of course it was a rough day, waiting in the car for me, or sitting in the hospital lounge while I made rounds. When I asked her what the trouble was, she said she'd lost her lady. Poor baby. She's been through so much disaster—and now there's not even her make-believe lady to cling to."

"Where is she now, Vinnie?"

Vinnie didn't speak for a moment. Then she took a long breath, which was something like a child's sigh of disappointment. "Asleep on your living room couch. I carried her in and put her down there. She was exhausted."

The sound at the doorway was very slight, but it drew the attention of all of them.

"Speaking of angels . . ." Vinnie got up and started toward the door.

A strange little figure stood there. The car blanket in which she had been wrapped trailed around her. Her tired little face was framed in a blue woolen scarf, knotted under her chin. She looked at the group around the table, her great black eyes masking as best they could her fear and weariness.

She looked from one to the other, the two seated at the table, and Vinnie, standing with her hand on the back of Tom's chair where she had paused, seeing the look on Amy's face.

Then, as though she could not believe what her own eyes beheld, the child stared at Amy. Slowly a look of complete joy and recognition flooded her face.

"My lady, my lady!" she cried, running and stumbling, the heavy blanket still around her, toward Amy.

She would have tripped and fallen had not Tom scooped her up, blanket and all, and put her in Amy's lap.

"We found her," the child called to Vinnie. "We found her! She was waiting for me!"

"What goes on here?" Vinnie's amazement was too real for them to doubt that this was a complete surprise to her.

Amy untied the blue scarf. The child sighed and put her head on Amy's breast. With a gentle hand Amy brushed the tangled dark hair back.

"That's a long story, too," she said. "Tom, warm a cup of milk, dear—and then, would you bring me a nightie and a robe, the pink one, from the chest in Carol's room?"

"Yes, darling," said Tom, stopping to lay his face for a moment on her hair. "I know the one you mean."

Vinnie looked at them. Then she picked up the car robe and folded it carefully, matching the edges and smoothing the fold.

Amy was humming to the child, whose lids were drooping.

> *There's a song in the air!*
> *There's a star in the sky!*

"MEDITATION" IN A MINOR KEY

JOSEPH LEININGER WHEELER

Could someone's life be dominated by a single piece of music? Even more improbably, *two* people's lives?

Before I write a single word of my stories, I ask God to give me both the characters and the plots. Once He has done so, I seek His divine wisdom each day as the story grows. Of all the stories the Lord and I have coauthored, this one, hands down, continues to elicit the most mail (even after fifteen years).

Eight minutes until curtain time, Mr. Devereaux."

"How's it looking?"

"Full house. No. *More* than full house—they're already turning away those who'll accept Standing Room Only tickets."

"Frankly, I'm a bit surprised, Mr. Schobel. My last concert here was not much of a success."

"I remember, Sir . . . The house was barely a third full."

"Hmm. I wonder . . . uh . . . what do you suppose has made the difference?"

"Well, for one thing, sir, it's your first-ever Christmas concert. For another, people are regaining interest—that Deutsche Gramophone recording has all Europe talking. But pardon me, sir. I'd better let you get ready. Good luck, sir."

And he was gone.

>┊◆┈◦┈◆┊<

No question about it, he mused as he bowed to acknowledge the applause, the venerable Opera House was indeed full. As always, his eyes panned the sea of faces as he vainly searched for the one who never came—had not in ten long years. He had *so* hoped tonight would be different. That package—it hadn't done the job after all . . .

Ten years ago . . . tonight . . . it was. Right here in Old Vienna. It was to have been the happiest Christmas Eve in his life: was not Ginevra to become his bride the next day?

What a fairy-tale courtship that had been. It had all started at the Salzburg Music Festival, where he was the center of attention—not only of the city but of the world. Had he not stunned concertgoers by his incredible coup? The first pianist to ever win grand piano's Triple Crown: the Van Cliburn, the Queen Elizabeth, and the Tchaikovsky competitions?

Fame had built steadily for him as one after another of the great prizes had fallen to him. Now, as reporters, interviewers, and cameramen followed his every move, he grew drunk on the wine of adulation.

It happened as he leaned over the parapet of Salzburg Castle, watching the morning sun gild the rooftops of the city below. He had risen early in order to hike up the hill to the castle and watch the sunrise. A cool alpine breeze ruffled the trees just above; but it also displaced a few strands of raven black hair only a few feet to his left. Their glances met—and they both glanced away, only to blush as they glanced back. She was the most beautiful girl he had ever seen. But beautiful in more than mere appearance: beautiful in poise and grace as well. Later, he would gradually discover her beauty of soul.

With uncharacteristic shyness, he introduced himself to her. And then she withdrew in confusion as she tied the name to the cover stories. Disarming her with a smile, he quickly changed the subject: what was *she* doing in Salzburg?

As it turned out, she was in Europe for a summerlong study tour—and how his heart leaped when she admitted that her study group was staying in Salzburg the entire week. He made the most of it: before her bus had moved on he had pried from her not very reluctant fingers a copy of the tour itinerary.

And like Jean Valjean's inexorable nemesis, Javert, he pursued her all over Europe, driving his concert manager into towering rages. Had he forgotten that there was the long and arduous fall schedule to prepare for? Had he forgotten the time it took to memorize a new repertoire? No, he hadn't forgotten: the truth of the matter was that his priorities had suddenly changed. Every midweek, in around-the-clock marathons, he'd give his practicing its due—then he'd escape in order to be with Ginevra for the weekend.

They were instant soul mates: They both loved the mountains and the sea, dawn and dusk, Tolstoy and Twain, snow and sand, hiking and skiing, Gothic cathedrals and medieval castles, sidewalk cafes and old bookstores. But they were not clones: in art, she loved Georges de La Tour and Caravaggio whereas his patron saints were Dürer and Hieronymus Bosch; in music, he preferred Mozart and Prokofiev whereas she revelled in Chopin and Liszt.

He knew the day he met her that, for him, there would never be another woman. He was that rarity: a man who out of the whole world will choose but one—and if that one be denied him. . . .

But he wasn't denied. It was on the last day of her stay, just hours before she boarded her plane for home, that he asked her to climb with him the zig-zagging inner staircases of the bell tower of Votivkirche, that great neo-Gothic cathedral of Vienna, paling in comparison only with its legendary ancestor, St. Stephens.

Far up in the tower, breathing hard for more than one reason, his voice shook as he took both her hands captive . . . and looked through her honest eyes into her heart—his, he knew, even without asking. She never *did* actually say yes, for the adorable curl of her lips, coupled with the candlelit road to heaven in her eyes, was her undoing.

The rapture which followed comes only once in a lifetime—when it comes at all.

Then the scene changed, and he stiffened as if receiving a mortal blow, for but four months later, in that selfsame bell tower, his world had come to an end. That terrible, terrible night when his nuptial dreams were slain by a violin.

Ginevra drew her heavy coat tighter around her as the airport limousine disappeared into the night. Inside the Opera House she made her way to the ticket counter to ask for directions to her section.

From the other side of the doors she heard Bach's *Italian Concerto* being reborn. . . . She listened intently. She had not been mistaken after all: a change *had* taken place.

Leaning against a pillar, she let the distant notes wash over her while she took the scroll of her life and unrolled a third of it. How vividly she remembered that memorable fall Michael's letters came as regularly as night following day: long letters most of the time, short messages when his hectic schedule precluded more. Her pattern was unvarying: she would walk up the mountain road to the mailbox, out of the day's mail search for that precious envelope, then carry it unopened on top of the rest of the mail back to the chalet, perched high on a promontory point 1600 feet above the Denver plain. Then she'd walk out onto the upper deck and seat herself. Off to her right were the Flatirons massed above the city of Boulder, front-center below was the skyline of Denver—at night a fairyland of twinkling lights—and to the left the mountains stair-stepped up to 14,255-foot Longs Peak and Rocky Mountain National Park. Then she'd listen for the pines—oh! those heavenly pines! They would be soughing their haunting song . . . and *then* she would open his letter.

So full of romance were her starlit eyes that weeks passed before she realized there was a hairline crack in her heart—and Michael was the cause of it. She hadn't realized it during that idyllic summer as the two of them had spent so much time exploring Gothic cathedrals, gazing transfixed as light transformed stained glass into heart-stopping glory, sitting on transepts as organists opened their stops and called on their pipes to dare the red zone of reverberating sound.

She finally, in a long letter, asked him point-blank whether or not he believed in God. His response was a masterpiece of subterfuge and fence-straddling for well he knew how central the Lord was to her. As women have ever since the dawn of time, she rationalized that if he just loved *her* enough—and surely he *did*—then of course he would come to love God as much as she.

So it was that she put her reservations and premonitions aside, and deflected her parents' concerns in that respect as well. Michael had decided he wanted to be married in the same cathedral where he had proposed to her, and as it was large enough to accommodate family as well as key figures of the music world, she had reluctantly acquiesced. Personally, she would have much rather been married in the small Boulder church high up on Mapleton Avenue. A Christmas wedding there, in the church she so loved . . . but it was not to be.

Deciding to make the best of it, she and her family drove down the mountain, took the freeway to Stapleton Airport, boarded the plane, and found their seats. As the big United jet roared off the runway, she looked out the window at Denver and her beloved Colorado receding below her. She wondered: could Michael's European world ever really take its place?

It was cold that memorable Christmas Eve, and the snow lay several feet deep on Viennese streets. Ginevra, ever the romantic, shyly asked Michael if he would make a special pilgrimage with her.

"Where to?" queried Michael. "It's mighty cold outside."

"The bell tower of Votivkirche."

He grinned that boyish grin she loved. "I really *am* marrying a sentimentalist, aren't I? Oh well," he complained good-naturedly, "guess I'd better get used to it. Let's find our coats."

An unearthly quiet came over the great city as they once again climbed the winding staircases of Votivkirche. She caught her breath at the beauty of it all when they at last reached their eyrie and looked down at the frosted rooftops and streets below. Michael, however, much preferred the vision *she* represented, in her flame-colored dress and sable coat.

Then it was . . . faintly and far away . . . that they heard it. They never did trace its origin exactly. It might have wafted its way up the tower from below or it might have come from an apartment across the way. Ordinarily, in the cacophony of the city, they could not possibly have heard it, but tonight, with snow deadening the street sounds, they could distinctly pick up every note. Whoever the violinist was . . . was a master.

Ginevra listened: transfixed. Michael, noting her tear-stained cheeks, shattered the moment with an ill-timed laugh. "Why you old crybaby, it's nothing but a song! I've heard it somewhere before. . . . I don't remember who wrote it, but it's certainly nothing to cry over."

He checked as he saw her recoil as if he had slashed her face with a whip. Her face blanched, and she struggled for control. After a long pause, she said in a toneless voice: "It's not a song—it's 'Meditation' by Massenet."

"Well, that's fine with me," quipped Michael, "I'll just meditate about *you*."

There was a long silence, and now, quite ill at ease, he shuffled his feet and tried to pass it all off as a joke.

But in that, he failed abysmally: "You . . . you don't hear it at all," she cried. "You just don't. . . . I never hear that melody without tears, or without soaring to heaven on the notes. Massenet *had* to have been a Christian! And, furthermore, whoever plays it like we just heard it played *has* to be a Christian too!"

"Oh, come now, Ginevra. Aren't you getting carried away by a simple little ditty? *Anyone* who really knows how to play the violin could play it just as well. . . . *I* certainly could—and I don't even believe in . . . in God—" He stopped, vainly trying to slam his lips on the words in time, but perversely they slipped out of their own accord.

Deep within the citadel of her innermost being, Ginevra felt her heart shudder as if seized by two powerful opposing forces. Then—where the hairline crack of her heart once was—there was an awful *crack*—and a yawning fault took its place.

The look of agony on her face brought him to his senses at last—but it was too late. She looked at him with glaciered cheeks and with eyes so frozen that he could barely discern the tiny flickering that had, only moments ago, almost overpowered him with the glow of a thousand love-lit candles.

She turned, slipped something which had once been on her finger into his coat pocket, and was gone. So quickly was the act done that at first he failed to realize she was no longer there. Then he called after her and ran blindly down the stairs. Ginevra, however, with the instinct of a wounded animal, found an unlocked stairwell door and hid inside until he had raced down the tower and into the street. Much later, she silently made her way out into a world made glad by midnight bells. But there was no Christmas gladness in *her* heart.

She determined to never see him again. Neither his calls nor his letters nor his telegrams would she answer; writing him only once: "Please do not *ever* try to contact me in any way again."

And he—his pride in shreds—never had.

Never . . . would he forget that awful Christmas when—*alone*—he had to face the several thousand wedding guests and the importunate press with the news that it was all off. No, he could give them no reasons. And then he had fled.

Since he had planned on an extended honeymoon he had no more concerts scheduled until the next fall. That winter and spring he spent much time in solitude, moping and feeling sorry for himself. By late spring, he was stir-crazy, so he fled to the South Pacific, to Asia, to Africa, to South America—*anywhere* to get away from himself and his memories.

Somehow, by midsummer, he began to regain control; he returned to Europe and quickly mastered his fall repertoire. That fall, most of his reviews were of the rave variety, for he dazzled with his virtuosity and technique.

For several years, his successes continued, and audiences filled concert halls wherever he performed. But there came a day when that was no longer true, when he realized that most dreaded of performing world truths: that it was all over—he had peaked. Here he was, his career hardly begun, and his star was already setting. But *why*?

Reviewers and concertgoers alike tried vainly to diagnose the ailment and prescribe medicinal cures, but nothing worked. More and more the tenor of the reviews began to sound like the following:

> *How sad it is that Devereaux—once thought to be the rising star of our age: the worthy successor to Horowitz—has been revealed as but human clay after all. It is as if he represents but a case of arrested development. Normally, as a pianist lives and ages, the roots sink deeper and the storm-battered trunk and branches develop seasoning and rugged strength. Not so with Devereaux. It's as if all growth ceased some time ago. Oh! No one can match him where it comes to razzle-dazzle and special effects, but one gets a bit tired of these when there is no offsetting depth.*

Like a baseball slugger in a prolonged batting slump, Michael tried everything: he dabbled in every philosophy or mysticism he came across. Like a drunken bee, he reeled from flower to flower without any real sense of direction.

And "Meditation" had gradually become an obsession with him. He just couldn't seem to get it out of his consciousness. He determined to prove to her that you didn't have to be religious in order to play it well. But as much as he tried, as much as he applied his vaunted techniques and interpretive virtuosity to it, it yet remained as flat, stale, and unmoving as three-hour-old coffee.

He even went to the trouble of researching the tune's origins, feeling confident that it, like much music concert performers play, would apparently have no religious connections whatsoever. In his research, he discovered that "Meditation" came from Massenet's opera *Thaïs*, which he knew had to do with a dissolute courtesan. Aha! He had her! But then, he dug deeper and discovered, to his chagrin, that although it was true that Thaïs had a dissolute sexual past, as was true with Mary Magdalene, she was redeemed—and "Meditation" represents the intermezzo bridge between the pagan past of the first two acts and the one-ness with God in the third act.

So he had to acknowledge defeat here too.

As for Ginevra, she was never far from his thoughts. But not once would his pride permit him to ask anyone about her, her career, or whether or not she had ever married.

He just *existed* . . . and measured his life by concerts and hotel rooms.

Ginevra too, after the long numbness and shock had at last weathered into a reluctant peace, belatedly realized that life had to go on . . . but just what should she do with her life?

It was during a freak spring blizzard which snowed her in that the answer came. She had been sitting in the conversation pit of the three-story-high massive moss rock fireplace, gazing dreamily into the fire, when suddenly, the mood came upon her to write. She reached for a piece of paper, picked up her Pilot pen, and began writing a poem. A poem about pain, disillusion, and heartbreak. The next day, she mailed it off to a magazine. Not long after, it was published.

She decided to do graduate work in the humanities and in education. She completed, along the way, a master's, and later a Ph.D.; in the process, becoming the world's foremost authority on the life and times of a woman writer of the American heartland. She also continued, as her busy schedule permitted, to write poems, essays, short stories, inspirational literature, and longer works of fiction.

So it was that Ginevra became a teacher: a teacher of writing, of literature—and life. Each class was a microcosm of life itself; in each class were souls crying out to be ministered to, to be appreciated, to be loved.

Because of her charm, vivacity, joie du vivre, and sense of humor, she became ever more popular and beloved with the passing of the years. She attracted suitors like children to a toy store. Yet, though some of these friendships got to the threshold of love, none of them got any farther: it was as if not one of them could match what she had left behind in Vienna.

The good Lord it was who saw her through: who shored up her frailties and helped to mend the brokenness.

Meanwhile, she did find time to keep up with Michael's life and career. In doing so, she bought all his recordings, and played them often. Yet, she was vaguely dissatisfied: she too noting the lack of growth—and wondered.

One balmy day in late November during the seventh year after the breakup, as she was walking down the ridge to her home, she stopped to listen to her two favorite sounds: the cascading creek cavorting its way down to the Front Range plain and the sibilant whispering of the pines. Leaning against a large rock, she looked up at that incredibly blue sky of the Colorado high country.

As always, her thoughts refused to stay in their neat little cages. She had tried all kinds of locks during those seven years, but not one of them had worked. And now, when she had thought them safely locked in, here came all her truant thoughts: bounding up to her like a ragtag litter of exuberant puppies, overjoyed at finding her hiding place.

And every last one of the little mutts was yelping Michael's name.

What would *he* be doing this Christmas. It bothered her—had bothered her for almost seven years now—that her own judge had refused to acquit her for her Michael-related words and actions. Periodically, during these years, she had submitted her case to the judge in the courthouse of her mind; and every last time, after listening to the evidence, the judge had looked at her stern-faced. She would bang the gavel on the judicial bench and intone severely: "Insufficient evidence on which to absolve you. . . . Next case?"

She couldn't get out of her head an article she had read several months before—an article about Michael Devereaux. The writer, who had interviewed her subject in depth, had done her homework well: for the portrait of Michael rang true to Ginevra. The individual revealed in the character sketch was both the Michael Ginevra knew and a Michael she would rather not know. The interviewer pointed out that Michael was a rather bitter man for one so young in years. So skittish had the interviewee been when approached on the subject of women in his life, that the writer postulated that it was her personal conviction that somewhere along the way Devereaux had been terribly hurt by someone he loved deeply. . . . And here, Ginevra winced. The writer concluded her character portrait with a disturbing synthesis: "Devereaux, his concert career floundering, appears to be searching for answers. But he's not looking in the direction of God. Like many, if not most, Europeans of our time, he appears to be almost totally secular; thus he has nowhere but within himself upon which to draw strength and inspiration. Sadly, his inner wells appear to retain only shallow reservoirs from which to draw. . . . A pity."

A nagging thought returned to tug at her heartstrings: what had *she* done— what had she *ever* done—to show Michael a better way? . . . "But," she retorted, "I don't want him to become a Christian just for *me*!" But this time that oft-used cop-out didn't suffice. She kept seeing that stern-faced judge within. . . . In the long, long silence that followed was born a plan of action. If it worked, if he responded as she hoped he might, sooner or later, she would *know*! For inescapably, the secret would "out" through his music.

She determined to implement her plan of action that very day.

Several weeks after Ginevra's decision, Michael had returned to his hotel after a concert, a particularly unsatisfactory one—and it seemed these days that there were more and more of this kind. Even the crowd had been smaller than any he could remember in years. He was increasingly convinced that his career and life were both failures—and that there was little reason to remain living. He went to bed and vainly tried to sleep. After an hour or two of thrashing around, he got up, turned on the light, and looked for the last packet of mail forwarded to him by his agent. There was something in it that intrigued him. Ah! Here it was.

A small registered package had arrived from New York. There was no return address, and he didn't recognize the handwriting on the mailer. Inside was a slim, evidently long-out-of-print book titled *The Story of the Other Wise Man* and written by an author he had never heard of: Henry Van Dyke. . . . Well, it looked like a quick read and he couldn't sleep anyhow . . .

A quick read it was not. He found himself rereading certain passages several times. It was after 3 A.M. before he finally put it down. He was moved in spite of himself. Then, he retired, this time to sleep.

During that Christmas season, he reread it twice more—and each time he read it he wondered what had motivated that unknown person to send it.

Three months later came another registered packet from New York. It too was obviously a book and, to his joy, another old one. To his relief—for he had an intense fear of God and religion—it did not appear to be a religious book. The author and title were alike unknown to him: Myrtle Reed's *The Master's Violin*. The exquisite metallic lamination of this turn-of-the-century first edition quite took his breath away. *Someone* had spent some money on *this* gift! He read it that night, and it seemed, in some respects, that the joy and pain he vicariously experienced in the reading mirrored his own. And the violin! It brought back memories of that melody, that melody which just would not let him go, that melody which represented the high tide of his life.

It was mid-June, three months later, when the next registered package arrived from New York. This time, his hands were actually trembling as he opened the package.

Another book by yet another author he'd never heard of: Harold Bell Wright. Kind of a strange title it had: *That Printer of Udel's*. But it was old and had a tipped-in cover; the combination was irresistible. He dropped everything and started to read.

He was not able to put it down. In it he saw depicted a portrait of Christian living unlike any he had ever seen before: a way of life which had to do not just with sterile doctrine but with a living, loving outreach to one's fellow man. He finished the book late that night. A month later, he read it again.

By late September, he had been watching his mail with great anticipation for some time. What would it be this time? Then it came: another book, first published in 1907, by the same author, with the intriguing title: *The Calling of Dan Matthews*. It made the same impact upon him its predecessor had. Nevertheless, Michael was no easy nut to crack: he continued to keep his jury sequestered—he was nowhere near ready for a verdict of any kind.

Early in December arrived his second Van Dyke: *The Mansion*, a lovely lime-green illustrated edition. This book spawned some exceedingly disturbing questions about his inner motivations. Of what value, really, was *his* life? When was the last time he had ever done anything for someone without expecting something in return? For such a small book, it certainly stirred up some difficult-to-answer questions!

March brought a book he had often talked about reading, but never had the temerity to tackle: Victor Hugo's forbidding *Les Misérables*: almost 1500 pages unabridged! He wondered: *Why?* Why such a literary classic following what he had been sent before? He didn't wonder long: the story of Jean Valjean was a story of redemption, the story of a man who climbed out of hell. The first Christ figure he could ever remember seeing in French literature. By now, he was beginning to look for fictional characters who exhibited, in some manner, Christian values.

At the end of the book was a brief note:

NO OTHER BOOK FOR SIX MONTHS. REVIEW.

He did . . . but he felt terribly abused, sorely missing the expected package in June.

By the time September's leaves began to fall, he was in a state of intense longing. Certainly, after *Les Misérables*, and after a half-year wait, it would have to be a blockbuster! To his amazement and disgust, it was a slim mass-market paperback with the thoroughly unappetizing title of *Mere Christianity*. The author he knew of but had never read: C. S. Lewis.

Swallowing his negative feelings with great difficulty, he gingerly tested with his toes . . . Lewis's Jordan River. As he stepped farther in, he was—quite literally—overwhelmed. Every argument he had ever thrown up as a barrier between him and God was systematically and thoroughly demolished. He had had no idea that God and Christianity were any more than an amalgamation of feelings—for the first time, he was able to conceptualize God with his *mind*!

Whoever was sending him the books was either feeling sorry for making him wait so long—or punishing him by literally burying him in print! He was kindly given two weeks to digest *Mere Christianity* and then began the nonstop barrage of his soul: first came three shells in a row: Lewis's Space Trilogy: *Out of That Silent Planet*, *Perelandra*, and *That Hideous Strength*. At first, Michael, like so many other readers of these books, enjoyed the plot solely on the science fiction level. Then, he wryly observed to himself that Lewis had set him up: woven into the story was God and His plan of salvation!

The Trilogy was followed by Lewis's *Screwtape Letters*. How Michael laughed as he read this one! How incredibly wily is the Great Antagonist! And how slyly Lewis had reversed the roles in order to shake up all his simplistic assumptions about the battles between Good and Evil.

A week later: another shell—*The Four Loves*. In it, Michael found himself reevaluating almost all of his people-related friendships in life. That was but the beginning: then Lewis challenged him to explore the possibilities of a friendship with the Eternal.

Two shells then came in succession: *Surprised By Joy* and *A Grief Observed*. At long last, he was able to learn more about Lewis the man. Not only that, but how Lewis, so late in life introduced to the joys of nuptial love, related to the untimely death of his bride. How Lewis, in his wracking grief, almost lost his way—almost turned away God Himself! Paralleling Lewis's searing loss of his beloved was Michael's loss of Ginevra: relived once again, it was bone-wrenching in its intensity. More so than Lewis's—for he had not Lewis's God to turn to in the darkest hour.

The final seven shells came in the form of what appeared to be, at first glance, a series of books for children: Lewis's *Chronicles of Narnia*. It took Michael some time to figure out why he'd been sent this series last—after such heavyweights! It was not until he was about halfway through that he knew. By then, he had fully realized just how powerful a manifestation of the attributes of Christ Aslan the lion was. By the moving conclusion of *The Last Battle*, the fifteen shells from Lewis's howitzer had made mere rubble out of what was left of Michael's defense system.

Then came a beautiful edition of the Phillips Translation of the New Testament. On the flyleaf, in neat black calligraphy, was this line:

MAY THIS BOOK HELP TO MAKE YOUR NEW YEAR TRULY NEW.

He read the New Testament with a receptive attitude, taking a month to complete it. One morning, following a concert the night before in Florence, he rose very early and walked to the Arno River to watch the sunrise. As he leaned against a lamppost, his thoughts (donning their accountant coats) did an audit of the past three years.

He was belatedly discovering that a life without God just wasn't worth living: in fact, *nothing*, he now concluded, had any lasting meaning divorced from a higher power. He looked around him, mentally scrutinizing the lives of family members, friends, and colleagues in the music world. He noted the devastating divorce statistics, the splintered homes, and the resulting flotsam of loneliness and despair. Without God, he now concluded, no human relationship was likely to last very long.

Nevertheless, even now that he was thoroughly convinced—in his mind—that God represented the only way out of his dead-end existence, he bullheadedly balked at crossing the line out of the Dark into the Light.

The day before Easter of that tenth year, there came another old book, an expensive English first edition of Francis Thompson's poems. Inside, on the endsheet, was this coda to their faceless three-year friendship:

> *Dear Michael,*
> *For almost three years now,*
> *you have never been out of my*
> *thoughts and prayers.*
>
> *I hope that these books have come*
> *to mean to you what they do to me.*
>
> *This is your last book.*
>
> *Please read "The Hound of Heaven."*
> *The rest is up to you.*
> *Your Friend*

Immediately, he turned to the long poem, and immersed himself in Thompson's lines. Although some of the words were a bit antiquated and jarred a little, nevertheless he felt that the lines were written laser-straight to him, especially those near the poem's gripping conclusion—for Michael identified totally with Thompson's own epic flight from the pursuing celestial Hound:

Whom will you find to love ignoble thee
Save Me, save only Me?
All which I took from thee I did but take,
Not for thy harms,
But just that thou might'st seek it in My arms.
All which thy child's mistake
Fancies as lost, I have stored for thee at home.
Rise, clasp My hand, and come!

These lines broke him . . . and he fell to his knees.

It was the morning after, and Michael awakened to the first Easter of the rest of his life. Needing very much to be alone, he decided to head for the family chalet near Mt. Blanc. How fortunate, he mused, that the rest of the family was skiing at St. Moritz that week.

Two hours before he got there, it began to snow, but his Porsche, itself born during a bitterly cold German winter, growled its delight as it devoured the road to Chamonix. It was snowing even harder when he arrived at the chalet, where Michael was greeted with delight by Jacques and Marie, the caretakers.

Breakfast was served adjacent to a roaring fire in the great alpine fireplace. Afterward, thoroughly satisfied, he leaned back in his favorite chair and looked out at the vista of falling snow.

He *felt*, he finally concluded, as if sometime in the night he had been reborn. It was as if all his life he had been carrying a staggeringly heavy backpack, a backpack into which some cruel overseer had dropped yet another five-pound brick each January 1st of his life, for as far back as he could remember. And now—suddenly—he was *free*! What a paradoxical revelation that was: that the long-feared surrender to God resulted in—not the dreaded straitjacketed servitude but the most incredible euphoric freedom he had ever imagined!

Looking back at the years of his life, he now recognized that he had been fighting God every step of the way, but God, refusing to give up on him, had merely kept His distance. He went to his suitcase, reached for that already precious book of poems, returned to his seat by the fire, and turned again to that riveting first stanza:

> *I fled Him, down the nights and down the days;*
> *I fled Him, down the arches of the years;*
> *I fled Him, down the labyrinthine ways*
> *Of my own mind, and in the midst of tears*
> *I hid from Him, and under running laughter.*
> *Up vistaed hopes I sped;*
> *And shot, precipitated*
> *Adown Titanic glooms of chastened fears,*
> *From those strong Feet that followed, followed after.*
> *But with unhurrying chase,*
> *And unperturbed pace,*
> *Deliberate speed, majestic instancy,*
> *They beat—and a Voice beat*
> *More instant than the Feet—*
> *'All things betray thee, who betrayest Me!'*

He turned away, unable, because of a blurring of his vision, to read on:

"How many *years* I have lost!" he sighed.

Years during which the frenetic pace of his life caused the Pursuing Hound to sadly drop back. Years during which he proudly strutted, wearing the tinsel crown of popularity. And then . . . that flimsy bit of ephemera was taken away and the long descent into the maelstrom had taken place. And it had been in his darkest hour, when he actually felt Ultimate Night reaching for him, that he plainly and distinctly heard his Pursuer again.

For almost three years now that Pursuer had drawn ever closer. There had been a strange meshing: the Voice in the crucifixion earthquake who spoke to Artaban, the Power that defied the Ally in the Dan Matthews story, the Force revealed through the pulsating strings of "mine Cremona," the Presence which—through the Bishop's incredible act of forgiveness and compassion—saved the shackled life of Jean Valjean, the Angel who showed John Weightman's pitiful mansion to him, Malacandra of the Perelandra story and Aslan in the Narnia series. As he read "The Hound of Heaven," all the foregoing lost their distinctiveness and merged into the pursuing Hound. They were one and the same!

Michael resonated with a strange new power, a power he had never experienced before. It was as if, during the night, in his badly crippled power station (a generating facility to which, over the years, one incoming line after another had been cut, until he was reduced to but one frail piece of frayed wire that alone kept him from blackout), a new cable, with the capacity to illuminate an entire world, had been snaked down the dusty stairs, and then: *plugged in*.

Then—from far back (even before his descent into hell), two images emerged out of the mists of time, one visual and one aural: the tearstained face of the Only Woman . . . and the throbbing notes of "Meditation."

Tingling all over, he stood up and walked over to the grand piano always kept in the lodge for his practicing needs, lifted up the lid, seated himself on the bench, and looked up. Humbly, he asked the question: "Am I ready at last, Lord?"

Then he reached for the keys and began to play. As his fingers swept back and forth, something else occurred: for the first time in over nine years, he was able—without printed music—to replay in his mind every note, every intonation, he and Ginevra had heard in that far-off bell tower of Votivkirche. Not only that . . . but the sterility was gone! The current that had been turned on inside him leaped to his hands and fingers.

At *last* . . . he was ready.

Michael immediately discarded the fall concert repertoire, chosen as it had been merely for showmanship reasons, and substituted a new musical menu for the old. Ever so carefully, as a master chef prepares a banquet for royalty, he selected his individual items. In fact, he agonized over them, for each number must not only mesh with all the others but enhance as well, gradually building into a crescendo that would trumpet a musical vision of his new life.

Much more complicated was the matter of his new recording. How could he stop the process at such a late date? Not surprisingly, when he met with Polygram management and dropped his bombshell, they were furious. Only with much effort was he able to calm them down—and that on a premise they strongly doubted: that his replacement would be so much *better* that they would be more than compensated for double the expected production expense!

He walked out of their offices in a very subdued mood. If he had retained any illusions about how low his musical stock had sunk, that meeting would have graphically settled the question. If his new recording failed to sell well, he would almost certainly be dropped from the label.

Then, he memorized all the numbers before making his trial-run recording; this way, he was able to give his undivided attention to interpretation before wrapping up the process. Only after he himself was thoroughly satisfied with the results did he have it recorded and then hand-carried by his agent to Deutsche Gramophone/ Polygram management.

He didn't have to wait very long; only minutes after they played his pilot recording, Michael received a long-distance phone call from the president himself. Michael had known him for years and knew him to be a very tough *hombre* indeed. Recognizing full well that he and the company lived and died by the bottom line, he was used to making decisions for the most pragmatic of reasons. And recording artists feared him because he had a way of telling the unvarnished truth sans embellishments or grace notes. And now he was on the line. Initially, almost speechless, he finally recovered and blurted out, "What has happened, Michael? For years now, your recordings have seemed—pardon my candidness, but, you know, blunt me—a bit tinny, fluffy, sometimes listless, and even a bit . . . uh . . . for want of a better word: "peevish," more or less as if you were irritably going through the motions again, but with little idea why. Now, here, on the other hand, comes a recording which sounded to us like you woke up one morning and decided to belatedly take control of your life and career; that there were new and exciting ways of interpreting music—interpreting with power . . . and beauty . . . and, I might add, Michael . . . a promise of depth and seasoning we quite frankly no longer believed was in you! *What has happened?*"

That incredible summer passed in a blur of activity. The long ebb over at last, the incoming tidal forces of Michael's life now thundered up the beaches of the musical world. Deutsche Gramophone management and employees worked around the clock to process, release, and then market what they firmly believed would be the greatest recording of his career. Word leaked out even before it was released; consequently, there was a run on it when it hit the market. All of this translated into enthusiastic interest in his fall concert schedule.

Early in August, before the recording had been released, Michael phoned his New York agent, who could hardly contain himself about the new bookings which were flooding in for the North American tour, spring of the following year. Michael, after first swearing him to secrecy, told him that he was entrusting to his care the most delicate assignment of their long association—one which, if botched, would result in irreparable damage. The agent promised to fulfill his instructions to the letter.

He wanted of him three things: to trace the whereabouts of a certain lady (taking great pains to ensure that the lady in question would not be aware of the search process); to find out if the lady had married; to process a mailing (the contents of the mailing would be adjusted according to whether the lady had married or not).

Meanwhile, Ginevra played the waiting game—a very *hard* game to play without great frustration. And for her, the frustration level had been steadily building for almost three years. *When* would she know?

Within a year after mailing her first book, she felt reasonably confident that he was reading what she had sent, but she had little data upon which to base her assumptions. During the second year, little snips of information relating to possible change in Devereaux appeared here and there. Nothing really significant, but enough to give her hope.

She had knelt down by her bed that memorable morning before she mailed Thompson's poems. In her heartfelt supplication, she voiced her conviction that, with this book, she had now done all that was in her power to do. The rest was up to Him. Then she drove down the mountain to the Boulder Post Office and sent it to her New York relayer—and returned home to wait.

It was several months before the Devereaux-related excitement in the music world began to build. Her heart beat a lilting "allegro" the day she first heard about the growing interest in Michael's new recording. She could hardly wait to get a copy.

Then came the day when, in her mailbox, there appeared a little yellow piece of paper indicating that a registered piece of mail was waiting for her in the post office. It turned out to be a *very large* package from an unknown source in New York.

Not until she had returned to her chalet did she open it. Initially, she was almost certain that one of her former students was playing a joke on her, for the box was disproportionately light. She quickly discovered the reason: it was jammed full with wadded-up paper. Her room was half full of paper before she discovered the strange-shaped box at the very bottom of the mailing carton. . . . *What* could it be? . . . *Who* could it be from? . . . . In this box, obviously packed with great care, were five items, each separated by a hard cardboard divider: a perfect flame-red rose in a sealed moisture-tight container, Michael's new Deutsche Gramophone recording, a publicity poster of a concert program which read as follows:

MICHAEL DEVEREAUX
FIRST CHRISTMAS EVE CONCERT
VIENNA OPERA HOUSE

(followed by the other data giving exact time and date), a round-trip airline ticket to Vienna, and at the very bottom, in an exquisite gold box—a front section ticket to the concert.

Fearing lest someone in the Standing section take her place before she could reach her seat, during the enthusiastic applause following Bach's *Italian Concerto*,

Ginevra asked an usher to escort her to her seat in the third row. Michael, who had turned to acknowledge the applause, caught the motion: the beautiful woman coming down the aisle. And she was wearing a flame-red rose. Even in Vienna, a city known for its beautiful women, she was a sight to pin dreams on.

How terribly grateful he was to the audience for continuing to clap, for that gave him time, precious time in which to restore his badly damaged equilibrium. It was passing strange, mused Michael. For years now, both his greatest dream and his greatest nightmare were one and the same: that Ginevra would actually show up for one of his concerts. The nightmare had to do with deep-seated fear that her presence in the audience would inevitably destroy his concentration, and with it the concert itself. And now, *here* she was! If he ever needed a higher power, he needed it now. Briefly, he bowed his head. When he raised it, he felt again this new sense of serenity, peace, and command.

Leaving the baroque world of Bach, he now turned to César Franck; being a composer of romantic music, but with baroque connections, Michael had felt him to be a perfect bridge from Bach to Martin and Prokofiev. As he began to play Franck's *Prélude: Chorale et Fugue,* he settled down to making this the greatest concert of his career. He had sometimes envied the great ones their announced conviction that, for each, the greatest concert was always the very next one on the schedule—they *never* took a free ride on their laurels. Only this season it had been that he had joined the masters, belatedly recognizing that the greatest thanks he could ever give his Maker would be to extend his powers to the limits, every time he performed, regardless of how large or how small the crowd.

The Opera House audience had quickly recognized the almost mind-boggling change in attitude. The last time he had played here, reviewers had unkindly but accurately declared him washed up. So desperate for success of any kind had he become that he openly pandered to what few people still came. It was really pathetic: he would edge out onto the platform like an abused puppy, cringing lest he be kicked again. Not surprisingly, what he apparently expected: he got.

Now, there was never any question as to who was in control. On the second, he would stride purposefully onto the stage, with a pleasant look on his face, and gracefully bow. He would often change his attire between sections: adding a visual extra to the auditory. His attire was always impeccable: newly cleaned and pressed, and he was neither over- nor underdressed for the occasion.

But neither was he proud, recognizing just how fragile is the line between success and failure—and how terribly difficult it is to stay at the top once you get there. Nor did he anymore grovel or play to the galleries. The attitude he now projected was, quite simply: *I'm so pleased you honored me by coming out tonight. I have prepared long and hard for this occasion, consequently it is both my intent and my expectation that we shall share the greatest musical hour and a half of our lifetimes.*

Ginevra felt herself becoming part of a living, breathing island in time. Every concert performed well, is that: kind of a magic moment during which outside life temporarily ceases to be. Great music after all, is outside of time and thus not subject to its rules. Thus it was that Ginevra, like the Viennese audience, lost all sense of identify: as Devereaux's playing became all the reality they were to know for some time.

These weren't just notes pried from a reluctant piano they were hearing: this was life itself, life with all its frustrations and complexities.

With such power and conviction did César Franck speak from the grave that they stood applauding for three minutes at the end of the first half. In fact, disregarding Opera House protocol, a number of the younger members of the audience swarmed onto the stage and surrounded Michael before he could get backstage. The new Michael stopped, and with a pleasant look on his face all the while, autographed every last program that was shoved at him. Nay—more than that: as one of these autograph seekers, jubilant of face, came back to Ginevra's row, she saw him proudly showing the program to his parents. Michael had taken the trouble to learn each person's name so he could inscribe each one personally!

Michael's tux was wringing wet. As for the gleaming black Boersendorfer, with such superhuman energy had Michael attacked it that it begged for the soothing balm of a piano tuner's ministrations; hence it was wheeled out for a badly needed rest. In its place was the monarch of the city's Steinway grands. Michael had specifically requested this living nine feet of history. No one knew for sure just how old it was, but it had for years been the pride and joy of Horowitz. Rubinstein would play here on no other, and it was even rumored that the great Paderewski performed on it. Michael, like all real artists, deeply loved his favorite instruments. Like the fabled Velveteen Rabbit, when an instrument such as this Steinway has brought so much happiness, fulfillment, meaning, and love into life . . . well, over the years, it ceases to be just a piano and approaches personhood. Thus it was that Michael, before it was wheeled in, had a heart-to-heart chat with it.

A stagehand, watching the scene, didn't even lift an eyebrow—concert musicians were *all* a loony bunch.

Only after a great deal of soul-searching had Michael decided to open the second half of his concert with Swiss-born Frank Martin's Eight Preludes. He had long appreciated and loved Martin's fresh approach to music, his lyrical euphonies. Martin reminded Michael of the American composer Howard Hanson. He often had a difficult time choosing which one to include in a given repertoire; but this season, it was Martin's turn.

More and more sure of himself, Michael only gained in power as he retold Martin's story; by the time he finished the Preludes, he owned Vienna. The deafening applause rolled on and on. And nobody appeared willing to ever sit down.

Finally, the house quiet once again, a microphone was brought out and Michael stepped up to speak.

"Ladies and gentlemen," he began, "I have a substitution to make. As you know, I am scheduled to perform Prokofiev's "Sonata #6 in A Major, Opus 82" as my concluding number, but I hope you will not be *too* disappointed"—and here he smiled his boyish grin—"if I substitute a piece that I composed, a piece that has never before been performed in public."

He paused, then continued: "Ten years ago tonight, in this fair city, this piece of music was born, but it was not completed until late this spring. I have been saving it for tonight." And here, he dared to glance in the direction of Ginevra.

"The title is . . . 'Variations on a Theme by Massenet.'"

Nothing in Michael's composing experience had been more difficult than deciding what to do with "Meditation." And the difficulties did not fall away with his conversion. He still had some tough decisions to face: Should his variations consist merely as creative side trips from that one melodic base? By doing so, he knew he could dazzle. Should the variations be limited to musical proof that he and his Maker were now friends? With neither was he satisfied.

Of all the epiphanies he had ever experienced, none could compare with the one which was born to him one "God's in His Heaven / All's right with the world" spring morning: he realized that he could create a counterpart to what Massenet had done with the "Meditation" intermezzo, a fusion of earthly love with the divine. Belatedly, he recognized a great truth: God does not come to us in the abstract—He comes to us through flesh and blood. We do not initially fall in love with God as a principle; rather, we first fall in love with human beings whose lives radiate friendship with the divine. It is only *then* that we seek out God on our own.

Ginevra was such a prototype—that is why he had fallen in love with her. And he had little doubt in his mind but that it was she who had choreographed his conversion. No one else had he ever known who would have cared enough to institute and carry out such a flawless plan of action. Besides, some of the book choices made him mighty suspicious.

Michael had also recognized what all true artists do sooner or later: that their greatest work must come from within, from known experience. If he was to endow his variations with power akin to the original, they must emanate from the joys and sorrows that made him what he was . . . and since she and God were inextricably woven together in Michael's multihued bolt of life, then woven together they must remain throughout the composition.

It would not be acceptable for her to distance herself and pretend she could judge what he had become dispassionately. No, Ginevra must enter into the world he had composed . . . and decide at the other end whether or not she would stay.

In Ginevra's mind, everything seemed to harken back to that cold night in the tower of Votivkirche, for it was there that two lives, only hours from oneness, had seen the cable of their intertwining selves unravel in only seconds.

Furthermore, there was more than God holding them apart. More than her romanticism as compared to his realism. That far-off exchange of words had highlighted for her some significant problems which, left unresolved, would preclude marriage even if Michael *had* been converted. Let's see: How could she conceptualize them?

Essentially, it all came down to these. Michael had laughed at and ridiculed her deepest-felt feelings. Had made light of her tears. Had shown a complete absence of empathy. Worse yet, he exhibited a clear-cut absence of the one most crucial character trait in the universe: *kindness*. Also, at no time since she had known him had she ever seen him admit in any way that he was wrong about anything—and compounding the problem, he had refused to disclose his true identity to her:

There had been a locked door halfway down to his heart.

There had been another locked door halfway up to his soul.

As far as she knew, both doors were still closed.

But if they ever *were* to be unlocked . . . "Meditation" would be the key.

As-soft-as-a-mother's-touch pianissimo, Michael begins to play. So softly that there appears to be no breaks at all between the notes, but rather a continuous skein of melodic sound. And, for the first time in Michael's career, there is a flowing oneness with the piano: impossible to tell where flesh, blood, and breath end and where wood, ivory, and metal join.

Ginevra cannot help but feel tense in spite of blurred fingers weaving dreams around her. Deep down, she knows that what occurs during *this* piece of music will have a profound effect upon the rest of her life. And the rest of Michael's life.

But she hadn't traveled so many thousands of miles just to be a referee or a critic. If their two worlds are ever to be one, she must leave her safe seat in the audience and step into the world of Michael's composition. Strangely enough—and living proof that it is the "small" things in life that are often the most significant—Michael's exhibition of kindness to the young people who blocked his exit during intermission strongly predisposes her in his favor.

How beautifully his arpeggios flow, cascading as serenely as alpine brooks singing their way down to the sea. All nature appears to be at peace. As Michael plays, she can envision the birds' wake-up calls, the falling rain and drifting snow, the sighing of her dear pines, and the endless journey of the stars. The world is a beautiful place . . . and love is in the air.

Suddenly, she stiffens: certainly those are bells she is hearing. Yes: Christmas bells, flooding the universe with joy. She listens intently as their pealing grows ever louder—*then that theme*! It begins to mesh with the bells, but only for an instant. Right in the middle of it, there is an ominous shift from major to minor key, and from harmony to dissonance. And the bells! In that selfsame instant, the pealing joy ceases and is replaced by tolling sorrow. How uncannily perfect is Michael's capture of that moment—that moment when all the joy in their world went sour.

The dissonance and tolling eventually give way to a classical music potpourri. Here and there she recognizes snatches of well-known themes, some of them from piano concertos. But the notes are clipped off short and played perfunctorily: more or less as if the pianist doesn't much care how they sound as long as they all get played in record time. Several times, the Theme tries to edge in, but each time it is rudely repulsed.

Now it is that Dvorak's *New World* Symphony thunders in. Aha! At last: Some resolution! Some affirmation! Not so. It quickly becomes apparent that this paean to a brave new world is, ironically, in steady retreat instead of advancing to triumph. Almost—it seems to her—as if it were a retrograde *Bolero:* its theme progressively diminishing in power instead of increasing. Once again, "Meditation" seeks entry; once again, it is unceremoniously disposed of.

By now, Ginevra is deciphering Michael's musical code quite well: vividly revealed has been the progressive deterioration of Michael both as a person and as a pianist. From the moment in the cathedral tower when the bells began to toll, every variation that followed has dealt with the stages of his fall.

Then, clouds close in, thunder rumbles in the east, lightning strikes short-circuit the sky, and the rain falls. Torrents of it. Darkness sweeps in, and with it all the hells loose on this turbulent planet. Ginevra shivers as Michael stays in minor keys, mourning all the sadness and pain in the universe.

The winds gradually increase to hurricane strength. Far ahead of her—for she is exposed to the elements too—she sees Michael, almost out of sight in the gloom, retreating from the storm. She follows, and attempts to call to him, but to no avail. The tempest swallows the words before they can be formed. Then the black clouds close in . . . and she loses sight of him altogether.

As the hurricane reaches ultimate strength, major keys are in full flight from the minors (Ginevra discovered some time back that Michael is equating majors with the forces of Light, and minors with the forces of Darkness). It does not seem possible that any force on earth could save Michael from destruction.

It is now, in the darkest midnight, when the few majors left are making their last stand. She senses that, for Michael, the end is near. Now, when she has all but conceded victory to the Dark Power, she again hears the strains of Thaïs's theme! How can such a frail thing possibly survive when leagued against the legions of Darkness? But, almost unbelievably, it does.

At this instant, Ginevra chances to look with wide-open eyes at—not Michael the pianist but Michael the man. He has clearly forgotten all about the world, the concert audience, even *her*. In his total identification with the struggle for his soul, he is playing for only two people: himself—the penitent sinner—and God. And his face? Well, never afterward could she really explain, but one thing was absolutely certain: there before her . . . was Michael's naked soul.

With Michael's surrender, the tide turns at last: the storm rages on, but the enemy is now unmistakably in retreat. Dissonance and minors contest every step of the battlefield, trying vainly to hold off the invading Light. Then victorious majors begin sweeping the field.

Ginevra discovers in all this a great truth: it is minors that reveal the full beauty of majors. Had she not heard "Meditation" sobbing on the ropes of a minor key, she would never have realized the limitless power of God. It is the minor key that gives texture and beauty to the major; and it is dissonance that, by contrast, reveals the glory of harmony. . . . It is sorrow that brings our wandering feet back to God. . . .

Finally, with the mists beginning to dissipate and the sun to break through, the Theme reappears, but alone for the first time. Now it is that Ginevra feels the full upward pull of the music, for "Meditation" soars heavenward with such passion, pathos, and power that gravity is powerless to restrain it.

And Ginevra . . . her choice made . . . reaches up,

and with Michael,

climbs the stairs of heaven to God.

Acknowledgments

"The Path to Christmas," (Introduction) by Joseph Leininger Wheeler. Copyright © 2006. Printed by permission of the author.

"A Few Bars in the Key of G," by Clifton Carlisle Osborne. First book publication of complete text
of 1904 story © 2006 (revised text). Text owned by Joe Wheeler (P.O. Box 1246, Conifer, CO 80433).

"Sea Anchor," by Marjorie Yourd Hill. If anyone can provide knowledge of earliest publication source of this old story,
or the whereabouts of the author or the author's next of kin, please contact Joe Wheeler (P.O. Box 1246, Conifer, CO 80433).

"A Girl Like Me," by Nancy Rue. Published in *Brio*, December 1990. Reprinted by permission of the author.

"Joyful *and* Triumphant," by John McCain. Reprinted with permission from the
December 1984 *Reader's Digest*. Copyright © 1984 by The Reader's Digest Assn., Inc., and the author.

"The Fir Tree Cousins," by Lucretia D. Clapp. Published in *The Youth's Instructor*, December 18, 1928. Reprinted by permission
of Joe Wheeler (P.O. Box 1246, Conifer, CO 80433) and Review and Herald Publishing Association, Hagerstown, MD.

"While Shepherds Watched," by Adeline Sergeant. Published in December 1898 *Nor-West Farmer*, Winnipeg, Canada.

"The Gold and Ivory Tablecloth," by Howard C. Schade. Reprinted with permission from
the December 1954 *Reader's Digest*. Copyright © 1954 by The Reader's Digest Assn., Inc.

"The Soft Spot in B606," author unknown. If anyone can provide knowledge of earliest publication source of this old story,
or the whereabouts of the author or the author's next of kin, please contact Joe Wheeler (P.O. Box 1246, Conifer, CO 80433).

"Santa Claus Is Kindness," by Temple Bailey. Published in December 1936 *Good Housekeeping*. If anyone can provide
knowledge of first publication source of this old story, please send to Joe Wheeler (P.O. Box 1246, Conifer, CO 80433).

"A Precious Memory," by David T. Doig. Published in December 1986 *Good Housekeeping*. Reprinted by permission of Rosalind Doig.

"The Tiny Foot," by Frederic Loomis. Story is included in Loomis's book, *Consultation Room*, (New York: Alfred Knopf, 1939).
If anyone can provide knowledge of Loomis's next of kin, please contact Joe Wheeler (P.O. Box 1246, Conifer, CO 80433).

"Like a Candle In The Window," by Margaret E. Sangster, Jr. If anyone can provide knowledge of the
first publication source of this old story, please contact Joe Wheeler (P.O. Box 1246, Conifer, CO 80433).

"The Bells Didn't Ring," by Isabel T. Dingman. Published in December 5, 1929 *Nor-West Farmer*. If anyone can provide
knowledge of the author or the author's next of kin of this old story, please contact Joe Wheeler (P.O. Box 1246, Conifer, CO 80433).

"Bethany's Christmas Carol," by Mabel McKee. Published in December 17, 1929 *The Youth's Instructor*. Reprinted by permission
of Joe Wheeler (P.O. Box 1246, Conifer, CO 80433) and Review and Herald Publishing Association, Hagerstown, MD.

"The Gift of the Magi," by O. Henry (William Sidney Porter). Included in O. Henry's collection
The Four Million (New York: Doubleday and Company, 1906).

"Meditation" in a Minor Key, by Joseph Leininger Wheeler. Copyright © 1991 (Revised, 1996). Reprinted by permission of the author.

"Secrets of the Heart," by Pearl S. Buck. Reprinted by permission of Harold Ober Associates Incorporated.
Copyright © 1968 by the Pearl S. Buck Foundation.

"There's a Song in the Air," by Katherine Reeves. Published in *The Christian Home*, December 1958 (The Graded Press,
Nashville, Tennessee). Reprinted by permission of Abingdon Press, Nashville, Tennessee. If anyone can provide knowledge
of the author or the author's next of kin, please contact Joe Wheeler (P.O. Box 1246, Conifer, CO 80433).